Chapter 1

"Cheer up, dude." Hania was trying to convince me to get over myself. She knew how much I hated myself, and the world, and the fact that both of us existed. "It's your birthday."

"I don't care about no fucking birthday."

Why would I even celebrate something as insignificant as my birthday? I mean, people get excited when they are living the moment exactly a few years after they were born. I didn't think people like us should even celebrate our birth, so long birthdays. July 31st should just be another normal day.

"There was nothing special in me being born, in fact, all I brought was misery. Plus, it's such a cliché to celebrate birthdays. Have a party, decorate the house, get each other gifts. I don't think I even have anyone that will ever love me, probably not even you. What's the point of birthday parties anyway? You all just waste money, and this is exactly why I asked you not to keep a birthday party for me; but no. You just have to be a pain in the ass."

"Hey, I do love you." She turned her green eyes at me, and looked deep into mine, "I love you so much, Javeria. You know that. And hey, how do you know about that party?"

"Do you really think I can't guess it when you ask to go to the *washroom* with Sana?" I rolled my eyes at her, "Plus, you were right outside the classroom. Sana really does talk loud."

"Come on, you're the queen today." Hania smiled at me, I didn't respond, "We're on top of the world today, okay?"

"Easy for you to say."

It really was easy for her, I mean, she was this tall 5'9 girl. She had naturally curly brown hair, and the best cheekbones. Not too round, and not too edgy either, she was perfect. Plus, she had green eyes, and everyone loves green eyes. Green eyes are like the ocean at sunset, I mean it's still an ocean, there's nothing different about it except that it's turning orange, or green in this case, and this somehow increases its beauty.

I, on the other hand, was unlike Hania: Ugly. I did not have green eyes: I had pretty ordinary brown eyes. I did not have naturally curled hair, they were neither straight nor curly, kind of frizzy, which was ugly. They were black, as black as my soul. My round cheeks were forcing my face to become a foot-ball, but at least I didn't care about it too much. Since I wasn't even that tall, no one even noticed me with Hania.

Hania pulled the strap of her bag, and laid it on the ground. The grass was a little wet, and probably was making her *beautiful* pink bag brownish-green. She was too dumb to realize that. She opened the zip, and started looking between the books, as I watched her bend over. God, she really was sexy. She had the perfect figure too, at least a C cup if not D, and an ass as perfect as a Kardashian's. I didn't have a crush on her, but I would be lying if I said I didn't want to make out with her at least once.

"Aha! There it is." She brought out a decorated pinkish box, with a red ribbon all over its cover. It was ugly, pretty kind of ugly.

"Woah, pinky. Slow down." I frowned.

Hania and I were completely different, anyone would notice that from a town apart. She was sexy, and hot. I was ugly and tragic. All she talked about was pretty things: unicorns, rainbows, and the perfect boys, but I was more suicidal: death, death, sad and suicidal music, death.

"Only the cover is pink." Hania smiled again, "I know your taste, Javeria."

"Cliché." I told her, but it didn't affect her a single bit.

"Just take it."

"Ugh, fine."

She handed me over the pink box with red ribbons, and it looked as if her dreams were poured into it. I decided to open it, and as I removed the ribbon, I was almost disgusted with the ribbon touching my hands. I wanted to just burn the thing down, and it would be so badass: Mission accomplished.

I opened it, and I was surprised. It was a wristwatch, I mean, that's a gift that can be expected. It's just too common, like wristwatches are the only real stuff left to gift, grow up people. I'd actually like a book, thank you very much. But, what was surprising about it was that I actually liked it. I liked it very much. It had a blackish strap, exactly the colour of T-shirt I was wearing, and I found it mesmerizing to look at. The gray dial was worth appreciating, and those silver needles, with diamond-numeric time figures in roman numerals. It was similar to what my brother had gifted me once, I guess, she really knew my style.

"I guess I have to thank you?" I was typically rude. I liked being rude. "Well, I'm not gonna."

"You don't have to." She had a cheerful way of talking. I hated it.

I don't get how people can be that cheerful. I mean, I know everybody is going through something, maybe even worse than me, but how come they are still so sprightly, and lively? I mean, do they not feel it? Is their situation so worse that they have gone numb? Would it kill them for being a little themselves?

I got home from college, and I was so tired I felt like I would die. We didn't even get any vacations except for those 20 days in Ramadan. Our exams ended on maybe 6th June, I think, and we were granted holidays 'till 27th. I mean, really?

I was kind of a just slightly above average student. I mean, I didn't want to study, who wants that? Not a sane person, but my parents were counting on me, even though I hated them. And even if I failed classes, or obtained bad grades, they'd still force me to study medicine. If I wasn't going to get grades good enough for a scholarship, they'd actually pay for my university fee, which was pretty expensive.

I don't really care about the money, but see, the thing was I would rather have that money spent on something else. Like, maybe on a new car, or a raise in pocket money, or on my biggest dream, singing.

I had been getting good grades, and one thing I had actually liked about my parents was that they'd get me anything as long as it's within their range and I was studying well. So, when I asked for a guitar exactly a year ago, they hesitated for a while. They thought it would actually make me lose interest in studies (little did they know I never had any). They did get me a guitar eventually, and I remember my dad's words:

"Look Jiya, if your grades drop, I will burn this thing." As he handed me over a medium (18 fret) guitar. I loved that guitar at first sight, there were only a few things I *actually* loved, and that guitar was one of them. It was an acoustic guitar, and I had no idea if it was any good when I started playing it. It was pretty *okay* in the end. It was lined with a black outline, and an orangish-red colour filled in. I liked it, it was exactly what I wanted.

"I promise dad, I'll get even better grades."

I kind of knew it was certainly going to be difficult, managing both college and my passion at once. But love does find a way somehow, doesn't it?

Learning the guitar was a pain, to be honest. It wasn't like one day: Oh Yes! I bought it. Next day: Oh Yes! I can play any song that has ever existed in the world. They got me that guitar right before Eid and I remember how excited I was, because for once it was off from my scary-ass college, and I had all the time in the world to practice.

I remember logging in to YouTube, and searching for guitar tutorials. Everything seemed so difficult, yet I somehow managed to get started. I can't even start describing the pain I felt in my fingers, before I had calluses. I think I practiced 5 hours straight the first day, and it fucking hurt. Anyway, It was a more amazing feeling playing the guitar to the ratio of the fingers hurting, so I bore it somehow.

"I know, you're not even gonna learn that guitar. It'll just be a show piece, hanging on the wall, a symbol of your quirkiness." My mom always used to say this to me, since after Eid, I wasn't really focused on learning the guitar. I was being pressured by parents to keep my grades good, and they were also teasing me for not learning the guitar *as quickly as normal people* do, but guess what mom? I'm not normal. I'm quirky, and I fucking like it.

Which brings us back to this day again. I looked at the watch Hania had bought me, and it was almost 6. There was no test the next day, so it was kind of a relief. I could practice my singing, and play guitar (which by now, I was playing good enough to sing any song with it), and chill for a while.

I started playing the first song I learned on guitar, and one of my absolute all-time favourites: *Hero by Enrique Iglesias.*

G7 chord shape, hit the bass note then strings E, B, G,

Em7 chord shape, hit the bass note then strings E, B, G.

Cadd9 chord shape, hit the bass note then strings E, B, G.

Dsus4 chord shape, hit the bass note then strings E, B, G.

And with the same chords, start singing.

Would you dance? If I asked you to dance?

Or would you run? And never look back.

Enrique was a Spanish singer, and copying his accent was a tough job. But I had a freaking awesome voice. I was ugly, I belonged to a mediocre background when it came to finance, I wasn't a topper, just slightly above average, there was nothing I could possibly like about myself, except for my voice.

Everyone has something special, you cannot be completely useless. I knew I was a good singer, I had a fucking potential to be one, and that was the only thing I was proud of. Out of the very few things I loved, I loved my vocal chords the most.

I just kept playing and singing, and recording on my mobile's recorder. I never realized how quickly time passed, and I wasn't feeling tired anymore. That's the thing about music, it rings something inside your heart that shakes your whole body. I didn't even realize when it struck 9, and I was still singing.

"Come out." Mom knocked at my door, "I have… uh… something to tell you."

"Mom, I know it's that *secret* birthday party." I stopped playing my guitar, which was the hardest thing ever to do. "I'm coming, but I would really appreciate it if you guys wouldn't interrupt me during my guitar session."

"Oh, darling." My *cool* mom is trying to make a *cool mom phrase*, "Party girls can't wait."

"Ugh."

I was down in a minute, and there they were. Fifteen or sixteen girls, 14 out of them I barely knew, and the rest of two: Hania and Sana.

"I hate this party already." I said as I walked down the stairs, looking at everyone in the TV lounge, "too many people. My insecurities hurt."

"We love you Javeria." Hania and Sana said at the same time.

"Well, I love my insecurities."

As I walked down the stairs, I watched this tsunami of girls. One good thing about all-girls college was that I had no male friends. I could handle girls, but I hated boys.

Hania came towards me, and spoke as she drank the coke in her hand, "Why aren't you dressed?"

"Can you see my butt or boobs?"

"Well, no." She took another sip and made a gulp noise, "What I mean is that, you are still wearing the same black shirt and jeans."

"That's because I like myself in this." Please stop judging me, "Black is better than any other colour. Makes you want to kill yourself."

"Stop being so depressed." She asked.

"I will stop, but only if…"

"If, what?" She questioned at once.

"If the gravity stops working and I fly into outer space, but not really since I'd die even before exiting the second layer of Atmosphere."

"There would be no layer of atmosphere if there was no gravity." Hania Rolled her eyes.

"Yeah, keep rolling your eyes. You might find a brain back there."

"Imma go talk to Sana."

And then she walked away from me. Sometimes, I didn't even get it how they could even bear me. People say I am not nice, and what I reply is *yes, I am not nice*. Because that is me, that is Javeria Sultan, the queen of her own world, who can destroy you anytime she wants, and who is not going to be nice no matter how hard you try.

It's not like I felt it was cool to be rude, but it kind of was one of my basic needs. It's cruel to be rude, but it's even worse to be fake. I am not fake, I am an honest person. The people who can't accept me like that are not accepted in my life. I'd rather be alone than with them.

"It's time to cut the cake." My mom almost shouted.

"Ugh, So cliché."

I got near to the arranged table, and there was a chocolate cake with icing stating *Happy Birthday Jiya*.

"You guys can't even settle for one name." I looked up, "Either call me Jiya or Javeria."

I cut a piece of my cake, and everybody started chanting *Happy Birthday to you, Happy birthday to you, Happy birthday to dear Javeria/Jiya, Happy birthday to you.*

"I think my life is full of colours again."

"We're trying to do that." Sana told me.

"Well, you're all moving in the wrong direction."

I hated parties. And it couldn't get any worse, or that's at least what I thought. It was still bearable, until my drunk step-mom entered the TV lounge.

You see, my father had two marriages. He married my step mom first, but she couldn't bear a child for my dad. My dad was furious, he, of course, wanted kids. He just wanted to make children, so he could make the children the slaves of the society. I had always wished I was never born.

My step mother was drunk. She was an alcoholic, and usually every night she'd be drunk. I mean, I don't really care if someone drinks, or smokes. That's your choice, but if you are gonna ruin other people's lives by getting drunk every night and fighting with their father, well they'd hate you.

Drinking is not common in a Muslim society, so when my so-called friends looked at my drunk step mother; I don't think they realized she was drunk until she did this:

"Everybody... is... here..." She couldn't even stand straight, and her eyes weren't opening properly. I had seen her like this before, and I knew she was drunk, "Having... fun... I... want to... have fun."

I facepalmed. She had started drinking 5 years ago, and I knew she was gonna keep talking bull-shit if I didn't send her back to her room.

"Someone please take her out of here!" I did not intend my voice to be this loud, but it felt like I was shouting.

"Someone's... being... bad..." She was still drunk, and she almost fell when she grabbed on to the couch for support, "Come... here... you..."

She got near me, and grabbed me as if to hug me. I wanted to get rid of her, but she was a big and fat lady. I couldn't understand why she had to grab me, until she did this. She reached under my waste, to my butt, and squeezed it as hard as she could.

Everyone just stood there watching, and I'm quite sure they had realized that she was drunk. When she squeezed my ass, I felt unprotected. I felt disgusted, and it felt as if she was just a nightmare, it all was just a nightmare. Because this wasn't all.

When I was 10 years old, I realized my sexuality. I was homosexual, because there was this pretty girl I had a huge crush on. Her name was Misha, and she was my class fellow. At first, I thought it was all very normal, but it was not normal, in fact it was all very wrong: according to my religion, according to my society, according to my family.

I used to be closer with my step-mom back then, she wasn't a drinker, she used to be more understanding, but she threw it all away. One night, I was crying my heart out when she came into my room:

"What happened dear?" She asked me as she sat by my bed, "Nightmare?"

I just shook my head, still sobbing. I was feeling the pain rising from my chest and going to my spine through my head.

"Then what?" She put a hand on my forehead, "Are you ill? Is it a cold?"

I shook my head again.

"What happened dear?" She tried to hug me, but I just pushed her away. I didn't want her to know anything, I had always been an introvert. I wasn't always this depressed weirdo, I was once a delicate little flower. People changed me.

"I'm a bad girl." I kept crying, but my shrieks became louder. I was choking, and she saw it. She saw me drowning in guilt, she was the only one ever to see me like this.

"Oh, no." She forcefully hugged me, "You can't be bad."

"No. I am." I wiped my tears, "I like girls."

"So, what?" She said as if she was oblivious to it all. Oblivious to everything.

"No. I mean I *like* girls."

"Oh…" She just exclaimed in surprise, "But why is it wrong?"

"Because girls liking girls is wrong."

"Oh dear, it is not." She just smiled at me, and for once I felt really comfortable around her, "Look Jiya. I love you, your father loves you, your mom loves you. You can't control who you like, now, can you? See? People judge, and they do it because other people judge them. It's like a chain, everybody tries to hide their flaws behind others, so they can all act good, be what people want them to be. You're good, okay? I know it's getting hard on you, but please, stop crying, okay? No matter what, I'll always understand you, and I'll always be there for you."

But then she started drinking just two years later, she never understood me anymore. She just left me alone, but it wasn't a real problem. I had grown too much in those two years, I had learnt to cope with my fears and handle my troubles. The only fear I ever had was her telling everything to my parents, because I couldn't tell anyone else about my sexuality. I would never fit in, and I knew what the consequences might be for trying to fit in. I couldn't let people know I was a lesbian.

My step mother had been molesting me since she started drinking, and she would always threaten me. I mean, it was a mistake to tell her about my sexuality, but it was even worse to trust her for a long period of time. I didn't know what was her deal, but she would always harass me; maybe she knew I didn't have a choice, because she knew I couldn't go anywhere with this.

Which brings us back to this day again, when she grabs my butt. I hear everyone gasp in the background, and I could feel a tear coming out of my eye, when I told her, "Fuck off."

I screamed so loud, I didn't even realize my birthday party was still going on. I realized quickly enough, and I turned to Hania and Sana

"See? This is exactly why I asked you to stop, but you bitches think this will help. Well, thanks a lot!"

My cheeks were red, hot with fear and anger. I was feeling catastrophic. I stormed out of there and went straight to my room. I did not believe what just happened, and as I locked the door, I kept hoping and saying to myself

"It's only just a dream."

"It's only just a bad dream." Because it happened very suddenly. It happened like a bad dream.

I kept crying all night. I was gay, and it wasn't my fault. I was rude, and it wasn't my fault. I had a pretty fucked up family, and it wasn't my fault. I still couldn't believe this just happened, and I grabbed my guitar once again.

I knew the pain was very real when the guitar wasn't helping anymore. So, I just plugged in my hands-free in my mobile phone, and started listening to all the sad songs I had sorted out in a playlist.

The pain was so bad, I thought it would actually burn my body. Like, you know when you're burnt, and you apply some sort of antiseptic or something on it, but it doesn't kill the pain as much as you'd hoped it would. Well, the songs were the antiseptic here, and the burns were just too deep to overcome. Not because it was just a butt grab, because I was all alone, I couldn't tell anyone how I was feeling. Feeling alone is by far the worst feeling of all.

I just came from my own birthday party, and I was all alone between those sixteen *friends*. Now I was laying here, and I was alone again. Suicidal and alone is never a good combination.

Hania started calling me, and I decided to ignore her. I mean, I didn't want to pick up. What would I reply? Like, "Hey, my step mom just grabbed my butt because she was drunk and I'm homo?" So, I tried to ignore her for as long as I could.

She started texting me.

Im sorry.

Hey?

Javeria?

Jiya, plz ans

Cum on, just pic up de fone.

I'm just trying 2 hlp

Luk, Javeria, I no exactly how u feel. Ive been embrrssd 2, u no – But bitch you have no idea how I'm feeling right now, because you are not homosexual, you don't have an abusive family. You are the queen of college, everybody loves you. I'm just another disappointment, even to my own self. I can't stand it when people try to be good to me, because the truth is no one has ever been good to me. They all act good at first, but then turn their heads away when I need them. Life is a ladder. Because no matter how hard I try, or how high I climb my ladder, I'm eventually gonna fall down, so, I never try to climb any higher. I'd actually like to never even try again, I just wanna try to not get myself hurt again. I'm always gonna fall down. For a part of my night, I had angry thoughts, but then came the beautiful part. I slept.

The college was supposed to start at 8 O'clock, but I never slept 'till 6 so when my actual mom tried to wake me up, I could never find the power to wake up.

"Wake up, sweetie pie."

"Go away, mom." I was still in my black outfit, which would have been scary if someone else knew I'd been wearing it for two days.

"But college?"

"Leave me alone." I was mad, mad at my real mom, mad at my step mom, mad at my college, but mostly mad at myself. "Just go away."

"Well, you're being granted today's day off only because it was your birthday yesterday…" She started explaining, and I was barely listening, "Also, try to get up still early, before Emaan comes back home from school and opens all the presents."

Emaan was my younger brother, and he was in the eighth grade. Out of all the people in my family: My parents, my stepparent, my aunts, uncles, cousins, he was the only person I truly loved, because he never judged me. He was too young to do that, and he always stood up for me. Even when three years ago my drunk step mom tried to beat the shit out of me with a cane, he stood up:

"Put that down. If you hurt Jiya aapi, I'll rip you apart in pieces."

I tried to get him away from this, I knew he could have been badly hurt. A drunk 30-year woman does not understand who is a cold 14-year-old teen ager or who is an 11-year-old innocent child.

I went to sleep again. I had always liked sleep, because there were only three things that helped me escape reality: Music, books and sleep. For once, I was the queen. And it was even better when I was writing my own songs or a short story or something, even though it was crappy, but in my own writings, I was the God. Yes, I wrote everything shitty, but I eventually was the God; and it felt good to have power.

Chapter 2:

I woke up at maybe 11 or 12 in the noon. I was still in my black outfit, when I decided to get off the bed. I saw my phone again, and Hania had texted:

I thought I was never gonna feel *like* it. But I had gone through worse times. This was just another ordinary thing, but I had never been harassed in front of my *friends,* and even though I disliked being fake, I didn't want people to know what kind of family I lived in.

I went down to the TV lounge again, and the decorations were now a mess. The party popper's ribbons were sprinkled all over the floor, and the balloons were still taped to the walls. The banner that said *Birthday girl rocks,* was still hanging, and it all somehow made my mood worse.

"Ugh." I said as I started cleaning the lounge. I didn't have to clean up the place, but I wanted to. Since, I couldn't clear up the mess I'd become, I could still clean up the mess that other people caused.

I played my favorite album of 2017 in the mp3 player I had bought from my own pocket money, and turned the volume to 100. Ed Sheeran's new album divide had fucking rocked me since I went to that trip to Ayubia with college.

My college finally decided to conduct an annual trip on March 3rd. I never liked to go on these trips, what's the point anyway? Just wasting money to waste time somewhere where the scenery might be just a little beautiful, or where the trees would call your name, and you could be on the top of a mountain and scream: I'm on top of the mountain, Cliché. So, when the college announced their trip to Ayubia, this hill station near Murree, it was the last thing on my mind.

I had told Hania I wouldn't go, so she never bought the ticket herself. It was 2000 bucks, why even waste that much money? Hania and I were like best buddies, but it all changed for a while.

There was only one girl I actually *liked* or had a *crush* on in college, and it was Zaib Abbasi. She was kinda like me, or at least she seemed like me. I never really knew her before that trip.

"Hey, Javeria, right?" She came up to me one day, and my heart started beating harder. She was just a little taller than me, and she was hot. She had the perfect curvy body, with her waist line emphasizing her ass, and her boobs were almost okay. She had a hot face, like that of Kristen Stewart, with her brows just a little thicker than average. She used to wear spectacles, and they looked awesome on her very light brown eyes. It was clear that I had no chance for her, since I was sure she was straight, and she was way hotter than me. "Look, I have this extra ticket. Bought it for a friend but she ditched me at the last moment. No one else wants it, will you please come with me? You don't even have to pay for the ticket, I just don't want to be alone."

"I don't want to..." I hesitated for a while. I had to think about it. I'm normally rude enough to say it straight away, but something got into me, "Maybe I can tell you about it later?"

"Oh, yes, thanks!" She looked a bit excited, "Please take this,"

She handed me over the ticket, and I refused.

"Woah, missy. I said I'll think about it."

"There is no one else I can take with me. If you still think the answer is no, you can burn the ticket up." She just smiled at me.

I tried to smile back but I'm sure it would have looked even creepier than usual, so I gave up.

"Ugh. Fine." I took the ticket, and took the rest of the classes.

I thought about it, again and again. I had already told Hania I wasn't going, and I didn't want to do this to her. If it was any other girl other than Zaib, I would have said "No" Straight away, but I guess I really liked her a lot. I would get to sleep with her, maybe cuddle her, Hug her. I mean, being homosexual wasn't easy, and I was a teenager. I just turned 17, how could I bear all of my hormones?

I decided to call Hania.

"Would it be bad if I decided to go on the trip, now?". I asked, as I realized what was coming.

"The tickets are sold out."

"Well, I got one somehow."

"What the hell?" Hania couldn't believe me, and her voice became louder.

"Zaib invited me, and it's free. It's just two days?"

"No. You called off the trip, I had no one else to go with. I couldn't go alone, and now you're doing this to me? What the hell?" I knew she was shaking her head behind the phone, I imagined her fury.

I didn't like her tone. She was getting offensive, I don't like it like that. So, I decided.

"I'm going, like it or not."

"If you go, we aren't talking anymore."

"I don't care," and I hung up the phone.

It was the morning of March 2nd, and I called Zaib to tell her I'm coming. It was just two days, it wasn't even a two-night stay. One day we'd go, and the next day we'd come back. There wasn't anything else to it, as I looked on the ticket:

- Departure: March 3rd 11 am

- Lunch at Murree (on house), estimated time 2 pm
- Tour of Murree Mall, until 6 pm
- Stay in tents: dinner and breakfast on the house.
- Trip to Ayubia in the morning, 10 am departure
- Stay at Ayubia 'till 2 pm
- Back to Islamabad, estimated time 6 pm

It looked reasonable, the price and everything, so I decided to pack my clothes. When a *sane* person opens my closet, they freak out. All I have in there is Black, black, black, white, grey, black, black.

All T-shirts, and only blue and black jeans. I knew it was gonna be colder in Murree & Ayubia, so I decided to pack a black zipper shirt and a *very* black Jacket too. They were supposed to keep me from getting cold, I guess. I didn't think they were warm enough.

By the time every other girl was busy with makeup and stuff, I was busy searching for songs. Music has some kind of special power, when you hear it, whatever you are feeling is stored into the music. It's like a gadget in a fairy tale. It takes away from your feelings, and gets it stored in itself, and whenever you hear that song again, all the feelings come back. Happy and sad feelings. Wonderful magic, music is.

I didn't just want any songs, I wanted songs to be good too. I came across the latest news. Ed Sheeran just released his new album. I had never been a fan of Ed's music, I still don't consider him the best, but his Album *Divide* really struck me. It just reached me, you know? It is my all-time favorite album.

I played songs one by one, and as I went through them, I thought, "Well, okay. Ed is a nice singer, but I'll download only those songs which I like. I need to have a memorable time, and surely songs will help." I ended up downloading all of the songs because they were all so good.

The trip was quite fun actually, when it started. Even though I was sitting next to Zaib Abbasi, I couldn't really throw my image in the gutter and start gossiping with her.

"Hey, you want bubble gum?" Zaib handed me a stick of gum, and I took it.

"Thanks." I started chewing gum, and plugged my hands-free into my phone, and started listening to Ed's album.

Zaib reached my left ear, and pulled one of the sides of the hands-free out of my ear.

"Here is a fun advice," I smiled sarcastically, "If you want to reach Murree alive, don't do that again."

"But I want to talk."

She brought her long arm from behind my neck, and tried to hug me. If it was someone else, I might have even killed her, but Zaib was different. She was also wearing a black outfit that day, which was attractive to say the least. I liked her a lot, and see, as hard as it is to say, it is the truth also: I did actually like her hugging me.

People tend to like each other for personal gains, even though I liked her because of how hot and attractive she was. I mean, even if we were *just* friends, I could spend at least some time with her.

I loved how my heart would go from beating at its fullest to so calm that it felt like I didn't have blood at all, when I was near her. Like an ocean, I was like an ocean. I never knew when the tide was coming, but it would eventually come, and then I'll be in waves. I'll be restless, and for once I'd be in pain without even feeling it. But then I'll go calm, and then even a single ripple would hurt me like it's the end of the world.

"Oh yeah? Let's see if you can find a topic interesting enough."

"Heard you can sing?" OH DAMN IT. SHE DID FIND A TOPIC.

Okay, here was my weakness. I mean, I was a good singer, and I liked that I could sing. And I liked to show off that I could sing. My Ocean wasn't calm now, and it was ready to roar.

"Kind of." I replied.

"So, what kind of music do you like?"

"I like everything long as it is good. I'll go from Pink Floyd to Eminem, Linkin' park to Ed Sheeran. I have no boundaries."

"I think I already like you." She smiled, but on the inside, I felt: NO BITCH, WE DON'T SMILE. but I decided otherwise, and I smiled back.

We just kept talking about music, until we were tired. Not like physically or mentally tired, but tired of talking about the same thing. So, we tried to open the conversation.

"What are your hobbies?" She asked.

"Umm… playing and singing and planning how to kill others. That's pretty much it."

"I see, you're a serial killer as well, huh." She smirked like she thought I was joking, "And hey, you play guitar?"

"I am kind of still in the learning process, but I kind of can play *Hero* on it, now."

"God, I wanna hear you sing so bad."

I wanted to sing, but see, no matter how much I liked my voice, and no matter how much I thought my voice was going to make me a star one day, I was still insecure. I couldn't sing in front of her. I couldn't open up that much to her. The moment I open up to people, is the moment tragedy starts.

"No." I said at once.

"Why not?"

"Because I don't sing to people."

"But you like to sing."

"What is your problem?" Now I was mad. I mean, I told her I wasn't going to sing, and she was resisting my decision. I am the queen, at least of my own world, I would kill you for trying to step into my kingdom. "Who told you I sing, anyway?"

She hesitated for a while, but then told me, "Hania."

I did not react to this. There were many questions, like, does she talk to Hania? Because Hania never mentioned that, or did she *specifically* talk to her, so she could find more about me? I just let it go and stuffed my hands-free back in my ears.

Zaib saw this, but this time she decided to ignore me.

Zaib didn't bother me, 'till we actually stopped for a while to get refreshments, and use the washroom. I hadn't realized how quickly time passed, until Zaib patted me on my shoulder.

"C'mon."

I looked around for a while, and I realized the bus had stopped. People were getting off, but they were leaving their stuff behind. I realized we had stopped on a rest-area.

"No." I told Zaib, "I would rather stay in the bus."

She left me again, and I kind of liked that. She wasn't faking anything, she was true. She let me be myself, and this was helping her gain my trust somehow.

She came back, sat next to me. Offered me a can of coke, and I took it. She also offered me salted Pringles, but I refused. I hated Pringles.

The trip seemed to get longer and longer. It was really uncomfortable to sit next to Zaib, and pretend not to notice whatever she was doing. People are the worst creations of God, and if demons really do exist, I'd loved to be one.

We reached Murree, after an uncomfortable trip of three hours, trying to get comfortable sitting; but the scenery, well it still wasn't worth it. I mean, so we are on top of a hill station, big deal?

As I walked across, I saw that the hills were getting steeper. I liked it only in one sense, If I jumped from there, I'd surely die. Probably, people won't even find my body. I'd finally be alone like I wanted to be alone.

Before Hania, or Sana or whatever, I was still alone. I was alone when they came into my life, and over all the years with Hania, I had still been alone. But I was never *really* alone, because being alone means having no one. I wasn't actually alone, I was just lonely, and loneliness is much worse than being alone. People are around you, but you still can't be around them. You do what they say, but they'll never listen to what you say. They just don't understand. I wanted to be alone, because when I'd finally be alone, I won't be feeling lonely anymore. I won't have my family or my *friends* with me, but I'll have my songs, and my books, and myself. I had always felt like running away, and never returning. I had always wanted to make people forget my existence, I just wanted a new life. I didn't actually want to die, I just wanted my current life to end, because if there was another life, I could hope to live that one better.

"This is beautiful." Zaib looked across the valley, over the trees. The sky was cloudy, but not like *rain* cloudy, they were white clouds. The air was fresher up there, and the view was taking *our* breaths away. Ugh, cliché.

"No. Death is beautiful."

"Sometimes I think, this beauty is what we really live for." She ignored me, "We all look for beautiful faces, beautiful places, beautiful music. We just want a beautiful life, but some of us' life is so tragic, that we can't find beauty anymore. Maybe that's why we find the concept of death a little more mesmerizing, maybe because there's nothing more beautiful than eternal silence." She just smiled at me, but this smile was different, this girl was different, and it felt as if she was saying something from behind her smile, as if she was saying, "Please help me."

Passing that beautiful hilly area, we reached the Mall. Mall was just this long road, which was slightly developed (and still underdeveloped.) I mean, there was nothing special about it, except that there was a market which sold different goods, and restaurants which sold crappy food, and charged extra money for it.

Zaib suddenly stopped at a shop, went inside and brought two tiaras on her way back.

"Try this on."

"No, not at all." I said at once, I was disgusted just by the looks of it. "Burn this thing down."

"Come on." She smiled, "It'll be fun."

And the most cliché thing happened, someone in the market played some sort of Irish music. It made me remember Ed Sheeran's Irish touch in his new album, which was amazing, but pure Irish music sucked.

Out of nowhere, Zaib started tap dancing. I'm not particularly a fan of dancing, but she was dancing quite well. It felt as if she had been taking classes, but still EWW.

"What the hell are you doing?" I moved away a little, trying to not make a fool out of myself standing with a dancer who was making a fool out of herself.

"Come on." She was looking pretty, and excited. She was enjoying this moment, and I was disgusted. I wondered how two *this* different people can still have a similar vibe. "It's fun."

"I think I'll pass."

I just continued walking, while I could hear people chanting in the background. Zaib was once again in the limelight. If this was *normal,* I was glad to be quirky.

I reached our destined hotel. I texted Zaib at once, because I didn't want her to be late, even though I was early. I think I just wanted some company, but I used the *be on time* BS.

She arrived in like five minutes, and then we sat there, waiting for everyone else to come. We ate the traditional *daal-chawal,* with cold-drinks, and then we were off to hang around again. It was boring, to say the least. Long day, and finally it was over, and we got to a meadow. It was just above six, and already getting dark. The management set up our tents, and a bonfire between the tents aligned in a circle. We just sat there, warmed ourselves on the fire, and cooked some BBQ over the bonfire. It was getting a little better.

When Zaib and I got into our tents, she pulled something out of her backpack. A complete case of an imported cigarette. It was expensive, it must have been expensive.

"Have some." She opened the pack, and faced it towards me.

I didn't want that cigarette, but I couldn't stop myself from taking it into my hands, "Why would people even smoke this?"

"No one is happy." She said as she went out of the tent. I followed her. It was late at night, and everyone was asleep.

Zaib just kept walking in the cold, and I had also left my jacket back. She just kept walking and walking, until she reached the end of a hill, and I knew if she had walked any further, she would fall down. I screamed, "STOP RIGHT THERE, ZAIB!"

She stopped, but she didn't turn. She was looking down the hill, and it almost felt as if she would jump from there. If she did have, I couldn't have stopped her anyway.

"What are you doing?" I pulled her away from the edge. I was afraid of heights, and I wasn't ashamed. Heights can kill people.

"No one is happy." She was crying, now. Her tears were hurting me, I was calm, but her tears were creating the ripples. She said again, under her breath, "No one is happy."

She sat on the ground, and lighted the cigarette. She put it in between her soft lips. Her lips were so pink, it was hurting me. Her eyes were so magical, it was hurting me. Her face was so beautiful, it was hurting me.

I had never smoked before, but when the *sad* Zaib handed me the lighter, I didn't give it too much of a thought. I just said, "Fuck it." And lit up the cigarette. As I touched the filter before my lips, something amazing went through me. I inhaled, and the smoke filled up my mouth. I could only take just a little bit of smoke inside, before I started coughing like crazy. I did that again, and somehow after the third or fourth try, I was smoking normally.

Smoking was like music, not songs, pure music. It made no sense, it had a sour taste and effect, and it actually killed people, but it was still so satisfying. It wanted me to smoke it again and again, until I had cancer or was dead any other way. I just wanted to keep smoking.

The night was getting darker, and at the point where the cigarettes couldn't keep us warm anymore, Zaib held me close. She just hugged me, and laid her head on my shoulder. She kept crying, and I could feel her tears running around my arms. This was the moment I decided to sing, and I sang the Ed Sheeran song, *How would you feel?*

You are the one girl, and you know that it's true

I'm feeling younger, every moment that I spend with you.

That song had a calming tune, and I loved how I could shape my voice into anything I wanted. From dead rock metal, to a soft Sheerio melody.

"You have a nice voice." She said as she closed her eyes. Breathing against me, her nose letting out faint smokes of water vapours. I was somehow mesmerizing, to watch her fall asleep

I didn't realize I was falling asleep too. I used to imagine death, every time before I fell asleep. I mean, there's more chance of never waking up than waking up happy the next day, for me. And it didn't really matter to me, until I saw her fall asleep. She was like an innocent soul, though I was sure she wasn't pure. No one is pure, just like no one is happy.

It felt nice, as I put my hand on her forehead, and felt the temperature being radiated by her head. The warmth was satisfying, with her breathing next to me. The air was cold, and her breaths were still spitting warm water vapors which were being condensed by the coldness of air, making a white *smoke*, like she was smoking in her dreams. I thought about it, only the smoke was less dense, so I thought it was harmless, and thus not credible.

And then I fell asleep, but in a split second, I was awake again. Moments are like sleep, you enjoy it while it lasts, but then it is gone. It's over. In a split second, and then you just remember the dreams, like it's some sort of magic. You never know the true value of a moment until it becomes a memory.

As I woke up, I noticed it was still dark, we were still almost to the edge of the clip, and Zaib was smoking again.

"Don't smoke." I asked her to keep *death* away from herself, even though I was always a strong believer that dying old is hypocrisy, and dying young is perverted envy.

"No one is happy." She claimed, again.

"I know." I wanted to ask her *what's wrong?* But then I gave up the idea, because to be fair, if I was smoking in the middle of night with some person I barely knew, on the edge of a hill, wanting to die, wanting to end all my problems right there, I wouldn't say a thing, even if the person asked, "That's the only thing you've said to me since you handed me the cigarettes."

"I want to die."

"We're on the edge of a hill, you know." And I swear, at that moment she had jumped, I had jumped behind her, because, why not? It would be crazy, but awesome. No awesome thing is awesome without a little crazy.

"That'd be nice." She looked at me, and then stared into the darkness of night, "But that's where you got me wrong. I want to die, but I cannot die."

"Why not?"

"Because I have to leave a mark before I go."

"Ugh. Cliché." I rolled my eyes at her, and I had to. Just when I thought we could be a little closer, she says the dumbest thing of all. *Leave a mark*, like it's painting a wall black, and then just put a white dot in the middle. "You know what? Just have a kid, name him Mark, leave him in the middle of a forest and be done with it."

"Puns." She almost laughed, not smiling somehow, but managing to laugh anyway, "I like you."

I just shook my head, and asked her to hand me over another cigarette. We smoked another cigarette, and another, and we continued, like there was no tomorrow.

And then came, what I recall, a beautiful memory. We stared into the horizon, over the valleys, over the mountain, and a beautiful orange sunlight just rising. It was warm, and it felt nice on the skin. After the cold night, a freshening sunshine had arrived.

"Let's go." I grabbed Zaib's arm as I stood up, and started walking back. She just kept following, walking at least 3 feet behind, and not uttering a single word.

I had not realized that we had come this long a way, last night. It was charming the previous night, but it was just tiring the next morning. It was an hour of walk, if not more, and it felt as if I would collapse any moment.

We reached our camping site, where people were coming out of their tents. A teacher saw us coming back, and started screaming his lungs about how worried he was, and I wanted to just punch him in the face. Of course, I couldn't, because I didn't care anymore after the first two minutes.

We had breakfast at around 8, and we were off to Ayubia by 10. I liked how they planned the whole trip, there were no time delays, everything was planned.

In the bus, for the hour-long journey, they decided to play Antakshari. Basically, this game where you have to start a song with the last letter of the song the opponent team had sung.

I enjoy music, and I could play Antakshari, only if I was playing only with my cat, alone in the corner of my room, also considering the fact that I did not have a cat. I do enjoy music, yes, but I don't enjoy a bunch of no-good-vocals guys singing the most cliché songs that have ever existed, so I decided to play *Divide* again, and as I listened to the songs, I realized how magical last night was, and how I want to hold on to Zaib, because even when she wasn't *that* close to me, she was still pretty right there with me.

As I listened to the songs, I reached out and held Zaib's hand. She had faced the other way, since she was playing a stupid game with no-sense-of-singing-or-choosing-songs, she did not turn around. She might have thought of turning around, because she moved a little, but she never actually turned around, and I kind of liked that.

Holding her hand was making my ocean all wavy and in unrest again, because that's what I was. A minute calm, the next minute not calm anymore. I was the ocean. But nothing could hurt me at that moment. It was a paradox, like Robert Graves' poem *In broken Images,* See, if a person is sure about something, he has clear images about it. He's never doubting them anymore, he trusts them blindly, but when it matters, he realizes he's made a mistake and trusted too much. A person who does not have clear images, will never trust them blindly, and they will make him reason. There is never certainty, even if you're sure, it can all go bad. And even if you're not sure, it is actually good that you reason. I was only hurt when I was calm, but when I was in severe unrest, and anxious, and everything seemed like it would hurt me, It never really did hurt me, until I was calm again, of course.

I had seen snow before, and I do remember how excited I was when I saw it for the first time. It's actually my earliest memory, when I stick my tongue out trying to let the snowflake fall on my tongue, so I could actually taste how nature felt. I stuck my tongue out, and I know that one or two snowflakes landed right on my taste buds, but it didn't taste like anything. There was no taste, not even like water or ice, I did not even feel it landing there, I just saw the snowflakes had flown over the people and into my mouth, but it having no taste was disappointing.

When I reached Ayubia, it had snowed there. The snow was all over the ground, like a white blanket on top of a sleeping child (and I almost thought as if the child would wake up, and everyone will be surprised, but not me, because that's me, I don't get surprised).

We walked to the ticket counter for a chairlift that would take us to the top of the hill station, and Zaib said as we walked.

"I like snow."

"Huh?" I realized she had said something to me, and it was about *liking snow*, so I replied, "Yeah, me too." Because I actually did like snow, but I liked it more when it was falling.

"I just hope it falls, too." She smiled at me.

"If nature wanted it to, it would fall." I talked in a tone that wasn't optimistic, because I wasn't optimistic, and didn't give a fuck about will it or will it not snow, or I didn't *hope* it would snow, I just *wanted* it to snow. Like, there's nothing I can possibly do about it, so why hope? Or why care? Just want.

"Yeah." She seemed upset.

We bought the tickets, and handed it to the ticket collector after a long line at the chairlift spot. It was kind of awkward getting on the chairlift, because the lift can't afford to stop. You have to jump on it while it's moving, so, when I jumped, I realized Zaib hadn't sat properly, and she was about to fall when I held her from her curvy waist, and pulled her back.

"Thanks." She sighed in relief, "I could have been hurt."

"Yeah, I figured out it won't kill you, so, I decided it wasn't going to be fun watching you fall and get *just* injured." This was exactly why I didn't have friends. I didn't want friends anyway.

"Thanks anyway."

As the chairlift rose, the ground grew further, and my fear of heights was there to battle my anxiety again. Zaib noticed my unrest, and asked at once, "What happened?"

"I am acrophobic." I replied, with trying to not look down, but each time I tried to look away, something in my brain decided that I should look down again, and the seesaw continued the whole *chairlift journey*.

"You don't look like an acrophobic, at first sight."

"I don't like a singer at first sight, either."

"Well, that's true." She held my hand, as if suggesting *I'm not gonna let go*, "I guess people really are mysteries, huh?"

"I guess."

As the chairlift kept rising, an area came where the ground below us started to rise too. It was where the hill started rising, and as we *flew* over it, I heard a beautiful voice, singing some kind of qawwali in the local language. I couldn't understand what he was saying, because I didn't understand Pashto, but his notes were on point. Acapella, between the mountains, and I knew it was hard to sing.

"This is beautiful." I almost screamed, I didn't *usually* scream.

"You think so?" Zaib took out a fifty Rupee bill from her pocket, and wrapped it in itself, and threw it as near the boy qawwal as she could, "I hope he gets the money."

I looked at the paper falling, like it was a snowflake, but will it reach the child? Does it have any taste? I could only wonder, but another thought hit me, such a beautiful voice, but for what? Will he spend all of his life there, just waiting for 50-rupee bills to be thrown at him, so he could get enough money to eat? And that's where I thought of Zaib's *mark*, but I guessed that mark did not have to be a mark of fame, maybe that mark was something like the mark of that boy. I don't know about anyone else, but he certainly left a mark in my heart, and I didn't even understand his words, but I think I understood his feelings. That's the thing about songs, or qawwalis, or music, it isn't meant to be understood verbally, it's meant to be understood emotionally.

Once we were on top, the view became pretty attractive. I never admired pretty places, or even pretty people. I just wanted, I never admired, or liked, or did anything else; I just wanted, either them or to be like them. I think I admired the top, though, not because of the look, but it had some sort of vibe.

The snow was everywhere, and it just made me remember my childhood maybe, it was simply mesmerizing.

"It's beautiful." I told Zaib, even though I didn't look at her. I was staring at the snow bed, and the trees that were covered in snow, and the rides that were covered in slightly less snow, and the people who were wearing big coats and jackets, and playing in the snow, covered in the snow.

Zaib looked at me, and smiled. I saw that from the corner of my eyes, and asked, "What?"

"Well, I don't usually say stuff. I am more of a thinker." The air was so charming up there, it actually made me start uttering true words. I don't usually say phrases like *it's beautiful,* or *I am more of a thinker*, but that was true.

"I like it when you stay stuff."

"You do, others don't." I slightly tilted my head.

"I'm sure they deserve a try." She smiled. She had a pretty smile.

"Sure." I started walking straight, and I did not realize the people I was passing. Were they looking at me? Was I something special, because I was feeling special and it hurt to only feel special, and not be special, like the times when I sit in the corner of my room, singing songs, just feeling special but never being special.

As I walked, something soft hit me on top of my head. It was cold and wet, and I at once realized it was a snowball. I turned around, and it was Zaib.

"I normally don't do this, but..." I picked up some snow from the ground, and started making a ball between my gloves. The gloves were getting wet, and I didn't care. I made a ball, and aimed it at Zaib's head, "Take this." I threw it, and immediately remembered taking aim wasn't easy with snowballs.

"Oh, you!" Zaib made another snowball, and we kept playing that game. I liked it, and maybe I even laughed. I didn't like laughing, but I can't control a few things.

We just danced in the snow, like snow would never be able to be seen again. It was magical, pure, and powerful, up there, with Zaib. I did not realize what was happening, but it was something different, it was something extraordinary.

All the time there, I wanted it to snow. But it didn't. It never did. *Wants* don't always become facts, and that's a fact. It's irrational to not accept that.

We were on our way back at exactly 2 o'clock, and on my way back, I thought about how this could all be a start with my friendship with Zaib, and how it felt to sit under the moonlight, on the edge of a hill. How beautiful it would be to do that again, maybe not in Ayubia, maybe in Islamabad, on top of *Damin-e-koh*.

We got back to college, already tired. I called my dad to pick me up, and he was the first one to arrive so I was the first one to go home. Zaib hugged me, and I would always remember that hug, because I thought everything was going to change.

Not everything, but something did change. Two days later, when I attended college, I noticed Hania was still mad at me. She wasn't even talking to me, and that was when she made Sana her friend. I did not care, because I was too excited about Zaib. I had not called her, because I didn't want to rush anything, but the day at college, she ignored me. She didn't want to talk to me, and she clearly said that. I was perplexed, confused, I didn't understand why. She wasn't my friend, no one became a friend in two days. And, I was alone again. I had lost Hania, and Zaib. To the moment when I actually cried in the bathroom of my college, I was torn apart. I was lonely, I didn't really mind being alone. But, Hania couldn't stand my pain anymore. Two weeks later, she came to me, and apologized. This is how I knew she cared about me. She didn't love me. It was stupid to think love existed, because it was not a thing. But she cared about me, and that is why I tried to be less rude to her. Hania was an incredible friend, but I was a terrible one. I didn't want people, because I didn't deserve them. I decided never to care again, never to sit and talk in an emotional time, I decided that there was only one part of my life I would ever care about: music. .

So, when the songs played the album while cleaning, it reminded me of Zaib, and smoking, and snow. It was saddening, yes, it was depressing. I had never smoked ever since, but whenever I played *Divide*, I felt as if I was smoking again. Brilliant thing, music is.

Hania texted me from the class.

"Dude?"

"Yeah?"

"Coming 2 colege 2moro?"

"college*"

"wutevr"

"I'll be there probably."

"k Im having dun

Fub*

Fun*"

"*laughing emoji*", I used to type *laughing emoji* instead of actually sending the emoji. Though both of them were cliché, saying it was more fun.

"itz difficult 2 typ under de table ok???"

"Okay", I thought. And then I sat with my *gifts*. I could already see what the gifts were, even from outside of the packing. *Clothes, clothes, clothes, books, perfume, and another book.* I guessed it absolutely right, a pink and a blue T-shirt, both of which I threw away. I black pair of jeans, which I kept. A book: *Men are from Mars, Women are from Venus*, which I never read because obviously men and women are both from planet Earth, a perfume whose smell wasn't even slightly likeable, and another book of poems which I started to read, but it was so boring that I even forgot the title.

Emaan came from school at around 2, just when I was finished cleaning, and as soon as he came, he didn't even change and brought me my guitar.

"Do you want me to sing?" I asked

"Yes." He smiled.

"Which song?"

"Fireflies!" He shouted, and his shouts were so pure, it was amazing. Like, he didn't want to listen to me just because I sang well, he loved me, and he wanted to spend time with his sister.

"Nice choice. Owl city."

> And then I began singing, as he sang with me.
>
> *You would not believe your eyes*
>
> *if ten million fireflies*
>
> *Lit up the world as I fell asleep*

It was amazing to see him enjoy my singing. I wanted to do that to a crowd, who'd just watch me sing. Who didn't care who I was, who believed that I could sing. Who wanted to spend some time with me.

Chapter 3:

The next morning, I went to college, and everyone just made it feel like they had totally forgotten about the incident. I was sure they had not, but that's how things would go. They'd talk about it behind my back, but never a word up front.

I met Hania at the gate, and she seemed pleased to see me.

"Yes!" She screamed so loud, the guard gave us a look saying *Go inside already, or let the wrath of God be upon you.*

"You are glad because I have come to a place of eternal misery?" Which was not true, college was better than home, but it was partly true because I could not play guitar or sing at the college.

"No, because I don't have to bear the misery alone."

"Yeah, right. I bring rainbows after the rain, and bring candies out of unicorns' hair." I rolled my eyes.

"Exactly." Her green eyes smiled at me again, and it felt cute but weird.

"Cliché."

"You say that a lot, you know."

I knew I said that a lot, because everything was super cliché. Literally, everything. Including people, and life itself.

"Guess what I found out?" Hania winked at me, and I knew it was going to be stupid.

"That I still hate you? And the world? And it would be amazing if the world goes to ashes?"

"Nope. Even better."

She took out her mobile, and showed me a picture. A girl, who had almost the same face structure as me, but was nowhere near like me. Uglier.

"I was surfing the web," Hania continued, "And then I came across this girl. She looks exactly like you."

"Eww." I said as we walked towards the class, "No way. I think she's the only person in the whole world who is uglier than me."

"SHE IS EXACTLY LIKE YOU."

"She is not!" I could have argued, with facts, but it's unwise to argue with a stupid person, because they won't ever accept that. "But I guess a bitch like you won't accept that she's the only person who is uglier than me."

"Even Sana thinks that." Yeah, like Sana is any less idiotic.

"Whatever."

We moved to the class, and English's lecture. Our teacher, Kamaal Khan was just another dumb guy, who knew a little bit of more English than me – er – I, and he would just dictate us the book. I could never focus on what he was speaking, even when he was dictating *good-bye Mr. Chips*, because a) He was too boring, and b) he had a tone that would make you fall asleep almost at once. I thought of recording his voice, so while those insomnia nights, I could finally be able to sleep.

The next Lecture was Pakistan Studies, which was basically the history and geography of *just* Pakistan. I never learnt about Cleopatra, or Tutankhamun, or Alexander the great from school or colleges, but I did know that Liaquat Ali Khan was murdered due to something I don't remember.

I liked Professor Hanif, not because he taught us Pakistan Studies, because he would go off topic every now and then. He didn't just teach us, he was one of the very few people I had known to actually make students think out of the box. He had these short sessions where he would answer any of students' questions, no matter what they were, about life, curriculum, people, it didn't matter. He also conducted those few speeches, where we would speak in front of the whole class. I liked him, though I never asked him any questions, ever, until that day.

"Why is homosexuality a sin, professor?"

Talking about sex, sexuality, even love openly was considered a taboo, and it was no surprise that the whole class gasped at my curiosity.

"Because that's what God says." He replied.

"But God made people like that." I continued, "If he didn't want people to be gay, why would he make them gay?"

"Homosexuality is a choice. Homosexuality is an influence."

"You are wrong." He was wrong. For a while, I thought being homosexual was wrong, I didn't know why. Until I came across an article, which had all the long words I couldn't understand when I was little, but it made me realize that being gay wasn't wrong. I was a lesbian, and it doesn't matter because I was, am, and will be a human being until I die. That article might have influenced me to come out, but not *be* gay. "Every person has a gay gene. It's an attachment to chromosome Xq28, which is why people are gay. It doesn't attach to every person's DNA, but the people's DNA it attaches, makes them gay. It's by birth, it's not a choice. It's a reality. People can't just run away from reality."

He remained quiet, and then asked me to sit down, as I did. "Fuck everyone," I thought. "Run away from reality." But then it hit me, run away.

Hania started texting me from under her desk again, and I was too busy thinking about running away, when she was texting *Numb*.

"Ive bcum so numb

I cnt feel u der

Bcum so tired

So much more sumthng-er"

"Stop ruining the song," I replied, "I have got A BRILLIANT Plan."

"………"

"Ellipses have only three dots."

"wutevr"

"I'll tell you about it after class."

"k"

"Why the hell are you obviously overexcited?" Hania asked me the moment I was out, and since Sana did not have a class, and somehow despite her studying pre-engineering, she was hanging around too, "Did Kodaline release a new single?"

"Or is it that all the guitar players have vanished and they want you to play?" Joined Sana. She thought she was funny, which was far from true.

The three of us remained quiet for a while, when Hania turned to Sana and said *chuss* (slang for lame) to which she laughed her lungs out and both Sana and I just watched her laugh, wishing it was going to be over soon.

"Okay, what is it?" Hania asked again, trying to get a hold of herself.

"It's a lifesaving plan."

"umm..." Sana hesitated a little, "Won't this be the time where you explain the plan?"

"Well, you both know the story of the tortoise and the hare." I begin explaining, "The thing is, I'm the tortoise, and everyone around me is either the hare or the animal community that expects me to lose. But here's the deal, my parents are the readers, and they think the tortoise will *slowly and steadily* win the race, but..."

"What's the difference between a tortoise and a turtle?" Sana asked.

"Don't interrupt me with your idiocy." I continued, "But, the thing is the hare is never going to stop here. I mean, the hare is going to win, so what can I actually do to make him stop? Because if he never stops, there is absolutely no chance that I can win. What do I do?"

"What?" Hania and Sana said at the same time, they almost jinxed.

"I play it by my way."

"err-?" They both looked confused, closing their cheek muscles like it was some sort of rocket science.

"I don't take the traditional path. I choose the path with a river between the finish and starting line, the hare can never cross it, and I am a brilliant swimmer."

"Meaning?"

"I run away." I smiled, "Literally."

"What?" Hania shouted, "Run away? Like – what the hell? Explain."

"I've decided to run away."

Sana kept quiet.

"Run away to where?"

"I don't know where. Just away." I raised my shoulders a little.

"That's ridiculous." Hania shook her head.

For a moment, I thought it was ridiculous, because running away from home was a big step. Hania knew exactly what I was talking about, because she knew how much I hated my family. Even though I didn't talk much, she knew I hated them, frankly, I hated every living soul on the planet. Well, maybe not every, but mostly.

"What about Emaan?" Sana broke the silence.

What about him? I thought. I had not thought about him when the idea first came to my mind, because surely, I was excited over being free for once. As much as I loved Emaan, I couldn't be a slave of my parents for life. It was going to come, sooner or later.

"He'll learn to live without me."

"This is madness." Hania claimed again.

"Hania, you're a bitch. I do whatever I want, with or without your help." I was offended, because for once I had a brilliant set-up in my mind, for once I knew that I could be independent. I liked the idea of running away, "You in or not?"

Hania looked at Sana, and Sana looked at her phone. Maybe a new message, maybe the time, and then she looked up, and both of them nodded at me, and I nodded back.

"What's the plan?" asked Sana.

"Okay, here it is." I had thought of the plan during the lecture. I thought It was perfect. "My step-mom, my dad, and my real mom are all going to Lahore next week-end at *Data Ganj Baksh*. Now, the thing is they are very less likely to take me, and also I can't ask them to me because that would ruin the whole concept of *me*. So, I still have to figure out how I'm going to get with them, and once I'm there, I'm free as a bird."

"Where will you stay?"

"I'll get a hotel, or a flat, or something. Heck, I'll live on the streets if I have to."

"This is a plan? This is barely even a thought." Hania was furious, because there were two things a) I didn't really have a great plan, and b) I was going away from her.

"It just occurred okay? Better than what your dumb mind could ever come up with." I raised my eyebrows a little, "I still don't know why I hadn't thought of running away from home before this seriously. I have thought about it before, but now I'm going to do it."

"You know what, Jiya?" Sana put her arm around my shoulder, and whispered into my ear, "You want to run away, and there's no reason why I won't help you with it, but the thing is, it's not the best of plans yet."

Hania brought out a water bottle, and pushed it against the palm of my hands, "Drink this. You need to relax."

"What the hell?" I got mad, because I was trying to discuss a life changing plan with two of my closest companions, and they were not even slightly interested. Why weren't they? Obviously because they didn't understand me.

"Chill, dude." Hania held my other hand, and laid it on top of the bottle, "Are you even sure what you're even gonna do there?"

"I don't know!" I screamed, and threw the bottle away, "Maybe I'll join a band or something, or do something else, I just don't want to be in this hell. It's more than I can take."

I pulled my bag back on my shoulder, and walked almost as fast as if I were running. I didn't look back to see if they were following me, but I was sure they were not. No one could ever handle my temper, even if they were Sana, or Hania, or even myself.

I took the rest of the classes, and did not talk to Hania. I guess, it was now a thing, if any of us were mad at anyone else, we'd just not talk. My ocean wasn't calm the whole day, and it didn't seem to get any better. Even Hania didn't try to talk to me, or text me, because she knew what I was thinking was complete and utter bullshit.

When I got home, I thought of sleeping for a while. Not because I had done a lot of physical exercise, my body wasn't tired at all, I think I was getting used to sleeping a lot. I rarely had any dreams, and I never told anyone about them, but some nights I wanted to have dreams, because dreams are the fantasies which are not real at all, but we still experience them. It's funny how that is even possible, even though it's completely normal.

At around 7 in the evening, a sudden thunder woke me up. It was my dad and my step mom fighting, and it was over something very silly. Everything was silly, the fights, the reasons for the fights, my step-mom's drinking habits, her molesting me, my whole life was just a silly point.

I walked out of the room, and let a big sigh. This was routine for me. I went out, and saw Emaan trying to stop them from fighting, and trying to calm them down, and I just stood watching. My real mum was also just watching, and we were both fed up with this.

"How long?" I asked my mom, without even looking at her.

"At least an hour." She just kept sipping from her tea, and never looked at me.

I looked at her now, "That means an hour more, eh?"

"Sure does." She took another sip, and gulped.

It was like I was immune to this all, like the world was screaming in front of me, trying its best to make my life miserable, but I had faced this for too long now. I still remember the times I hoped everything would be normal, and I would have a normal life again, but I gave up the hope way back. I never really understood why out of 7 billion people around the globe, it was me who had to suffer. I had never really understood that *no one is happy.*

At last Emaan was tired, tired of trying to stop what couldn't have been stopped. He came up to me, and spoke

"I tried my best." He looked down, making a fist and pressing it hard enough to hurt himself.

"Again." I smiled at him, "What you did was the best anyone can do. They just won't stop arguing."

I didn't really ask him to give up trying to stop our parents, because he had hope that one day our step mom and dad might get along. I was sure it wasn't going to happen, but killing hope is worse than the truth factor.

"Hey. Don't cry." I started wiping the tears flowing out of his eyes, and pressed the palm of my hands against his cheeks, "Don't worry. One day, everything will be alright, and then you'll know the true value of things. Trust me." I smiled.

"You promise?"

"I pinky promise, bruh."

And Finally, Emaan smiled back.

Emaan and I got back into my room, and we could hear the screaming and shouting no more. The *argument* was finally over, and I sat down next to Emaan.

"Sing me a song!" He held my guitar.

"Which one?"

"A happy song."

"Okay." I smiled, "let's make a deal. You strum and I'll play the chords on the fretboard, okay?"

"Okay."

And Emaan strummed while I made chords with my left hand. I sang *Smile by Mikky Ekko*

Smile, the worst is yet to come

We'll be lucky if we ever see the sun

Got nowhere to go, we'll be alright

But the future is forgiven, so smile.

"Hey, you're playing so good." I spoke and began singing again.

"Thanks!" he said, and then we sang the chorus together.

It was all good. Maybe Emaan was why I had not been practical about running away before, and maybe his presence was why I was restricting myself to not overthink it. Frankly, Emaan was my favorite person, and I couldn't leave him behind with these monsters, I didn't want him to turn out like me. Alone, rude, and dangerous.

I thought about running away again, and I thought about the consequences. The only consequence that was holding me back was Emaan, and how would he turn out, would he miss me? Would he accept the fact that I finally had to go? Or would he never understand why I left him behind? I thought about it. It was about my freedom, or Emaan's. I didn't want to be selfish, because I did care more about Emaan more than I did about myself, but *running* away from home wasn't just about my freedom, it was an opportunity to prove that I can stand alone, I can do incredible stuff on my own. Definitely, running away was the right choice, but somehow, I was not ready to accept it yet.

Hania called me later, and I decided to pick up.

"Dude?"

"Yeah?"

"I'm sorry about today, but running away is not really a good plan, especially when you don't know where to go."

"Ugh." I rolled my eyes even though I knew she couldn't see me. She did have a point though, running away from home without a proper concept of *how* to run away, and *where* to run away was stupid.

"So, Sana and I checked out for places you can stay at in Lahore." She smiled, she must have smiled, I could feel it.

"What?" I said calmly. "You're actually with me on this? That's... that's great. I think I might be a little merciful now before feeding you to the piranhas."

"Please be nice to me sometimes."

"Shut up."

"Anyway," She let out a tiring sigh, "I searched, and Sana searched and we have found someone whom you can talk to if you want to find a place in Lahore."

"Thank you?"

"But wait, it's like 10k per month, for a flat that accommodates two people, how will you afford it?"

"Then we also need to look for a job."

"Exactly."

"..."

"So, I looked up the jobs and that's where we have an issue. They won't accept female workers everywhere, I suppose you can work at a coffee shop or something, where you could actually serve and wait, but I couldn't come across anything."

"Thanks."

"Not my fault, okay? You're the one running away."

"Also, I'm the one feeling all the pain." My voice started to get louder, and I realized it quickly enough, "You go to hell and let me know if something comes up." It got pretty bad pretty quickly.

"Woah?" She seemed mad herself, and hung up the phone. I didn't feel any regret, like I said, it wasn't hurting, it was just simple unrest.

I fell asleep, and woke up in the middle of the night. It would happen sometimes, I would wake up in the middle of the night and just stare at the dark ceiling. It was just mesmerizing to look into the darkness, so much that it was haunting me. I was calm at that time, and hence the ripples were creating hallucinations. When I was little, I was afraid of the dark. When I grew up, I became dark myself. It wasn't something I could help, but it was the truth. It was like my future, dark and uncertain.

As I started into the darkness, I did what I usually did: thought about how everything went wrong. It all started when my parents decided to mate, and a gene decided to make me gay. And then I was born, crying, and the crying never stopped, people just forgot how to listen. Things were never okay, and they were never going to be okay since the problem was I myself.

I thought: What if I wasn't gay? Or what if my other mom had never started drinking? what if she did not have infertile ovaries? What if the world was okay? what if I was okay? I guess it could all be true, in a land of myths.

It's almost impossible to go back to sleep once you have woken up, and the weird part is there is not even a real reason for it. I just lay there, but then I decided to listen to a few songs. I listened to songs that would help me fall asleep, which included songs like *Snow Patrol - Chasing cars*.

I usually listened to old songs, and I could listen to new songs too, if they were good, but the thing is usually the older songs would make me feel like the person I was, maybe because I was getting older myself. I wondered how strange it was to be sometimes sleepy all the time, and sometimes waking up in the middle of the night thinking about the horrors that ruined my past and were terrorizing my future.

For a moment I was calm, but then I had a mental breakdown. My ocean, something strange happened, and it started hurting even when I was uncalm. This happened very rarely, and I couldn't feel anymore if I was breathing or not, if I had my eyes closed or not, or in what position I was lying, or if I still had my mobile in my hands. I crossed my arms, as if hugging myself, and the only thing I could feel was the ache in my head, and the ache in my heart, both simultaneously hurting me so bad that my whole body was shaking. It felt like the Earth was shaking with me, like an earthquake, and then I tried to sit straight. But I couldn't breathe, and I tried to scream. My vocal chords couldn't make any sound, and the only sound I could exhale was a muffled cry, and it felt like I would die at that moment, and if I had, it was going to be painful. But it would be all happy in the end, like that would be the summary of my life, the legend of Javeria Sultan in a nutshell, dying on her bed out of pain in the body, wishing to die too, but somehow, I didn't die. I made it out alive, in the end, and everything was calm again. I started breathing heavily before it got the *usual* calm, and my heartache was gone, but my headache still existed, which kind of wasn't letting me to sleep.

I stopped playing the songs, even though I wanted to listen to them, I guess I thought the music was giving me a headache so I decided to put my mobile and earphones aside, lay down again, and closed my eyes. But I couldn't sleep, so I opened them, and closed them again, until I eventually went to sleep.

I woke up, when my mom decided to shake me harder than last night's quake, and for a moment I couldn't open my eyes. Even when I sat up, I didn't know what was happening around me, until I realized that I still had to brush my teeth, brush and braid my hair, BUT wash my face first.

"Come on sweetie pie." My mom said as she left the room, and I didn't even look at her, "we don't wanna be late."

"You're not going to be late, even if I do."

"Get fresh, breakfast will be ready in a minute."

I did it all, washing, brushing, brushing, braiding, looking, getting disgusted, looking again, wearing black, and then I went downstairs to have breakfast.

"What the actual hell?" I almost shouted at my mom who was in the kitchen probably washing dishes while I was mad while standing in the living room, "you know I don't like French toast. NO FRENCH TOAST.

I looked at the table, with a plate with three yellow-ish french toasts lying in front of me, as if hypnotising me into being nauseous.

"We were out of jam." My mom replied from the kitchen.

"What about simple toasts with eggs?"

"You would have complained about it too."

"I hate how true that is."

I sat down, but I couldn't eat. I was very choosy about my food, and I couldn't tolerate anything that I didn't like, even if I had to starve the rest of the day.

"I'm going."

I went outside, without eating my food, without wishing anything else, cursing upon the college which was eternal misery, like my house, like my family, like myself, in fact the whole world.

Chapter 4:

I got to college from the usual bus, and at the gate I met Sana. I usually didn't meet either of Sana or Hania at the gate, unless they're already waiting for me, because I was always either late or just on time. So, having to meet Sana and Hania on the gate, on alternate days, it was funny but seemed fishy.
"My whole day is going to be great." I hinted sarcasm at Sana as I got behind her, when she was looking away at the college building.
"Oh," she turned around and hesitated for a moment, "Hi. Didn't see you there."
"I really wish I would disappear, wouldn't have to face you people." I was looking at the building myself, now.
"I'm sorry." She turned to me, and looked down.
For a moment I didn't answer, but then I looked at her, nodded and said, "See, that's why I wanna run away."
She did not reply, and we started walking towards the gate, and then finally into the place of misery.
"I really can't take it anymore." I started the conversation again, I normally liked being quiet but I did want a plan, a plan that ensured my freedom. "Did you think of anything?"
"I tried…" She stopped, and I stopped just ahead of her, and she looked straight into my eyes, "You cannot run away. You cannot leave her…"
"Leave who?"
"Hania."
"Ugh." I rolled my eyes, "Cliché. I don't care about Hania, and Hania doesn't care about me. I'm a loner, I'm different from you all. I don't like you or Hania at all! So for God's sake, stop using the *don't leave me and Hania* BS, because IT IS ENOUGH."
"You know what, Weirdo?" her expressions changed like ocean tides, and now it felt as if she was mad, pretty mad. "I don't like you, either. You're a bitch, you will always be a bitch. I wouldn't even care if you'd run away, but Hania is a nice person. She likes you, she loves you, and she wants to stay your friend. I know you're a dumb fuck who can't see that, but I'm not an idiot."
Sana was mad as hell, and I knew she couldn't stand me anymore. Honestly, her words didn't affect me a bit, because she didn't matter to me at all. No one mattered to me but myself, I didn't care about Hania, Sana, or even Emaan for that matter, because what I wanted, was freedom.

I leaped near to her face, and then to her right cheek, I almost whispered, "Go to hell." And then I decided to walk away, and this time I did look behind to see if she was following me, she wasn't. She just took out her phone, and started texting someone, Hania, perhaps. It didn't matter, nothing mattered.

I walked straight, and saw the door of my classroom was closed, that meant the lecture had started. I decided to look from the window, and it was Professor Kamaal, whom I hated so much I decided to bunk the class. An attendance? Big deal.

I continued walking, hoping no body saw me from the window, and sat down at a bench. I thought about running away, and then I realized I did care about Hania, and Emaan. My mind is a maze, everything gets lost in there. Sometimes I thought I cared about Hania, and sometimes I didn't. It was all just silly. As I sat there, in my usual black Tee, and jeans, I felt a slight vibration in my pants. I took it out, and it was Hania texting me:

"Dude, no colege again?"

"College*, and I'm in college, I just don't want to die listening to a boring lecture. I would like to die trying to escape."

"Yo

Datz kool"

"Ugh."

"Clishey???"

"Cliche* you dork."

"I didnt no u were bunking clazzez now."

I didn't reply, and put my mobile back into my pocket. I just sat there, took a deep breath, and stretched my shoulders. I looked around a college block, surrounded by at least two dozen classes, none of which were giving us education, none of which making the most out of our potential. Then I took out my mobile again, took out my hands-free, plugged it in, and started listening to songs. I never really sang along to songs, even when I was alone, but this time I was silently humming them.

I felt a tap on my shoulder, and thought it was the proctor. *Normal* people were more afraid of the procter than I was, so it wasn't really freaking me out. I stood up, and when I turned around, I fell deep into shock. It was Zaib Abbasi.

I didn't even take my earplug out, I just shook my head, and sat down again. I didn't want to face her, but why all of a sudden is she here to talk to me? I was curious, because she didn't even want to see my face after we came back from Ayubia, she didn't want to talk, she wasn't a friend. Now, she's here again, patting my shoulder and all, why?

Zaib did the same annoying thing again, and took out one of my earplugs, "I need to talk to you."

"Well, I am not a big talker." I pulled the earplug back, and stuffed it into my ear.

She took out both of the earplugs out at the same time, threw them down, and held my round cheeks with both of her hands, as if she was about to kiss me, and if she had, I would have kissed back.

"Look…" She looked into my eyes, her eyes were a little watery, and the spectacles magnified the brown-ness of her brown eye-lense, "I know how to run away."

"Normally, I'd fall for that." I got her hands off my face, "but I have no reason to trust an asshole like you."

"Not trusting is stupid, so is trusting. It's just about letting go."
I kept quiet for a moment, and looked away. I didn't want to have eye contact with her, I was still mad at
her, "Why didn't you talk to me? Why did you shut your doors up? I mean, what the hell happened? I
thought you were like me." I looked back at her, "aren't you like me?"
"Precisely." She smiled. "Let's be friends." She let her hand out, offering a handshake. I did not accept
that, and stood up, "I guess I have class." And I walked away.

I got back into my classroom, and after listening to my professor, trying to embarrass me for coming
late, I sat at the last bench. Hania texted me.
"Gud 2 c u."
"Not at all good to see you, though."
"Sowwy."
"Cliché."

Throughout the lecture, I kept thinking about the same thing, what got into Zaib recently? She didn't
want to look at my face just a few months ago, we hadn't talked since, I was almost over her. Now, she
wanted to be my friend? She should know I don't make friends, because that is what I am, a non-friendly
weirdo.
        I decided not to talk about this with Hania or Sana. So when the nightmare of the lecture was
finally over, I decided that I was ill and I needed to go home. I took the permission slip from the office,
and got out of the college. I walked up to the bus stand, and was confused again, there was Zaib Abbasi
standing there, leaning against a side of the pillar that held the bus board, waiting for a bus herself.
        I walked up to her, and asked, "are you following me?" I shook my head real fast, "I don't like
you. I hate you, and this isn't working - "
"Dude," she interrupted me, "Chill."
She remained quiet, and I stood with her. I thought of saying a thing or two, but I decided to remain
quiet myself, because there was no point. I just wanted to go home, I still had to explain why I was home
this early.

A little while later, a bus came by. My bus was still to arrive, but this was Zaib's. The door opened, right
in front of her. It was the middle of the day, the whole bus was almost empty, and she walked in. Just at
the door, she turned around and said, "Well, are you waiting for an invitation card? Hop on."
        I didn't know what I was thinking, but I wanted to go with her. I didn't hold back, and followed
Zaib into the bus.
"Where to?" I asked. I was curious, because I wasn't the type of girl who'd call college off early and be
hanging around with other girls without knowing what's happening.
"You'll see." She smiled, "Do you want bubble gum?" She offered me a stick, and I took it.
"Strawberry's cliché." I said as I chewed the gum between my teeth.
She didn't reply, and remained quiet for the rest of the journey. It was amazing to watch her observing
things out of her window as we passed parks, and buildings, and trees, and coffee shops, and movie
theatres, not saying a thing. Something was about this girl, and I thought of the questions she had asked
before, and in a moment of silence, I decided she was going to be my friend. My only true friend. Of

course she had to answer why she closed on me, but I knew there was going to be an answer, a pretty good one.

We reached a bus stop, and after thirty minutes at least, Zaib spoke for the first time.
"Okay, here it is." She got excited and jumped from her seat, pushing my legs trying to get out, "Come on. Move it."
"Yeah, yeah." I got up lazily.
"It's Margara Hills, Daman-e-koh, Pir Sohawa, what else can you be excited for?" She had a delightful charm in her eyes, and it was beautiful, her eyes were beautiful.
"Umm…" I replied as I followed her off the bus, "Death. Music. Guitar. Singing. Way better."
"Sure." She didn't care much about what I said.

We walked a hundred metres from the bus stop, and a big sign board said:
Daman-e-koh: 3.6 km above

Zaib continued walking, but I stopped and asked, "Why are we not taking a coach to the top?"
"What's the fun in that? Let's walk." Zaib turned around, and smiled while I went blank on the thought of walking more than 3 kilometres, because the road was ten times the hill, including the fact that I'm acrophobic. A moment later she laughed, "Only joking. Come with me you coward."
"So laugh I forgot to be funny." I rolled my eyes.
She started walking again, and I followed her.
A while later, she just stood at the side of the climbing road, where we were walking, and I asked, "what now?"
"We wait for a lift."
"What the hell?" I opened my eyes, "why wait for a lift? We could have easily taken a coach, and just go to the top. It would also be less scary."
"And also less fun." she looked at me, "Javeria, sometimes you do stuff not because it makes sense, not because it's right or wrong, not because it's good or bad, because it's nothing at all. It's not even fun, it's just happening."
She raised her right hand, and pointed her thumb to ask for a lift. A couple of cars passed by and no one noticed, but then came a convertible Bentley, with two well-built boys riding it. They were wearing some sort of sport zippers, and one of the guys winked at me.
"Eww." I exclaimed at once, "No way."
I shook my head, but when I saw them again, I realized Zaib had already gotten in the car. "Not a reason." I smirked, "I see." And then I followed her in the back of the car.
"So, which of you pretty ladies wants me?" the guy at the passenger seat turned back, and put his hand at my thigh.
"Have you ever even seen yourself in the mirror?" I was disgusted, "If Satan had a face, it would be yours."
Everybody else laughed, but his dirty smile faded, but then Zaib texted me:
"Dude, these guys are tokens for free food, and everything."
"Ohh."

"Yeah, follow my lead."

As the creeps kept flirting with us, I didn't bother too much. I noticed what was happening around: outside the car, we were entering a more steeper slope, swirling around a mountain. The long pine trees were getting shorter to my left, and the mountain was getting rockier to my right. The road was getting bumpy, and now the height was scaring me a little.
"What's that look on your face?" Zaib turned to me.
"I… uh…" I looked down the trees, "acrophile, remember?"
"Exactly." She winked at me like it was nothing.
The car kept moving, until we reached an area where the road was blocked by at least seventy monkeys. Just staring at us, and not moving a muscle.
"They live here." Zaib spoke to the driving guy, "It's amazing."
"Hey, move it." The driver kept honking at the monkeys, but didn't seem to move a muscle, "Fuck away."
I patted the passenger guy from the shoulder and said in amusement, "Oh look! how familiar." No one noticed, but the guy winked at me. "cliché", I leaned back to my seat.
Zaib took out a bag of popcorn from her backpack, and started feeding the monkeys from where the roof must have been.
"They can die." I told her, "popcorn is too salty. they might choke."
"Not as salty as you though." The passenger seat guy turned back, "I don't think I have introduced you yet, I'm Danish, Danish Ali."
"Oh… I'm Mahnoor." I gave out a fake name. "Mahnoor not-interested-in-you."
"I'm Adil Kamran." The driver turned back, and stopped honking for a minute, "You can call me Adii."
"I'm Zaib Abbasi." Zaib smiled, "You can call me Zaib Abbasi."
In a moment, the monkeys started to move away, and we were back on track.

The guys were *typical handsome men*, and Hania would have killed to be girlfriend of one of them. Danish was a tall guy, with a nice buffy chest. He had nice biceps, and I knew he was a show-off. He had a nice build, but the problem was his face: it was ugly.

Adil was more fat than well built, but he was prettier on the face thing. He had a nice trimmed beard, with long black hair, turned to one side. But he did not have biceps, or abs, or a nice chest. Anyway, if I would have been straight, both of them would've been out of my league. They both stopped just for Zaib.

As we continued, I noticed we were getting higher and higher from sea level, and it wasn't a really big issue since there was no death threat if the boys don't be jerks and be cool to drive around at an over-limit speed, I realized it was fine.

We reached the top, and parked the car. The guys offered us Ice-cream, and normally I wouldn't have accepted that, because I didn't need jerks to buy me ice-creams, I can do things myself but I still told them yes because a) I didn't have any money, b) I wanted ice-cream, c) Zaib was getting free ice-cream too, and since I thought it's the first and last time we're hanging around with the douches, I let them be douches.

From the parking lot to an ice-cream parlor, it was all nice. But Zaib then decided to show me Damin-e-koh, and as she walked I followed her. She walked across a small family restaurant area, the restaurants were closed right now because it was about 1 in the after-noon, and walked over a very small park. Everything was almost empty, even though we saw a few cars passing while we were coming up. I wondered where they were. Zaib continued walking, and I asked her, "Hey! Slow down!" but she decided to ignore me and continued even faster. And then came a sign *tourist spot*, and I could see a little fence maybe 100 metres away, and I knew it was the end of the mountain. She reached there in no time, and I followed her. I looked over the fence, and because it was protected and I couldn't really fall until I jumped over, I wasn't too afraid.

I looked, and looked at it again. It was beautiful, and it spread through the horizon. The whole city could be seen from up there, linked with a main double road in the centre, and little homes spread on both sides. Much more city-like from up there, with the only prominent building being plazas and the three Centaurus skyscrapers.

"Are you afraid?" Zaib asked me while looking down at the view, "does this scare ya?"

"Not really…" I didn't look at her either, the view really was beautiful, "It could have been different without a fence."

"Cute." She must have smiled, I saw from the corner of my eye.

"Shut up, you're cute." I finally looked at her. "Eww. None of us is cute."

She laughed, and then finally said, "remember this moment, 'cause now we're going somewhere else." And she turned and started walking back, and I shouted behind her, "where?" I started following, as she ignored me, "Hello? … Tell me? … Come on! …"

We were united with Adil and Danish again, and Danish started flirting with me again but I didn't care. I tried not to burn him up, but he was getting on my nerves.

"Girls like you make me believe in angels."

"Yeah… no… third eye of Satan." I was disgusted by his creepiness.

"So, where are we going?" Adil asked as we were getting back into the Bentley, and Zaib decided that she should drive.

"Pir Sohawa." She answered, just when I was about to sit in the backseat, "Hey, Jiya. No, sit at the front."

"Okay." I raised my shoulders, and sat on the passenger seat. "Where's that Peer Suwuwuwuwu?"

"Sohawa." she corrected me, "at the top."

"So, this isn't the top?" I asked her, swallowing my thoughts, my adam's apple bobbing, "I'm acrophobic, girl."

"It'll be fine." she smiled as she drove off, and Danish kept flirting with me from the backseat.

Now came the horror part, the hills had just begun. I looked across, and I saw a very narrow road that led to the top, circling around the mountains. There was no side fence, there was no protection if the car went out of control, there was nothing at all that would have prevented us from dying if Zaib had panicked and pushed the accelerator instead of brakes, but the thing was, Zaib never panicked.

Zaib was driving at 40, which was clearly too fast and I was so scared I had tears in my eyes.

"Oh God, Oh God, Oh God!" I kept screaming as Zaib drove the car on the circling path, with each turn my heart in my mouth, "Oh God, Oh God." I tried not to look.

"That's what I make girls say at night too." Danish winked at me.

"Shut up!" and then I turned to Zaib, "For God's sake Zaib! SLOW THE FUCK DOWN."

"Why?" She smiled, and lifted her both hands from the steering wheel for a split second, "Look, no hands."

"I swear Zaib, if I get out alive somehow, I'm gonna kill you."

"Cliché." she laughed as she put her hands back on the wheel.

"UGH." I screamed very loud, louder than what I intended it to be.

Every Time she'd put her feet on the brake of the accelerating pedal, it'd make me feel like I'd throw up, even when the rest of them just kept laughing. It was scary, not because it was a fact, because I was just a coward. Scared of what the world had for me, heights and falls.

I somehow managed not to die of a heart attack, when we finally reached the *actual* top. It was a lot similar to the place earlier, only it was smaller and had only one restaurant, which was open, somehow. There wasn't much of an area to hang around, it could all be seen in one view, a single restaurant with a large area for *outside* eating.

"Okay, guys, order whatever you want." Zaib asked them once we parked the car, in a very small but empty parking lot, "Mahnoor and I have something to talk about."

"Do we really?" I thought.

She walked across the restaurant, and there was a fence again. The view was similar, only that everything was smaller and all I could really notice there were the three scrapers and Faisal Mosque. I hadn't got near to the fence, before Zaib jumped over, and a very strong pulse went through me. She jumped, *no one is happy*? What happened? I ran as fast as I could, and leaned over the fence before I saw a very small piece of land just before a very steep abyssus, and there was no way if she had tripped over, she would have lived.

"Are you crazy?" I shouted from above.

"Yes." she smiled, "Jump."

"No way." I shook my head, as I looked past her, further down. "No way in hell am I going to jump. I haven't gone insane yet, thank you very much."

"It's amazing to be insane."

"It's idiotic to be insane."

"It's poetic to be insane," and she smirked, like she knew I wanted to jump, "jump. Please. Nothing is going to happen."

I thought about it for a second, why do I jump? Well, obviously because Zaib is telling me to. What if I do jump? Zaib jumped, and nothing happened. It was a six feet height at least, and any mistake could result in serious injury if not death, but then she said again: *jump*, and the voice kept echoing in my brain. I wouldn't have jumped, but I felt like I needed to jump. It didn't make sense, it was idiotic, it was insane. "This is insane." And I jumped, I jumped like the time a bird is freed from its cage, like the time a kid fell from his bicycle and kept running and crying in the rain, like the time the world keeps calling your name. I jumped, and in mid-air I realized what it really was. It was life, scary, but everything was going to be alright in the end. I felt free, I wondered if it would be the same if I ran away from home, and would it be this coming to come to know yourself? To be a successful singer? I landed very strongly on my feet, and they hurt for a millisecond, but the whole concept of jumping was amazing as a whole, and yes, insane. "What's the point?" I asked, before she started to singing a few lyrics of a song:

'Cause you told me that you'd never be afraid of heights again
Nobody ever thought that we could make it this high
You're the only one I'd follow 'til the end of time
If we fall, we fall together baby, don't think twice again

"Billy Talent." I laughed, "nice. I appreciate the song, but your voice sucks."
"Thank you." and then she reached her backpack once again and while opening the zip and looking in it, she asked, "Do you want - err - ?"
"No." I interrupted her, "As much as I want to die, I don't want to die of lung cancer or falling."
"Wha-?" She laughed, "Not a cigarette, fool. I only smoke at night, because that's when I'm vulnerable the most." She took out two lollipops, and handed me one, "Have a lollipop."
"Cliché." I told her, but I liked the idea of having a lollipop at a height God knows how many metres above the ground. I tried to open the wrapper off the lollipop, but it was tight, and my fingernails weren't long enough.
"Give it to me before you hurt yourself." She took the pop, and opened it for me, "here."
"Okay."

We just sat there for a while, behind at the edge, without realizing our clothes were getting dirty, because we were too excited to live the moment. Enjoying the view, and never worrying what might happen.
"You know why no one is happy?" Zaib asked me, without looking at me again.
"Huh?" I was too involved in the scenery, because I thought that was the first and last time I was going to enjoy the scene from there, even though I didn't care about *beauty* and stuff. It was all cliché. "Oh, yeah, why?"
"Cherophobia." She turned to me, "the fear of happiness."
"Ugh, relatable."
"You'd think everybody wants to be happy. No. Cherophobia is not as simple as the fear of heights, or the fear of cats, it's logical. We are afraid of happiness, we all are, it's the fear of what comes after happiness, because what comes after is pain. There is never going to be happiness without pain." She continued as I thought about it as my ocean, it was never going to be calm but non-hurting, "and there is never going to be happiness without pain. It's all linked, like, you can't play guitar unless your fingers hurt, your fingers won't hurt if you don't play guitar, but you know guitar brings you happiness. That's cherophobia. We all have it at some level, and thus in the legendary words of Zaib Khan Abbasi: No one is happy."
She stood up, and walked right to the edge. This time, I wasn't afraid to go to the edge. I was scared, because that's what my mind wanted me to be, but I wasn't afraid of falling.
"Look at this." She opened her arms wide, as I looked across, and it felt as if I was the queen of the whole city. "Tell me, Javeria. What do you see?"

I looked at it again, and even more intensely.

"Islamabad?"

"No. That's where you're wrong. This is height, your worst fear. But do you see what you should see? What if you jump? You would never come back. You would die, but do you understand why it was important to not stop at Daman e koh and show you why *this* is important? Because where you are is Daman e Koh, and where you must be is the literal area here. The road is tough, but you somehow made it, didn't you?" She turned to me, and looked deep into my eyes, moving ever so slightly to the edge, like she's about to jump, "Tell me Javeria, are you ready to fall? Are you ready to climb? Are you ready to jump? Are you ready to run away?"

I looked in her eyes, through the spectacles, and there was only one answer in my mind. And that was the moment I realized I didn't care about Hania, I didn't care about Sana, I didn't even care about Emaan as much as I cared about my freedom and what I wanted to do.

"Yes."

She held my hand, "We're running away tomorrow night. Are you with me?"

"Yes." I nodded. I didn't think much about it, it was like a reflex.

"Glad. How much money can you get?"

"I don't know." I thought about it, "Maybe 20, or 40 thousand? Can't really say. My own money is zero, but I think I can sneak dad's ATM card."

"Great, and what stuff do you need to take with you?"

"Umm… clothes, my guitar, my mobile and my laptop. My tooth brush, like everything you need to take with you during a tour or something."

"Exactly."

"So, how are you making me escape?"

"Oh, we both are escaping." she winked at me, "I need to run away too."

"That escalated quickly." I tilted my head a little.

"Sure did." And we both sucked on our lollipops, and hoped for the best, staring into the wind.

The guys bought us some kind of mexican food, and we in return gave them fake numbers. The ride coming down was just as scary, but it was more fun this time. I was too excited about the fact that I had decided to run away, and that too with Zaib. My life was almost about to begin.

I reached home and was still confused about Zaib leaving me very suddenly, and even more abruptly asking to help me out, and not just help me out, run away with me. I called Hania and told her that Zaib met me, and we went on a trip but didn't really tell her about the whole *run away* plan.

"Oh…" her voice sounded a little down, "Javeria."

"What?"

"Promise you won't be mad."

"I will be mad if it's something that deserves to be mad on."

"Well... I..." she hesitated for a moment, "the thing is, Zaib and I talked before you went on that college trip with her. I asked her to go on that trip with you, and we already had a deal to... that she'll stop talking to you when she comes back."

"What the hell?" I got mad. What the hell is she talking about, Zaib never wanted to go on the trip with me? And it was Hania who asked her to. And when she came back, she could have talked with me, we could have been friends, but Hania had already told her to ditch me? What the fuck was she talking about?

"Look... I just wanted you to know it's not nice to hurt people, and we are friends, and I'm sorry."

"WHAT THE FUCK?" Why would she even do this? She knows I am not nice, and what she did was what I deserved, but it didn't make sense to call me her friend now.

"Please don't be mad. I was trying to protect - no, I'm not gonna lie. I don't know Jiya, I was hurt that you were not being a good friend... I... I'm sorry. Please, I didn't mean it, I even tried to tell you.. but..."

"You think? You bitch. A whore. A psychopath heartless..." I realized I was calling her all that stuff, but I was defining myself too, "you know what, Hania? I hate you, I'm not your friend anymore, I never was. Don't call me."

I disconnected the phone, and blocked her number. I blocked her from all social media websites at once. This was a lot more sudden than what I expected it to be, because even though I knew Hania and I were never going to work out, I didn't think it was going to be like that. I thought it would be more like *we have different universities* or like *I'm engaged with a very ugly but rich fella so I'm moving to LA, bye*. I didn't think it was going to be like this, but every painful thing is like that, sudden, abrupt, and hurting, like a needle. I thought I was overreacting, and it was just a fight, but I was running away, and this was probably the last time we talked.

Just a little while later, Sana texted me:

"Javeria. We are sorry."

I didn't reply and blocked her number too. I still didn't get the whole point of this, I thought they were playing a prank on me. It just didn't feel like Hania, it didn't feel like Zaib. I was mad at all of them, and I was mad at myself.

I decided to calm myself down, and a little while later I thought about it. But my thoughts were too messed up, so I decided to write it all down.

What I want → My freedom
Who can help → Zaib
Can I do it without Zaib → Nope
Do I know anything about Zaib's plan → Nope
Is Zaib trustworthy? → Meh
Is my freedom worth taking a high risk? → DEFINITELY

Graph of of Risk and Result

During Trip → Risk high ⇒ Result high
After trip → Risk low ⇒ Result low
Today → Risk high ⇒ Result high

Expected plotting as the situation has been

Running away → Risk high ⇒ Result high

Okay, now this is sorted out, also:

HANIA IS A WHORE WHO IS JUST A BITCH WHO CAN'T UNDERSTAND WHAT I'M GOING THROUGH AND MAYBE NEVER WILL BECAUSE SHE DOESN'T KNOW WHAT IT FEELS LIKE TO BE ME OR MEET SOMEONE LIKE YOURSELF WHEN YOU'VE BEEN ALONE YOUR WHOLE LIFE. I WISH SHE WOULD DIE.

I was mad at myself because of the fact that I had to trust Zaib again if I had to run away. But I needed to run away, because it was enough. I hated everything, I hated everyone. In the excitement of trying to run away, I had forgotten a little about how much I really hated my dad, my mom, my step mom, everyone. I decided it was my last night in this filthy house.

I decided to Call Zaib, and talk about the plan, as Zaib picked up:
"It's going to be tomorrow in the evening, or night. I'll text you and you'll come at the corner of your street."
"What do I pack?"
"Pack anything you want, just have some money, and even if you pack nothing, it'll be fine."
"I'll pack my toothbrush for sure."
"What's with your toothbrush?" She laughed, "Pack whatever you want, just be there when I text you and not a second late."
"Okay."

I waited for the routine *argument* to happen at night, and there it was again. My dad and my step mom are fighting again, but this was my golden chance. I looked across the living room to see if Emaan was still trying to stop them, and he was. I sneaked into my Dad's room, and saw his wallet on the side table. I carefully took out the ATM card, and got out. Now, here was the tough part, I had to go through the living room to get out, so I decided to call Dad on his mobile so they'd all go inside the room when dad goes to check his phone.

I realized I shouldn't call, because he'd ask me why I called him then, and it would definitely be a mistake. I was about to text Hania, before I realized I had blocked her and she was a bitch. I texted Zaib, and asked her to call my dad. As soon as the bell rang, my dad went inside, so did my step mom, so did my real mom, and so did Emaan.

I sneaked out, and walked in the coldness of the night to a nearby bank. I walked very slowly, with the ATM card and my hands in my pockets, I felt the breeze blowing through my hair. It was going to be my last night, or second last, in Islamabad. I was going away, and I was never going to return. It all felt irrational, and felt like I was moving too fast. It was a leap, a big one, but it was also blindfolded. I didn't know where I was going, I didn't know what I was going to do, hell, I wasn't even sure if it would be any place better, but I had to do this. I couldn't live in fear of never getting where I wanted to be, just to live in a place that's already hell.

I got to the ATM, and made a transaction of 20,000 RS twice, and put the money in my left pocket. I put the ATM card in my right pocket, and started walking back towards home. I thought about it once again, is it all really necessary? Is it happening too fast? Should I go through with it? Something inside me told me again: DEFINITELY.

No one except Emaan even noticed me when I was gone from home, and somehow I put the ATM card back in its place after the fight was over. I got into my room upstairs, and Emaan rushed back in again. He pointed at my guitar, and asked me to play a song. This was probably going to be the last time I was going to play for him, and I had to go away, I was never going to sing for him again. I decided to sing a song I used to sing him even before I played the guitar, *Hey Brother by Avicii:*

Hey, brother, there's an endless road to re-discover.

Then he sang the next line:

Hey, sister, know the water's sweet but blood is thicker.

And then we sang together:

Oh, if the sky comes falling down for you,
There's nothing in this world I wouldn't do.

And it continued like this for the whole song, verses and chorus, it was amazing to sing with him. We kept singing the same song over and over. Once he got back into his room, I thought about it once again, *should I do this? Should I leave him?* The answer was the same: *I have to.*

I just went to sleep after having my lungs out, because I was too tired. It took me long to sleep, because I knew it was going to be my last sleep here, and the excitement was not letting me rest, it was making my ocean un-calm, but then tiredness finally won, and the tides faded away.

My mom woke me up the next morning,
"Hey sweetie, wake up."
I woke up at once, and I told her, "I'm not going to college today."
"Why not?" She smiled at me, "college is good."
"Ugh, no it's not." I rolled my eyes, "I can't bear it one day more."
"Fine, Jiya." She winked at me, "but don't tell your dad." And then she put her index finger on top of her lips, like I was going to tell dad if she hadn't done that.

I texted Zaib at once, "Hey dude, I'm not coming to college, so tell me when you're coming."
Just a moment later Zaib replied, "be ready by 8. Exactly by 8."

I talked to mom once again before she went off to work, "Hey mom?"
"Yeah?" she spoke as she read a James Hilton Novel, "what is it Jiya?"
"Umm… I was thinking." I hesitated for a little while, "what if something happens and Emaan disappears, what will you do?"
"He won't." She didn't even look at me, her eyes were always on the novel.
"Fine."

It was 11 in the morning, and I thought I had a lot of time so I decided to leave packing for a little later. I thought about it again, why did I really need to go, because there were many reasons. For five years, I had taken enough abuse of my step mom. I couldn't take it anymore, I knew something like this was coming. I was finally going to a new place, new people, somewhere people didn't know me, and that's where I belonged, a place where people didn't know who or what I was, and I could finally be myself. A musician, a singer, not a puppet of my parents, or the college, but the person I was: A star.

About 2 in the evening, Zaib texted me again:

"ALERT ALERT. BE THERE IN AN HOUR! PACK YOUR STUFF UP. NO TIME TO EXPLAIN."

I panicked at her text, ONLY AN HOUR? I took out my clothes, *black, black, black, black, grey, white, black,* and my jeans, and stuffed them into my backpack somehow. I took my laptop, and checked my money. I took my deodorant, and a broken wrist watch which was once gifted by Emaan, but it was a fake Rolex so it broke, but I always kept it. I decided to wear it, even when it wasn't working. I took my guitar, and put it in its rugged bag, and I looked at the time when the bell rang. I still had half an hour when Emaan came home.

There wasn't much time to talk to him, so I decided to not see him at all, and it was hurting me. My ocean was not calm, but it was somehow still hurting me. Because I was leaving him, I was finally leaving him. I decided to write a note, So he'd know how much I loved him, but I couldn't face him otherwise because the idea of leaving him was like my voice gone forever. I didn't want to leave him, but I had to. I guess that's what life is: tough choices.

Mom, Dad, Step-mom, Emaan:

I'm sorry I have to go. Yeah, that's right, this is a letter by a girl who is running away, and not just some girl, your daughter. I know you're all probably thinking why, well, there's not one answer to that. I'm sure you all know somewhere deep inside your heart that why am I doing this. I hate you all, other than Emaan. I hate you guys because you weren't there when I needed you, because even if you could have understood me, you didn't try to. Because you all were just too self-absorbed and didn't care about me. Well, That's me, I'm gone with the wind now. I have nothing to say to you, because you don't even deserve these words.

But, Emaan, Emaan dear I love you. I love you so much it hurts to leave you alone, because you deserved a better sister than me, and I don't know what I did to have a brother like you. For all my life, there was only one person who actually stood for me in everything, and it was you. And It hurts to leave you alone with these monsters, but I hope you understand what I'm doing. I hope you understand that I wouldn't have done any of this if it wasn't over the line. It's not a sudden decision, I thought about it, I really did. Anything that could have stopped me from going away, was you, and even though I know I am stupid, I can't do it. I can't stay here. I have to go. You know? It'll be like the times we sing together, yes! Only now, when you open your eyes, you'll only hear the music, you will only hear the guitar, you will not hear my voice, but you will hear me play, because I won't be there physically but I'll always be there in your heart. I know it sounds super cliché, but trust me, it's not. Every time you're sad, just remember me. Take a look at our pictures, and remember the times when we used to sing together. Also, remember, no matter where I go, or whatever happens to me, I'm always, ALWAYS thinking about you, because that's what brothers and sisters do, and I know I'm a pretty bad sister, but I love you, and I know you'll remember me too. Don't wait for me to return, okay? Because I'm not going to. It all sounds so sudden and abrupt, na? Well, even I think that. At the moment, my heart is racing like it has never raced before, but you know what? It's gonna be alright. In fact, take a diary, and name it "Jiya Aapi". I'll be it, and you can write whatever you want in it, and I swear I'll hear it, even songs, okay? I have to go now, and Remember, I love you so much. Bye. Bye forever.

Love, and mostly hate,
Javeria Sultan.

I looked at my broken watch, and pictured Emaan. I went to Emaan's room, and saw him sleeping. He looked cute, and him breathing, just breathing, was enough for me to give me enough courage to go. I kissed him on the forehead, and went back into my room. I was crying, I knew I was crying, and I tried to hold back my tears but I couldn't. Suddenly Zaib texted:
"Come out."

And this was it, a beginning of a new life. My bad times were going to be over soon, and I took my backpack, and my guitar, and got outside. As I got to the corner of my street, I was perplexed once again, it was Zaib and I was pretty sure she was in the same Bentley that belonged to Adil and Danish.
"What the hell?" I asked her holding the guitar in one hand, and having the backpack on my shoulder.
"No time to explain." She told me, and sweat was pouring out of her forehead, "Get in."
I threw my stuff on the back seat, and jumped over the door. I could notice the way Zaib was driving, she had definitely stolen the car.
"Did you steal it?" I asked her, "wow."
"Just borrowed it." She tried to laugh but couldn't, "okay, so you sure you wanna do this?"
I kept quiet for a while, I didn't know what to answer when Zaib asked me again, "Don't do this to me. You're sure, just say it!"
"I'm sure. Yeah. I'm pretty sure."
"Good." She nodded, "now, throw away your sim from your mobile."
I pinned my mobile from the side, and the sim case came out. I was really doing it, wasn't I? I threw away the sim, when Zaib took one out from her pocket. I took that and placed it in.
"Good." She said again, "In half an hour, we will no longer be in Islamabad. Think of a fake name."
"Mahnoor?"
"Sure."
And she continued driving, while I noticed her suddenly get calmer.

About in half an hour, we got nearer to the motorway, and once we were going to be on the motorway, there was no stopping us.

"Oh shit." I pointed through the car screen.

"What?"

"Police blockade."

"Dude!" She let out a big sigh, "you scared me. This ain't nothing. Just be normal."

"Double negative is positive, dumbass." I told her even though I used to use double negative. Though it sounded cooler.

We drove past the blockade, and the police did notice the Bentley, of course, but he would have thought that we did own this car, which was far from reality, and my heart was racing, but somehow we did get past them. And now, it was finally it. We were officially out of Islamabad, and now we were on the Lahore-Islamabad motorway. It was it, finally, I was free. Finally, I was going to live. Questions after questions popping in my mind, but they were nothing to the freedom I felt.

Chapter 5:

On our way, I was feeling a lot. I didn't know what was happening, and it all still seemed a lot sudden. But it was it. I was going away, and a lot of questions were popping in my mind. My ocean of unrest, tides all over my heart beat. I finally had to ask her:

"So…" I looked at her, but she seemed focused on the road. She looked a bit too uncomfortable, I guess it was because of the glasses. "Are you going to tell me anything?"

"Yeah." She said, still focused, not moving a muscle, "Ask."

"I guess the question should start from the car." I raised my shoulders a little.

"I told you." And now she looked at me, and gave her signature smirk, "Borrowed."

"Okay." I raised my eyebrows a little, "what about the rest of the plan?"

"What about it?"

"Where are we going to stay? what am I gonna do?" I tilted my head ever so slightly, "how am I going to get involved in the music industry?"

"Oh." She straightened her glasses with her right hand, this was the first time I saw her do that, "We'll go with the flow." She smiled, still looking at the road.

"Cliché" I rolled my eyes, "No, seriously. What is going to happen."

"For now, we are not going to Lahore."

"Where?"

"Hafizabad." She turned and smiled. I got worried for an instance. What if she goes and hits into a truck.

"Focus on the road." I shook my head, "Where's Hafizabad?"

"It's just before Gujranwala. You'll see."

"Okay." I thought. And that was all I knew of what was happening. I thought about why Hafizabad, or what would happen there. But I gave up the idea, because there was no point. I didn't care. I wanted to be free, and I was free.

In the passenger seat, the air was going through me like I was flying. Maybe I was, maybe I was a bird. A bird finally out of the cage. Maybe I was a breeze myself, getting a push by the wind. Maybe I was nothing, maybe I was just me, but it didn't matter. What mattered was the air, what mattered was the speed at which Zaib was driving, what mattered was what I wanted, and how bad I wanted. Maybe it was foolish, maybe it was crazy. Maybe it was insane, but it really is poetic to be insane, isn't it?

Still on the road, there was a large silence. A silence I liked. A silence, filled with the scent of Zaib's hair, and the smell of fresh air. A silence filled with a mixture of Zaib's tension, and my relief. A silence filled with a maze of my thoughts, coming together one by one. A silence, as true as my heart beat. I decided to stand up. I let the air through my hair, I let my hands in the air. I let out a scream, a joyous scream. I let people know I was in love, I was in love with this. For the first time in my life I felt — not me.

"Hey, uh… Mahnoor." She reached into her bag with her left hand, trying to look both on the road and into the bag. I noticed how she called me Mahnoor, and not Javeria or Jiya. Maybe that was it. Maybe I didn't just leave my family behind, I left myself behind too. I left Javeria behind too. "Want a gum? Or a lollipop?"

"Lollipop, please."

I put it in my mouth. Strawberry. It used to be cliché, and suddenly it didn't feel cliché anymore. It felt amazing, the taste. Just having a lollipop in my mouth, and watching Zaib have a lollipop in her mouth, it made me wonder: is this what is like to be normal? What was something that I was missing all these years? Whatever it was, it was incredible.

I decided to turn on the radio, and the song was amazing. I had heard it before, but I didn't like it the first time. But now listening to it again as Mahnoor, gave it a new charm.

Ed Sheeran – Castle on the hill

I'm on my way

Driving at 90 down those country lanes

Singing to tiny dancers

And I miss the way you made me feel, and it's real

Where we watched the sunset over the castle on the hill.

It was amazing, because it was relatable. I loved how much my heart resonated to this one, and how much I wanted to keep listening to it again and again.

"Hey Mano. Can I call you Mano?" Suddenly Zaib turned down the radio volume, and patted at my shoulder as I nodded, "Yeah. So, Mano. I just want to say I'm sorry."

"Sorry for what? And don't call me Mano, please."

"About after Ayubia." She turned her eyes to me, and made them round somehow. She looked cute. She looked prettier all of a sudden, "I have to tell you the truth. I never even knew about you, before Hania came up to me. She told me about you. She told me you were sad, and suicidal, and disgusted by everyone else. She told me you liked singing, and the color black. She told me you were special, but she made a mistake. She asked me to go on the trip with you, and then break your heart. I wouldn't have agreed to it, I swear, but there was only one reason I wanted to go there with you: I am like you. You asked me, and here is my exact answer – I am sad, suicidal, disgusted with everyone else too. And for a long time, I was stuck in a dead end, but then I met you. You make me believe in things, Mahnoor. You really do."

"Cliché." I told her it was cliché, but it wasn't really. I forgave her, in fact I was never mad at her, because I wasn't the only one who made her believe, she made me believe too. She laughed at my reply, and so I followed her laugh. It felt nice to laugh after a long time.

And the road continued, and we sang along the songs on the radio. I was enjoying every bit of it. And in the excitement, I looked at Zaib. I saw her brown hair going backwards and forwards, falling on her face and then going back. I noticed how she was flexing her shoulders, and how she was straightening her glasses. I watched as she tilted her head, and comforted her hands on the steering wheel. I saw her jaws, clenching and relaxing. And then I realized I was staring for too long, and so I decided to take a break from looking at the pretty girl.

I looked at myself in the side mirror, and immediately realized how ugly I was. No makeup, no fancy haircut, no pretty earrings. It was Javeria, still. I decided to change it. I promised myself to change it as soon as I get to Lahore, if not in Hafizabad.

"What are you thinking?" Zaib noticed me staring into the side mirror, "everything alright?"

"No. I'm ugly." It came out a little more seriously, but I didn't mean to make it awkward, so I decided to follow it with a laugh, which just made it even more awkward, but in a second Zaib laughed too.

"Anyway. We're stopping at a rest area in about half an hour. Do you want anything?"

"Not really." I shook my head, "how long have we been on the road anyway?"

"about two hours now." She smiled, and straightened her glasses again.

Two hours – I thought. I had been free for almost two hours now, and it was already good enough, except the realization that I was very ugly. My heartbeat was steady now, my ocean calm. I started imagining now, I could feel myself in a million different lights. I could understand what was happening to me, I could know that I was getting what I deserved.

In a moment, we were there. The rest area, kind of like a very large plaza. Zaib turned in, and started driving towards the parking lot. I watched the large banners of McDonald's and KFC passing by, and we reached the parking lot.

"Do you want anything?" She asked, as she pulled up her hand break. I just shook my head, but just as she closed the door of the car, I asked her, "actually get me a soda and a chicken burger. I'll pay you later."

She just smiled, "no need to pay, yet."

I sat there, still listening to the songs on the radio. I felt the songs getting into my head, and then into my heart. I felt the beat of the songs calling me. I kept smiling, tearing up a little now. I fucking liked this all. I fucking wanted this.

For a moment I thought what would happen if I didn't become a successful singer, and the thought was horrific. Because I still had to find a job in Lahore, which was going to be very hard considering I was seventeen and a girl. And also, I didn't have any working experience anywhere. And I thought about what if nothing good happens after the real troubles come?

Zaib finally came back. Barely holding all the plastic bags, juggling them on her hands and shoulders. I just laughed, while she kept screaming *IT'S NOT FUNNY*. I got out and helped her, still laughing. We put everything in the car, and got in. She just sat with me, and said, "Well eat your burger."

"Sure." I smiled, and I opened the McDonald's bag. It was delicious.

"I got you something." She smiled at me, "I have it somewhere between these bags… ugh… let me look."

And she got into looking, while I got into eating. Just when I was about to finish, she almost screamed, "AHA." And she came back with a black bracelet. Thread bracelet, almost all black. But it was detailed, and designs were made on it. It was good, actually it was amazing. "Have this." I held the bracelet, and noticed the last detail on it: three stars. Very little, but very close.

"Thanks…" I tilted my head, "I guess." I clenched my cheek muscle.

"Pleasure."

And then we got the car tank filled. I paid 500 bucks, and now I had 39,500 Rupees. Which was still enough, but the lost 500 bucks made me a little anxious. And as Zaib drove, I thought about my fear again.

"Hey, Zaib." I decided to ask her about that, because as far as I remembered, she had an answer for everything, even when she didn't tell me. "what if I don't succeed in music? Or what if I fail completely, even in running away?"

I knew she heard me, but she didn't reply. Maybe she was thinking, maybe she decided to ignore me, or maybe she really didn't have an answer to everything. It stung me a little, but I had already come too far. And then I thought about my family, had they read my letter by now? Are they searching for me? What is happening back there? I got a little nervous, and a lot anxious. I tried to hold it in, but it had now spread to my spine, and I wanted to call them. But of course, I just got a new number for a reason: to cut away everything from family. I was not to log in on the internet either. But it was worth it, it had to be worth it.

And the journey continued, and I started feeling a little sleepy. I had not touched my guitar once on the trip, and I didn't think I was going to either. I decided to close my eyes for a little bit, and just relax a little. But it was comfortable, sleeping next to Zaib, with her still driving. I knew we were moving, and the wind was still rushing through me, but finally it all ended – I went to sleep.

I woke up when I felt a sudden shaking. The car had stopped. The air was going through me no more. I felt tired, even though I had just slept, I didn't know for how long but it felt like a good nap. Zaib was trying to wake me up, "wake up Mahnoor."

"I'm up, I'm up." I yawned, and forgot to put my hand on my mouth, "Are we there?"

"We are there." She smiled, "but first, I want to ask you, what's your surname? It's killing me."

And I thought about it, what should be my surname? I can't have Sultan anymore, she is gone. I can't choose anything from my past, even though I wanted to keep it. Emaan Sultan and Javeria Sultan, a link. A connection. I'd miss him, I was missing him. But this was a new start, a new start meant a new everything – from scratch. I decided.

"Mahnoor Ahmad." I smiled, "Yeah. Mahnoor Ahmad it is."

"cute."

She started picking up the bags, and trying to hold all of them at once when I told her to wait. I got up, and even though I was tired, I got a hold of her, and then the bags. I hadn't noticed it before, but we were in front of a very big house. It was on the main road, and it was the only house as far as I could look. This was more of a country area, but the air felt fresher here.

"where are we?" I asked Zaib pointing at the house, still trying to figure things out.

"You'll see." She smirked again. Something was about her smirk, about her smile, about her everything.

"Thanks for the information." I rolled my eyes.

"Pleasure."

And then she pulled out her phone, and started texting. I wondered if she had changed her sim too, maybe she hadn't. Why would she? Unless she gave her number to Chania, or Sana. I didn't think about it too much, because I knew Zaib was always prepared. Always.

As soon as she put her phone back in her pocket, a boy came to the door. And to much of my surprise, it was Danish. The same guy from our little Pir Sohawa journey. Just standing there, probably smiling at my facial expressions. What the hell?

"What the hell?" I asked Zaib as she started walking towards the gate, "what is he doing here?"

"He's my cousin." She smirked again.

She and her mysteries. Her mysterious smirks and her mysterious words. "WELL? EXPLAIN?"

"Greetings." Danish bowed, "our true angel has come."

"Please. No. Yukh."

"The pretty girl. Symbol of beauty."

"Shut up" I remembered his name, but I still went for not-remembering-the-name trick, "Mr. whatever your name was."

"It's Danish Ali, thank you very much."

Zaib walked in the door, and I realized I had to follow. Danish got in too, and I was out there, alone for a while. The dust was rising, and I decided to walk in too. They were talking about something, just standing there in the front yard. I scanned a quick look around the house – a nice yard, the garage was large too. A small black gate was right there, that led to the actual house. But some stairs were right there on its right side, rounded and went upstairs. There were only two floors.

"So, umm… Mahnoor." Danish chuckled at the word *Mahnoor,* and it felt annoying, "We are staying upstairs."

"Cliché."

"Also, you cannot come downstairs until I tell you to." Danish told us both, "My parents will kill me if they find out I'm keeping some girl here."

"Umm… okay? I guess?"

"Yes."

Zaib and I climbed the stairs, still holding our bags and my guitar. With slight difficulty, and I almost fell when somehow Zaib held me, we finally climbed. I looked across, more porch than rooms. We could play football there, If I knew how to. Zaib went straight into the room, and I followed.

I noticed how there was only one room for us, the rest of the rooms were locked.

"I better take a shower." Zaib told me, as she removed her shirt. I saw her bra, I saw her body. Half-naked. She was always pretty, but she was suddenly being sexy now. I wanted to kiss her, but then I thought about it again. I recalled looking in the side mirror, I remembered how ugly I was. Even considering she was homosexual, she was way out of my league.

Zaib noticed me staring at her, at her shoulders, at her chest, at her stomach. But I wasn't just staring, I was understanding her concept. People's bodies can tell you a lot about them. I noticed all the marks over her shoulder, and her chest. Freckles. They were looking pretty and not at all ugly.

"Are you in love with me or something?" she laughed, and I replied with an eye roll.

And she took off her pants, and turned around to go to the bathroom. I watched her go. I noticed the curviness of her ass, and her gait. I noticed how she turned, I noticed how her back curved ever so slightly whenever she walked. She didn't seem nervous, I wanted to hug her. I wanted to cuddle her.

Just before she was about to enter the bathroom, she asked me something. Out of the blue, "you're gay?" My heartbeat rose dramatically, my ocean was uncalm. Something happened. I felt chilling through my spine, I felt my hair rising off goosebumps, "You're gay." She smiled. She came up to me, and she got her head near me. My breathing was fast, but she was calm. Her lips were very near mine, and I thought she was going to kiss me. But she didn't. She just said, "amazing." And sighed. And walked back. Got into the shower, but just before she got into the shower, she turned back, "Now I know how you feel. I'm a lesbian too." She smiled, and she left me confused.

All the time she was in the shower, I kept thinking about the same thing over and over. She is gay too? Wow. But it didn't matter too much, because even if she was homosexual, she was way out of my league. I looked at the mirror in the room, and I looked at it still trying to figure out a way to make myself less ugly. My face was always going to be round, I was always going to have stretch marks on my body. My belly would always be a pouch. I wasn't very fat, but I was still fat enough to be ugly.

I heard Zaib singing in the shower, and her voice suddenly became better. She sounded horrific the last time, but now I wanted to hear her sing. I wanted to sit beside her, and hear her as I played the guitar. I wanted to kiss her. I could kiss her. I should have kissed her. Ugh, why didn't I? I really, really should have.

When she came out of the shower, I asked her one more thing. "So, you were telling the truth when you said *Borrowed?*"

"What did you think?" She smirked, and winked at me. "Anyway, I like how you didn't ask a question about my gayness."

"It doesn't matter to me." I said it like it was true, but it wasn't true. I did care if she was a lesbian too, because the truth was I wanted her to be gay. I wanted to be her girlfriend – or maybe that's going a little too far.

"Why doesn't it?" She said, still in the bathrobe. The towel on her hair, and just a little cleavage off her chest, "I want to talk about homosexuality with someone who truly understands it. Don't you?"

"Well," I looked at her. I looked at her curvy body, I looked at her brown eyes, her blushed cheeks, her pretty lips, I kept looking at her, "yeah, but… isn't it kind of personal?"

"Maybe." She smiled. "Okay, so you wanna go outside for a while or do you want me to change in front of you?"

Obviously, I wanted her to change in front of me, but I couldn't say that – could I? So, I just nodded and got out of the room. It was getting colder out there. It was night, and it was a very dark night. Despite, when I looked up, the stars were shining, and the moon was magical, and everything seemed a lot better suddenly. It felt as if the sky was calling me, and I wanted to fly away. Wanted to fly far away.

Zaib came, and I didn't hear her footsteps until she was right behind me, and hugged me. She hugged me like she meant it. I wanted to stay there, I could stay there the whole night. Between her arms, her boobs on my back, her face on my neck. Her legs touched mine. My hair rising to the edge, I wanted to turn around and kiss her. I just wanted to. I could have, but I didn't. For the second time, I made the same mistake.

"Hey?" She said, very softly. I could barely hear her, even though her mouth was right next to my ear, "Do you wanna sleep outside tonight?"

I turned around, and I saw her lips right in front of me. I saw her eyes, and I looked deep into them. I saw the universe, I saw something I cannot describe, maybe I saw my reflection. Maybe I saw my future, or my past. I didn't know, I can never know. "Sure." I said, and she walked back in. Perhaps to fetch a mattress or something, and I realized quickly enough she couldn't get that thing alone, so I went after her.

She was trying to hold the mattress straight, but it kept falling. It was too big for both of us, but it was good enough for me to have a laugh.

"SHUT UP AND HELP ME." She almost screamed, when I decided laughter isn't the best option here. So, I tried to hold the mattress from the other end, and somehow, we were able to get it in the right position and get it out of the room.

Zaib placed it right on the dusty porch, and we didn't much care about that. We just wanted to lie down, but someone had to go and get the blankets and the pillows. I went in, and came back with two blankets and two very fluffy pillows. I saw Zaib, already lying there. She looked pretty even in her night dress. I couldn't wait to be with her, sleep with her again. I almost jumped on the mattress, and she let out a little squeak followed by a laughter. Her laughter was pure. I tickled her, and found out she was just as ticklish as me. I put my hands around her waist, she put her hands around my back. We pulled each other closer, and the laughter was now over. I was breathing heavily again, and now she was too. She said it again, "amazing." And this time she didn't hold back. She put her lips on mine, and I suddenly felt my breath being taken away. My body got warmer, especially my neck. She put her hands around my face. And she kissed even more, she kissed me like she meant it. And finally, when none of us could breathe anymore, she pulled her mouth away. I could hear her breathing, I could feel the air from her mouth falling on my face. I could smell her, her hair, her breath, her scent. Chocolate, strawberries, mint. Everything which was supposed to be cliché, was turning out to be the best dream ever. We kissed again, and just as good. Better. We could have done that all night. I had never kissed before, and I wasn't sure if she had either, but it felt like something different than anything else I had ever done. We were both tired, tired enough to stop the kissing. We just lay there, she had her arms around my body. I had cuddled with her chest, because she was a little taller than me. But it was amazing. And then she reached down to her side of the mattress, and brought an unopened pack of cigarettes.

"Oh no." I looked at her face, and it was wet. She was crying. She hadn't made a single sound, but her face was filled with tears, "What happened?"

"No one is happy." She said it again, just as powerfully the first time. "Why the fuck won't this open?"

Her hands were shaking, her whole body was. She was trying to remove the transparent cover off the pack, but she was hurt too badly. I took the pack from her. At first, I thought of throwing it away, I didn't want her to smoke. I did not want her to smoke the poison, I didn't want her to die of cancer. I wanted her to live, because I wanted more nights like this one. I wanted more kisses. It was all very naïve, so I decided that I should help her. I opened the pack for her, and pulled out two cigarettes. Put one in my mouth, and one in hers. I signed, asking for the lighter, and she gave me one. I looked at it, it was designed with the Van Gogh painting. The starry night. I looked at the sky, the stars. I looked at my bracelet, which I was still wearing. I looked at her face, and she pulled out the cigarette.

"I like stars." She smiled. And she pointed towards the sky, I followed her finger, "Look."

And I looked, and it was amazing. The stars, the night, the moon. It was amazing. I had changed, that was when I truly realized I had changed. I really wasn't Javeria Sultan anymore – I was Mahnoor Ahmad.

I lit up my cigarette, and then I lit up Zaib's. And we smoked, we smoked like it was the last time we were smoking. Like there would be no tomorrow, and we would die. And if we did have, It would have been the happiest death ever. But I didn't die, and Zaib didn't die either.

"You're a star." She smiled, "you really are."

"Distant and dying." I replied, and she laughed.

"Everyone is dying. Life is just the beginning of death." She kissed my cheek, my round ugly cheek, "but you're not distant anymore. I swear you're not."

And we smoked. We just kept smoking, and we never stopped. One after another, we smoked the whole pack. It was amazing, the taste, the nicotine, the relief, the beauty in it. Everything was amazing, just like Zaib, just like Mahnoor, just like the entire universe.

I had thought about crushes, and I had thought about having feelings for someone. I had thought about heartbreaks, and even about death, but I had never thought about love. How would it be to fall in love. You can't control your exceptionally high rate of heartbeat, or your breathing, or your thoughts. I always thought it was just some hormones, some oxytocin, and that is it. That is love. But it felt greater than that, and I didn't know it would come like this. But it did come like this – I was falling in love.

When we were finished smoking, Zaib looked at me again. And I didn't know what to do, I just stared back. Then she faced her eyes towards the sky, and I followed her.

"Look." She said again, and I did as she said. Then she pointed at a few stars. I tried to look where she was pointing, "See those three stars?"

"What three stars?" I tried to look harder, and finally I did look at them. The three stars, very close to each other. I didn't know any technical names, but I had noticed them before. "Oh."

"Orion's belt." She smiled. "We are like Orion's belt, okay? These stars are always close to each other, they never fall apart. And they're usually the brightest to shine. We three are like the belt of Orion, always together, always shining, always *amazing*."

"We three?" I was confused. But aren't we just two? What did she mean?

She just smiled, and took a long, "you'll see. Tomorrow." I raised my eyebrows a little.

"Okay, I guess?"

She nodded, and closed her eyes. And I looked back at the sky. Orion's belt. The three stars, always together and never apart. Who's the third one? It didn't matter. We were the three stars, always together and never apart. Just like my ocean, just like myself, just like Zaib. Always together and never apart.

Chapter 6:

I slept, and it was the best night I ever had – at least as far as I could remember. I woke up next to Zaib, who wasn't asleep. When I opened my eyes, she was looking at me.

"Come on." I saw her smile, and then she lowered her face a little more. She kissed me. I didn't care if she had brushed, or washed her face, or anything else, I just kissed back. "Glad you're up."

"I need a shower." I told her. I realized it wasn't morning yet, it was still dark. "Or, maybe after sunrise."

She smiled, and held me. I sat straight. It was still cold.

"Cigarette?" I asked her, and she almost laughed. She still hadn't had her glasses on, and I liked her that way. I liked her with glasses, I liked her without glasses, I just liked her every way.

She shook her head, and reached to her bag, and took out two lollipops.

"Want a lollipop?" She offered me one of them, and I took it. Obviously.

"I wonder if they're poisonous." I stared at the wrapper, still trying to figure out how to open it. "I wouldn't care even if they are." I looked at Zaib, she looked back, and we smiled. "So, are we waiting for sunrise?"

"Yeah." She closed her eyes for a second, and then opened them again. I couldn't figure the meaning out of it, "Just a minute."

The air smelt like her, it smelt like her hair, it smelt like her breath, it smelt like her scent. I liked it. I wanted to stay there forever. And then we kept quiet. We used to do that, we used to keep a little while of silence every now and then. Sometimes, it made me wonder, how could a silence that usual could make me feel different?

And there it was. My second sunrise with Zaib, just like the first one. The sunrays just fall on our arms, and shoulders, and then our chest. We held each other in our arms, and we could feel the warmth of every inch of our skin. Maybe it wasn't the sunrise, maybe it was something else. Whatever it was, it was amazing.

"Hey, Mahnoor." I liked that I wasn't Javeria anymore, but I wanted her to call me by my real name. I didn't know why, but I guess I could work it anyway, "you know what really is my plan?"

"What?"

"Just this." She smiled, or smirked. I couldn't tell the difference, "just this."

"I hope this is metaphorical." And we both laughed. I liked the way she laughed, I liked the way I used to laugh with her.

"Totally." She pulled her glasses out of her bag, and wore it on. Still beautiful, still pretty, still sexy. "We're going Lahore, and I know a guy who can get you into this music thingy."

"What guy?" I raised my shoulder a little. I was suddenly a lot more curious, because it was about the real thing I had come to do. Sing. I had come this far, not to be with Zaib, but to be a star. Not the *distant and dying* kind, the *always together and never apart* kind.

"Akmal." She smiled, as she put on her socks. I didn't notice she had slept without socks, it was too cold for that. Did she feel as cold as I did? Or is she immune to that too? Such a mystery. "The third star."

The third star? Wow. Some dude, who can get me into singing is the third star from Orion's belt. He had to be special, I started imagining him. He had to be a big guy, handsome, sexy. Not very intellectual, but the kind of guy who knows where what is. Who could smuggle you a bag of meth if he wanted to – but I thought about it again, how could a guy like that be our third star? I mean, he had come before me, there had to be something very special about him. *Akmal*. I liked the name. *Akmal*. I smiled.

I got into the shower. I couldn't take off my shirt or my pants in front of Zaib, like she did. I wasn't that sexy, I didn't have that great of a body. I didn't know what to do. When I took off my clothes in the bathroom, I couldn't stare at myself in the mirror for much long. It made me cry – stretch marks, chubby cheeks, lose belly. I wanted to work out, but what was going to be the point anyway? I was still going to be ugly on the face. I wonder if I had anything better to do than maybe sing a little. I hated myself. But not so much anymore, since Zaib. Whenever I kissed her, she made me feel worth it. We couldn't kiss in public, but when there was no one watching, we could kiss as much as we wanted to.

Guess what I realized just before running the water on? I forgot to pack my toothbrush. The water ran over my face, and I kept thinking the same thing over and over. Who is Akmal? What is happening between me and Zaib? Is she in love with me too? Or is it all just another ordinary relationship? The more I thought about it, the more intense it got, because there were no clues to answer any of these questions except that when she kissed me, I could feel she was reaching my heart and whispering *I love you*. But was she whispering? Or was it just another illusion?

I got out of the shower. Looked at my clothes – black, black, black, black, grey, white, black. I didn't want to wear black that day, I wanted to wear something more freshening. I remembered seeing an orange kurta once, it had little jasmine and tulip flowers printed on it, the colors didn't match much – but it was pretty. Ugly, yes, but pretty. The pretty kind of ugly. I used to think it was very cliché, but now I wanted to wear that kurta. I wanted to try it on, and hug Zaib. I wanted to ask Zaib how I looked in that. But I couldn't, of course. So, I just decided to wear the white shirt. A very rare occasion. I wore my blue jeans. I guess the outfit was okay, I mean, it was cool by Jiya's standards – but by Mahnoor's? I don't know.

When I looked in the mirror, and started brushing again, I decided what I am going to change when I get to Lahore. First thing – the hair. I had to get a haircut, I would have looked way better in a shorter haircut. I wanted to have a tomboy hairstyle. The dress. I was still not going to buy any kurtas, but I decided to widen my range of Tees and Jeans, maybe of different styles, and designs. I had to start working out, definitely. I had gotten way fat. No more extra fast food, or ice cream, or anything. Everything is limited. It was always going to be limited anyway, since I knew I was going to have money problems. I was missing out on something... what should it be. Ugh. And then I realized, I needed a tattoo too! Yes, a tattoo. But of what? What was going to be special enough? I had no more thoughts. Always together and never apart.

When I was done with thinking about my ugliness, and what I had to do in order to fit in, in order to make myself worth Zaib. I was just about to call Zaib, to ask where she was, because she wasn't there when I had come out of the bathroom. But then I heard a roar, Zaib came in from the door, and banged the door behind her as quickly as possible.

"Quick." She looked tensed, sweat pouring out of her forehead, "hide as much of your stuff as you can. NOW."

And she and I both started packing things, put it under the bed, behind the cupboard. I was still confused as to why, maybe her aunt had figured out that Danish was hiding girls here. Very carefully, we slid in our every item. The hair brush, the ponies, the socks, my deodorant. Everything. And I hid them all under the bed, with the suitcase.

"Get in the cupboard with me." In the same hurried tone, she almost ordered me to get our asses saved, "NOW."

And we got in the cupboard. Barely enough room for both us, our bodies almost collapsing, and we could barely hear what was happening outside. I can't think for sure, but I guess Zaib put her finger between her lips, and asked me to keep quiet, and I did keep quiet. I tried to listen, and it in fact was Danish's mom.

"Mom! I swear there was no one here." Danish's voice was shaky, and nervous. Kind of like what mine gets just before I go to sleep. "I don't lie to you."

"I saw someone, mister." By the confidence in her voice, I could tell she had seen at least one of us. Probably Zaib when she was not in the room, "And not just someone but a girl. And you tell me, Danish. You say I can't believe my own eyes? I know somebody's hiding here."

I didn't think it was going to be this big of a deal, but it was. Danish's mom didn't take anything for granted, not even letting someone sleep in their house for a single night.

"Mama." Danish's voice was still shaky, "If there really was someone, wouldn't they be here? I guess you saw the neighbor's boy, and thought he was a girl. He's always sneaking on the roof. Always fooling around."

Here mom didn't answer, perhaps she believed him. But I can bet she looked for us, or at least Zaib. She would have turned even the mattress over, thank God, we brought it back in the morning. It's a miracle she didn't look under the bed, and when finally, we could hear no more voices than Danish's telling us to get out, we indeed came out.

When she was with me in the cupboard, all I got to think other than not being caught, is how close she is to me. Because every time she touched me, everything made sense. I liked how she was colder one moment, and then got very warm the other. She was only cold when I needed her to be, like the time we were smoking on the edge of the cliff, and warm when she had to be, like every time the sun would ask us to fall in love, and fall hard.

"Okay." I asked Zaib as soon as we caught our breath again, "now what?"

"We'll take a bus. To Lahore. And live our life to the fullest." She smiled. That damned smile. Beautiful but mysterious.

And we started packing, for real. I had almost forgotten about the bracelet, and when I looked at it again, just before I wore it, I noticed the stars. Orion's belt. Always together and never apart. I smiled. I usually never realized that I was smiling, but whenever I saw that bracelet, each time I knew I was smiling. It was a reflex.

When we were just about to leave, Danish was seeing us on the bus. We walked, on the highway. The bus stop was just around the corner – according to Danish, but I didn't know where it was *just around the corner*. It felt long enough, though.

My head was still hurting with the thought of Zaib kissing me. It was anxiety, and even though I loved it when she did that, for a moment I wanted to be alone. But of course, I couldn't be. We kept walking.

"Where is it?" I got fed up with walking with all those bags on me. I was tired.

"Just around the corner." Danish pointed his fingers towards the far stretching road, and I couldn't see any corner. "What? You're tired? Do you want me to hold your bag for you?" He said. It makes me look pitiful.

"You can't even hold your life together, how can you hold my bag?" I rolled my eyes, and pulled the bag closer to my shoulder. Zaib laughed, and I smiled. I liked to make her laugh.

"Stop fighting you guys." Zaib kicked me very lightly, "We're gonna do amazing things, okay Mahnoor?"

"Nothing could be more amazing than killing this douchebag." She laughed, and I laughed too. I wanted to kiss her, but not with Danish watching.

"What's your plan anyway?" Danish looked down at his shoes as he walked beside us. His hands in his pockets, barely moving his shoulders.

"She's a singer." Zaib told him, like it was very normal. "A pretty good one."

"Really?" He looked at me like it was something very unusual. I mean, as unusual it could get, seeing a singer shouldn't be that fascinating. "Sing something."

I thought of not singing – Javeria would have never, but this wasn't Javeria. This was Mahnoor. Mahnoor likes to show off her singing to common people, she doesn't hold back when people ask her to sing, she in fact loves it when people ask her to sing. So, I sang *Passenger*:

Here's a simple song

Won't stop the rain from coming down, or your heart from breaking

Here's a simple

Never gonna turn this day around, or stop the Earth from shaking

"Wow." Danish shook his head a little, not in denial, but in appreciation. His eyes wide. "Fuck."

"Really?" I creased my brows, something smells fishy, "you're just saying."

"No." He shook his head again, "nothing."

I looked at Zaib, and noticed she was smiling. Again, mysterious. I wanted to know what was going on. There was silence, except when Danish was talking to himself. Or was he? I don't really know. He was speaking very softly, I couldn't hear him.

We finally got on the bus, after having listened to the repeated phrase of *Take care* by Danish. He made travelling on the bus look like some job only Martians could do – I think he would still have mistrust. It was not an actual bus, rather a coach.

"Hey, Mahnoor." She patted me on the shoulder as we walked towards our seats, "would you mind if I take the window seat?"

"Oh." I smiled, "Not at all." I could expect her to ask me this, she was always this cheerful girl who liked window seats, sunrises, and snowfall. She was special, and a special girl always likes special things – and maybe that was the only part that made me special.

She sat on the window seat, and I sat beside her. The chairs were uncomfortable, and I had to rearrange my position every five minutes, like I was getting some kind of punishment. The bus ride was very different from the Bentley ride. Less air, less comfort, less independence. Couldn't play guitar, even though I didn't play it the first time either. But anyway, the excitement was greater – Many reasons: A new life, singing career, Zaib, and of course, Akmal.

"Do you want bubble gum?" She asked me. Her eyes were not at all tired, but I guess they were down for some reason. I couldn't understand what that reason was, but she seemed sad. I wanted to kiss her, I wanted to cheer her up, but I realized the best way to do that was to accept the bubble gum.

"Strawberry?" I raised my eyebrows, and my shoulders. I tried to smile.

"Strawberry." She nodded with a quick jerk, and smiled back. I took the bubblegum, and put it in my mouth. I chewed a little, and focused on the flavor. I let it melt, I let it please my mouth.

"I like strawberries." I smiled again, and grabbed her hand. Her hands were cold, even though it was unusually hot outside. I noticed as far as we got from Islamabad, the atmosphere started getting hotter, but not Zaib. She was as cold as they get. But she had the warmest heart.

For a while we remained quiet. She was looking out of the window as we passed trees, and fields, and different houses. She was thinking about something, she definitely was. I decided to talk to her.

"Hey, Zaib." I knocked her arm with my elbow, "Tell me. Why do you eat so much sugar? Lollipops and bubblegum. They can give you diabetes. Maybe not as early an age as now, but later."

"Do you want me to smoke, rather?" She looked serious. I hadn't seen her this serious in a while, not even when she was kissing me. She was a little mad, it couldn't be about this question. She was mad at something else. I shook my head. "Then fucking let me have gum."

I wasn't angry at her for being mad at me. I simply held her hand again, and slid my thumb over her wrist slightly. I knew she was getting calmer. Maybe she was like my ocean too – only hurts when calm, because as calm as she got, as sad she was getting. I had another idea, and I pulled out hands-free from the corner pocket of my bag. I had to stand up and awkwardly bend to get it out, but I did it for Zaib.

"Do you wanna listen to something special?" I asked her, she didn't react. So, I got near her ear, and asked again. "Zaib, do you want to listen to something special?"

She nodded and sighed. I plugged my hands-free in my cell, and put the nodes in head ears. And then I played the songs I had recorded back in my room. They were not just songs, they were my feelings, and she was the first person to listen to them beside me. I noticed the change in her expressions, she wasn't mad or sad anymore. She was finally getting better.

"You sing so well." She grabbed my hand, and I grabbed back. "you're awesome."

"I know that." I laughed, and she laughed back. Finally.

Chapter 7:

We didn't talk very much on the bus, maybe because Zaib didn't want to, or maybe because I didn't want to. Not because I didn't want Zaib to not tell me why she was sad – Oh God forbid, no. I just wanted her to take her time. It was just as likely that this was her first relationship with someone. Or, I wanted her to tell me, but I didn't know how to ask.

I kept chewing on the gum. I liked the smell and the sound it made when I popped the bubble, and how it tasted like Zaib's kisses. I looked at Zaib again, she was beautiful. I could say that a million times and it wouldn't have been enough – but, yes, she was beautiful. She was amazing.

Finally, the bus stopped. I grabbed my guitar, and my bag. Zaib didn't realize the bus had stopped, so I had to pat on her shoulder like she used to, to me. She smiled.

"Day dreaming?" Her head was resting on the window glass, and she tried to turn her head around but the hair got stuck, so she had to jerk it, "Don't tell me it was a nightmare."

"Nightmares aren't real." She tried to stand up, "but the past is."

I understood. Something from her past was still bothering her, but what was it? She hadn't told me, but of course I hadn't asked either. I didn't want to ask her out of curiosity, I decided I would ask her when I would be able enough to help her. I wanted to hug her, hold her in my arms, kiss her. But I couldn't do that on the bus, so I somehow just grabbed her bag too, and started walking ahead of her. She followed me out of the bus, and now I finally realized. I'm in Lahore. Freedom. Independence. Dream. Love. I let out a very loud *WooHoo,* hands in the air putting the bags down, very unlike Javeria.

"Wow." She looked at me like I was a mad person, maybe I was. "Told you. Poetic to be insane."

My ocean was very uncalm, I couldn't believe the time was here. The time when I will finally do stuff I was made for. I wasn't born in the right place, but I was going to do the right thing. "Poetic to be insane indeed." I smiled.

"I should write a book." She looked around a little, and cracked her knuckles slightly, "How to motivate people: 101."

"I bet it would be a bestseller."

And all of a sudden, she got serious. Her eyes were focused, her fingers on her chin, "Maybe I should." For a moment I felt stupid to think she was joking in the first place, but then she laughed at my stunned look and it made me feel stupid all over again.

"You know what would the title of a book if I ever write one?" She folded her arms in front of her chest, and her shoulder muscles tensed. I wondered.

"What?" I shook my head slightly, and lifted my shoulders in curiosity.

"How to fail at writing a book: 101." She smirked, and I burst out laughing. It was good to see her cheer up a little. For a moment I forgot about everything, even Akmal. All I wanted to do was kiss her. But only for a moment, and I started thinking about Akmal again.

"Why are we waiting here?" I looked at my broken watch, and I remembered Emaan. How is he doing? Is he okay? Has he understood that I had to go? I just shook my head to myself. Don't think about it. "When will we go to Akmal?"

"Why are you so impatient?" She said it like it wasn't normal to be impatient. I was dying to know who he is, what he looked like, what made him our third star. "You just came. Let me show you my city."

"Your city?"

"Don't you know?" She smirked again. Mysterious. Tragic. Beautiful. "I am in fact a Lahori. I came to Islamabad only to study."

"Explains a lot."

It did. Her family was here. Explained everything. She was ready to run away, because she wasn't really running away. She was going back. Maybe she had already told her family about me. Maybe I was going to stay with them. That is why no one at college knew about Zaib's background, because she kept it low key. No one ever came to pick her up, or drop her off. No one ever came to her parent-teacher meetings. It all made sense.

"Ugh." In my thoughts, I didn't realize she was holding her phone in her hand. She was texting someone. Who? Oh, I knew! Akmal. "Akmal is almost here."

"Isn't that a good thing?" I jolted my head a little, and she just shook her head.

"Not when I had to show you around a little."

"It's a whole city, even bigger than Islamabad. What could you have shown me in mere a couple minutes?"

"I don't know." She rolled her eyes, and I saw myself in that, "at least something."

Akmal was coming to pick us up. He was almost here. Who could he be? What did he feel like? Did he smell like Zaib too? Or did he like sweets too? And then I thought about another thing – Did he even know he was a star? I didn't know I was one until last night, could it be the same with him? Whatever it was, I knew one thing. There was no scenario where I didn't picture Akmal as someone special. He had to be special too. He had to be *Amazing*.

Zaib walked around for a little while, because Akmal was late. Her hands tied behind her back, she kept walking in the same circle over and over around the bench I was sitting on. I couldn't keep looking at her because my head would hurt, but I wanted to keep looking at her, because somehow she looked prettier when she was mad. Serious. Intense. God, I loved how she walked too, leg after leg, and her hips moving ever so slightly. She was so sexy, in every way. Unlike me, and suddenly the thought of my ugliness put me down a little. I wish I were that sexy.

"Ugh." She put her hands in the air, forcing a claw and looking at the sky as she continued her walk, "where the hell is he?"

"And you say I'm impatient."

"Ugh." She rolled her eyes, and then I had the perfect idea. I decided to sing a song. That would cheer her up a little, yes it definitely would.

I put my guitar in my lap, and started strumming just before she realized I was playing the guitar. She stopped, turned around in a flash. Her eyes were sparkling – like a star. I knew how much she loved my voice, and I knew how my singing could make her feel better. I decided to sing a song by Grace VanderWaal. A song I could always relate too.

I don't know my name.

I don't play by the rules of the game.

So, you say I'm just trying, just trying.

She was smiling. Her cheeks were wide, her lips were together. Her face was calmer, there was no anger, and I decided to continue. People started gathering around me – listening to me without uttering a word, and I kept going – song after song, chord after chord, note after note. I enjoyed it. I enjoyed people listening to me, admiring me, seeing my potential. But most of all, I enjoyed Zaib listening to me.

I enjoyed how she dramatically changed when I was singing, like I wasn't me. I wasn't Javeria, or Mahnoor. I wasn't Hania, or Sana. I was something different, someone else, someone like Zaib herself.

I kept playing, 'till I was tired. And the moment I was tired, I realized that Akmal was very late. I let out a very slight sigh just after I finished, and said under my breath, "That's it, folks." I smiled a little, and the people cheered. Claps, and chanting. I felt special again, not the kind of special I used to feel, but the kind of special that made me special too. If I would have told them to follow me on social media, they probably would have. That kind of special. But doing that would have made me weak, because that was deflecting myself from my real purpose – the top. Even though I had no idea, I knew Zaib had something special going on. She just left all the suspense to me, and to be honest – I didn't even mind it that much. I just smiled.

And then came a car, and parked right in front of us. A grey Santro, Old. Dented, and scratched all over. It must have been around ten to twelve years old – but it was a car, and what mattered more was Zaib's reaction on the arrival of the car. She stood up with a flash, sharp, quick. Same sparkling eyes, and she almost shouted, "AKMAL!" I could see the joy in her smile. She put her arms wide open, as to hug the car, but then came out of the car a teenager. About our age. He was skinny, almost as tall as Zaib, but he had a light beard. 5 0'clock shadow. His face was pointed, like a wizard hat, but it was somehow cute. Handsome. He looked an awful lot like Zaib, and at once I realized – brother.

"It's been so long." He took off his shades, and I saw his eyes. Brown. Zaib brown. His voice was a little shady, but high somehow. Not the kind you're afraid of, the kind you like enjoying listening to. The only thing is unlike Zaib, anyway I liked both of their voices.

Zaib kept her hug on Akmal for a minute, but then she pulled back, and hit him forcefully on the chest. She didn't intend the punch to be light or anything, she meant to hit him just as hard as possible. Akmal let out a little *Ow,* and asked with sheer innocence, "What was that for?"

"Two years." Zaib said angrily, and with even more passion, "TWO YEARS. And you're late?!"

Two years? What about two years? They hadn't met for Two years? I thought about not meeting Emaan for two years, and it would have killed me. Sure, I had run away, but I was going to go back someday, and I hoped that someday would come within a year or even six months. But leaving Emaan wasn't a choice, and these guys did it voluntarily? No. There was something, there had to be something I didn't know.

"I was hungry." Akmal smiled. Smirked, in fact, exactly like Zaib. "Had to grab a bite. Priorities."

"I covered half Punjab for you." She frowned, "and all you can think of is food?"

"Ahem for me ahem." He said it with enough sarcasm to make Zaib bite her lip.

"And also, Mahnoor." She shook her head a little, making me insignificant in comparison to Akmal. To be honest, it made me a little angry. Why not? I was a fucking star too. She told me she was running away for me, with me. Did she? She did, even if not directly. God. But then I got over that, because Akmal indeed was a star with her, since her birth. I mean, I just came along, but Akmal was there for her for her whole life. Life is a mysterious term, it can start at one moment and end at another.

Akmal walked towards me, and I smelled honey. And tobacco, and nicotine. He smelled like honey and cigarettes. Made sense. Or maybe still not. The pieces were being put together little by little – Zaib has a tragic backstory, she has a brother she loves, she smokes and eats sweets, she is homosexual, she believes no one is happy because everyone is afraid of happiness. Okay, maybe the puzzle was still not any clear, but I had to know. I really had to.

"Wow." Akmal was taller than me, just like Zaib, so he bowed a little, "I'm Akmal. Akmal Abbasi." He smiled, and pulled himself a little closer to me. I stared into his eyes, "And you are Mahnoor. Mahnoor Ahmad."

I nodded. Maybe to myself, maybe to make myself confront once more that I'm Mahnoor now. Mahnoor Ahmad. Not Jav- Oh forget it. I vowed to never take that name again – and stop others from calling me that too. I was Mahnoor Ahmad, only Mahnoor Ahmad. Who was in a fantastic relationship with the most perfect girl in the universe: Zaib Abbasi.

"I'm hungry too, you know." Zaib cried from the back, and Akmal smirked still looking at me.

"I'm not." He turned his head, and I saw a little tattoo on his neck. Just above his black shirt – A star. He knew he was a star, and judging by the confidence with which he talked to me, I concluded he knew I was a star too.

The tattoo was more than a star, a bolt going through it. The whole thing was covered in lining, and it looked like it was done by an expensive tattoo artist. I decided right then. I was going to get a similar tattoo.

They argued a little, not the serious kind even though Zaib seemed pretty mad. My ocean was uncalm, it hadn't been calm for a while now. I looked at my watch again, and it had been two hours since we arrived on the station. That was late, and finally they ended their little argument.

"Okay Mahnoor." Zaib winked at me, and smiled. Much more cheerful now. "We are going to McDonald's. Are you just gonna sit there?"

"I hope not." I smiled and rolled my eyes at the same time, and winked back. "Let's go."

I realized Zaib was a shotgun even if she didn't call it, so I just helped myself to the back seat. It was just as bad on the inside as it was on the outside. To face it, it was pathetic. The seat covers were all messed up, and the floor had litter, and it stink. Of cigarettes of course. But I liked it, because for once all three stars were under the same roof. It was amazing, the feeling, to know that all you could have was there, and the only thing left, was music.

"Heard you can sing." Akmal looked at me through the back mirror, with slight awkwardness, "sing."

I thought of playing guitar, but it was too congested. I couldn't, so I decided to sing Acapella instead. I thought about what song to sing, I had never thought about it before, but I did this time. Because I had to build an impression, and these were actually my first words to him. So, I finally sang Halsey – Gasoline

You can't wake up this is not a dream

Your part is a machine, you're not a human being

I think it did the job, judging by the look on his face. He was stunned, and Zaib gave him an *I told you* look. I was stiff, and moved my eyes around them for a millisecond, and then understood it all. I smiled. But I knew, that look on Akmal, that look meant something.

I stayed quiet in the back seat, but Akmal and Zaib talked a lot. About everything that had happened, like they hadn't talked for years, even though that could not be possible because I saw her texting him. Maybe they just liked to talk to each other.

As the car moved, I kept thinking about their family. What Would their parents be like? Do they know I'm coming? They had to know – you can't sneak a person forever. I was sure I was going to stay with them, Zaib knew I couldn't survive on my own. Or maybe their parents were to be a little different than mine, maybe they understood their children, maybe they knew that sometimes, helping is okay. Maybe. It had all to be answered.

Akmal took a sharp turn, and suddenly out of nowhere we were in some sort of slums. Ghettos. It was barely enough space for the car to drive through, and bumps were constantly making the car jump like on a trampoline. And it stunk. It was nasty, I had to hold my neck and keep myself still as Akmal tried not to scratch the car. And suddenly, the bad condition of the car made sense. So much for the fresh air of freedom.

"enjoying your ride?" Zaib turned back and smirked. I just made a funny face of disgust, as if teasing her, and she laughed slightly. Akmal laughed too.

"Please tell me your house is not here." I barely spoke, with my hand still on my nose, "PLEASE."

"Do you think I'm the CEO of Amazon?" She frowned a little, "it's all I can afford."

"yikes."

"It's not that bad." Akmal jumped in, trying to break the tension, "once you get used to it, you'll understand all that matters, lies within."

"Thou shalt not act like Shakespeare." I said in a fabulous tone, "thee shalt only listen to Mahnoor Ahmad."

"Thou shalt shut up when thee don't know how to use thee."

"Confusing." I nodded, finally lifting off my hand, "but cool."

"I'm still hungry you know." Zaib shook her head slightly, "I still need food."

"I have a bag of fries from three days old."

"Eww." She put her hand in front of Akmal and turned her head the other way, "gross." Akmal just gave an evil smile.

And for the next five minutes, I let them talk again. I was too busy thinking I was going to stay here. I wasn't used to facing any situations like this one, I had always had a house in a *respectable* place, if that's the right word. But I thought, if Zaib used to live here, I could too. The houses were small, I guessed her family was small too. Maybe they could accommodate me.

And then the car finally stopped. I looked at the house, it was small. Like, half as small as my old house. It was packed, no front lawn, no porch, no balcony, nothing. There were only going to be rooms inside. We took our luggage, and walked in. Okay, there was a little porch, and a hole above it making a way for air and sunlight, but the rest, only rooms. There were two floors, and when Akmal walked upstairs, Zaib followed and I followed. I noticed the rooms downstairs were occupied, as the lights were on. Upstairs was one less room, but that gave a space for some area you may call a *balcony*, but it wasn't visible from the outside. It had two rooms, but there was no differentiation between them. You could hang a curtain between them, but I didn't think there was any need. There was no one upstairs, so I assumed their family was downstairs. I wondered when I would meet them. I so wanted to meet Zaib's parents, how come they were able to give birth to an angel.

Akmal unlocked the door, and almost shouted, "home, sweet home!"

"Sweet for sure." I rolled my eyes. I knew I was being rude again, it had changed for a while, but maybe I was programmed like that. I was a little rude with Zaib when I first met her too, and I was a little rude with Akmal too. It was going to take some time to get used to Akmal. "It's like a hen farm. Small. Stinky."

"No house is small." Zaib kissed on my cheek, "and no home stinks."

A sudden shiver went through my skin, like lightning hit me. I needed that, I needed that kiss. I needed her lips to touch me, so I turned around quickly enough and kissed her on the lips. Strawberries again. And between our lips, there was a feeling. I can't really put it into any other words but: it was like *Always together and never apart.*

Akmal jumped on the bed without taking off his shoes, and the mud off his snickers made the bed sheet slightly dirty. Zaib's face got red, and her eyes red. "AKMAL." He smiled, and realized it as soon as she shouted. He took off his shoes, and the smell just mixed with the already present stink and somehow almost made me throw up.

"How do you guys live here?" I put my hand again on my nose, this time covering it, "are you even human?"

"No." they both said at the same time, "we're stars."

Those words made me smile. Akmal knew. I knew. Zaib knew. I took my hand off, and hugged them. They hugged back, like a trio meant to be. Of course, meant to be. *Always together and never apart.*

There was only one bed, king size. Two people could sleep on it easily, but how could three people sleep on it? I didn't know. The rooms were smaller, in fact the two rooms combined made enough for the one I used to live in. The paint was hanging off the wall, like it had been years before it actually got painted. The smell didn't faint, but I was getting used to it. It was okay, I guess. It was livable.

The whole Zaib deal was getting onto me, so I had to ask her what was so tragic in the past, and when would I meet her family. I finally decided, I would ask her at dinner. I was tired from all the travelling and singing, so I fell on to the bed at once. I hadn't changed, I hadn't done anything yet. I just slept. I remembered Zaib before I fell asleep, I pictured her falling asleep next to me again. And then I thought *Does Akmal know we are in a relationship with each other? If he does, it will be awesome.* And then I fell asleep.

When I woke up, Zaib was shaking me. "Get up." Her voice sounded soft, and it seemed as if she would kiss me. She did, twice. "Get up, now." I groaned, and shook my head. She told me again, "Get up. Dinner." I stretched my arms and my legs, and took a big yawn. From the very narrow opening of my eyes, I looked at her smiling at me. She left the urge to wake me up, and lay down with me on the bed. We both remained quiet for a while. And then I finally gathered the guts to ask her, "Zaib?"

"Yeah?" Her voice was still soft, her eyes closed. Her breathing rate is normal enough for me to feel it, her hands are mine.

"Why aren't you happy?"

"Cherophobia." I looked at her, and she smiled. "Fear of happiness."

"No." I kissed her on the cheek, and she blushed, "tell me the real thing. Why aren't YOU Happy?"

"I think it's time." She nodded, and sat up. Her back was curvy, and I grabbed her from there. I kissed her on the neck, and then I slowly grabbed her cheeks. "My mom's name was Ishrat."

I pulled myself back, and felt a sudden jerk in my chest cavity. "Was?" I asked her, swallowing the fear of inevitable.

She looked at me again, put her hands on my hands again, "do you know what Ishrat means?"

"What?" I was stunned. Her mom was dead. She didn't wanna say it. Oh God. No, that couldn't happen to a person this good. No, please, no.

"Happiness." She told me, and the ground moved below me, and suddenly the air seemed grey. I couldn't breathe. "Happiness is… is dead." She focused her eyebrows on her glabella, and straightened her eyelids. She couldn't breathe either.

I didn't know what to say, I just stared at her. She was just as stunned as me, even though it was new to only one of us. "When she was alive, she was happy. I was happy. And now, no one is happy." She started crying, tear after tear. She didn't put her head between the palm of her hands, like I cry, no. She just sat still, let the tears come. This was the second time I saw her cry, just as the first time. The air felt cold again, and I wanted to kiss her, I swear I did, I should have, but I didn't. I did nothing. I felt like an idiot, this was exactly why I thought I should ask her when I was able enough to help her. But then again, when was I going to be able enough? I can't bring people back from the dead.

I had to know what happened, so trying hard not to drown in our sadness, I wiped her eyes. "Hey?" She looked at me, and I smiled very subtly, "Look at me." I nodded my head a little, "tell me what happened."

"Car accident." Her voice wasn't shaky, it was confident. Like she knew she was going to tell me. "Let me tell you everything. Before I was born, my mom wasn't very rich. Of course, but she was pretty. She had wonderful eyes, a wonderful face, everything about her was amazing. But of course, no money, no *Ishrat*. Her parents were poor too, but they had realized the beauty of their daughter, so, when my grandparents came across my dad, that rascal, they gave him my mother. Just for the sake of money. He, well, didn't treat her well, he didn't treat us well. He was an asshole." She shook her head again, and stood up, "Of course he was rich, and we did need money. But three years ago, my mom and my grandparents died in a car accident. My dad disowned us, and here we are. Do you know how I got this house? If it weren't for Akmal. We used to live on the streets, but Akmal got a job. The manager gave us both a single room. He was giving us two, but Akmal said that he wanted me to study, and that he may get me into a college, and he doesn't even need a salary. Just food. I wanted to study in Islamabad, in your college. I did. All thanks to Akmal. And I think I've studied enough, and now I believe in you. I want you to be my next third star."

"Next third star?"

"Alnitak." She nodded, and tried to smile, "My mom told me and Akmal, that we were the three brightest stars of Orion. There are a total of seven, but the belt only has three. Alnitak, Alnilam and Mintaka. She was Alnitak, I am Alnilam, and Akmal is Mintaka."

"I..." I couldn't find any words. I just saw the sparkle in her eyes, I couldn't believe she was actually bringing me this close to her, "I don't know what to say. I had no idea... I mean..."

Zaib put her finger on my lips, *shh*. She kissed me slightly, and my hair stood on end, "All I want you to know is, you're very special."

I nodded. And then I asked, "who are the people downstairs?"

"The manager."

"He's letting you live in his own house?"

"Yes." Zaib took out her phone, and started walking. I followed her as she texted, probably Akmal. "He's a very nice person, you know. He's helped us a lot."

"Hey Zaib." I held her hand, and stopped her with a sudden movement. "I just wanna say, you've made my life a lot better."

Zaib smiled. She finally did. Of course, she was still sad, sad on the inside, but I realized I meant a lot to her, and to know it made me happy. "Hey Mahnoor. You're the best girl I've ever come across."

I followed Zaib downstairs, where I saw a large fat guy. He was bald, and had freckles on his cheeks, he looked funny, and his face was way rounder than mine. His eyes were small, which might be a little cute. Typical manager. She had a wife, almost as fat, and looked just like him but they made a beautiful couple. They looked cute together.

"Hey, hey, hey." The Manager lifted his hand to High-five Akmal, "How's my beast?" Akmal high-fived him with just as enthusiasm, and replied, "doing great, chief. This Sunday's championship is definitely ours." And they talked about that a little, I didn't know what they meant. They couldn't have been talking about sports, but the guy was too fat to be a chief. I didn't care about it too much. Zaib went into the kitchen, and I followed her.

"Zaib."

"Yeah?" She asked me, still looking into the food being cooked. She stirred it smoothly. It smelled like Chicken.

"What championship?"

She looked at me, and opened her eyes a little, and then she relaxed, and smirked. "you'll see, tomorrow."

"Is that a catchphrase?" I shook my head, but she laughed, "could have been better, like *I'm a mystery*."

"Aren't mysteries cliché?" She winked and I noticed the sarcasm in her voice.

"You're a mystery, Zaib. And mysteries are beautiful." I nodded and she nodded back. No one was watching, I kissed her again. I had to stand on the edge of my toes to reach her forehead, but it was one of the best feelings I had ever felt.

And we sat at the dinner table. I introduced myself to them, and they introduced themselves

"I'm Akbar aka the chief." The fat guy told me, "and this is my lovely wife Zainab. I see you're a friend of Akmal."

"Yes, sir, I am."

"You see, we work-" Zaib gave Chief a sudden look, and he stopped telling me about the work. I loved how Zaib used to keep mysteries. It was cute, sometimes killer, but mostly cute. "Anyway, Akmal told me you can sing. I could use a good singer. You see, there's a championship coming up, and I need a host and a singer."

"I can host!" Zaib almost shouted. I liked the idea of me and Zaib working together, "Since I have no college, I would like to help."

"Sure." The chief nodded, and turned back to me, "Can you sing a little for me?"

"What is this championship?" I ignored the chief's invitation to sing, even though it was tempting, "I'll sing just as you tell me." I smirked at Zaib. I wanted to know what they were on, and I also wanted a little challenge with Zaib.

"Forget it." He waved his hand, and turned away.

"Sorry, sorry." I laughed and begged, at the same time, "I can sing, I can sing." Zaib and Akmal laughed, and I gave them an angry look. The chief told me to go on, and I sang Justin Bieber – Cold water

Everybody gets high sometimes, you know

What else can we do when we're feeling low?

So, take a deep breath and let it go

You shouldn't be drowning on your own

The chief's face was something to see, his small eyes as if popped out, and I could see his thoughts admiring me. "WOW" I didn't know I was this good. I mean, okay, I could sing, and sing very well, but really?

"What did I tell ya chief? Akmal hit his elbow on the chief's arm, just before he realized he was lost, "Like a freaking angel."

Chief couldn't say anything, he just nodded. I got some self-confidence, I was an amazing singer. I was the next big *wow*. I thought about how he was offering me my first professional job as a singer. Yes. It was all going alright for me! Even Zaib didn't smoke that night, all three of us slept on the bed somehow. We kept cuddling and all, it wasn't exactly how I imagined, but it really was turning out to be the best decision I had made for life. Life was amazing in Lahore.

Chapter 08:

Okay, did I tell you we slept fine? We didn't. Well, for once we were together, sleeping in on the same bed, but the bed was small. So, it was really a tussle to find your space. In the middle of the night, when I woke up after being hit on the face by Akmal's elbow, I groaned forcefully, but he continued his snorts. I smiled, and lowered my face next to his ears very slowly, and then all of a sudden shouted.

"WHAT THE HELL?"

Akmal woke up like a soldier, opened his eyes, didn't turn even a little, and sat still. "What happened?" Just as his mind was over the shock, his eyes went bloodshot, and yawned, "why shouting?"

Zaib woke up behind me, and trying to keep her calm said, "what's wrong?"

"Apparently… Akmal has a real liking of hitting my face with his elbow, and fists, and legs." Akmal chuckled, and I turned to him, leaning my eyebrows a little more, "Oh, you think it's funny?" I hit him straight into his stomach, and only then I realized how hard it was. It could have even been abs, but he was so skinny on the rest of his body.

"Oww." Akmal grabbed his tummy with both of his hands, "geez, what was that for?"

"For laughing at my plight."

"You deserved it, though." Zaib kicked in, and we both smirked at each other. I thought maybe it could be a thing, but Akmal was hurt worse than I thought. He got off the bed, and I started feeling a little sorry for him.

"Hey, are you okay?" I asked him as I got closer to him, leaning on the bed. I put my hand on his shoulder, but then he saw the chance and I realized he was faking it. He pulled me, and I fell off the bed just as hard. Zaib laughed, and at the end, I laughed too. It was fun, I wasn't actually mad at him.

Zaib grabbed my hand and pulled me back on the bed, and we lay next to each other again. Just before I fell asleep again, she held my hand. It made me feel warm and comfortable, "We'll do something about this tomorrow." And even though her eyes were closed, I nodded. Maybe she somehow knew I nodded, because she smiled.

The morning was pretty simple. When I woke up, neither of them were there, so I had to help myself to understand what was going to happen for breakfast. I stood up, realized I hadn't brushed my teeth for one day and two nights now. It made me feel sick, because even though I was unhygienic, I was still human. I texted Zaib that I needed a toothbrush, and she replied with *I know. It's in the bathroom.* There was a small bathroom in the corner of the adjoined rooms, and even though it was just as clean as you want it to be, it stunk. Maybe it was in the air, anyway I somehow brushed my teeth, took a dump, and had a shower. I played songs on my mobile phone during my shower, and when I came out, Zaib was standing there.

"What do we have for breakfast?" I asked her.

"I don't know, what do you want?"

"Anything." I sighed, "Anything would be okay. Are we eating with the chief?"

"No. The chief is at work, and so is Akmal, and so should be us. But I asked him to give us a day off, since we needed to shop and teach you everything you need to know about Lahore."

"Aye."

Zaib walked in front of me, and my stomach was having hunger pangs so loud I bet Zaib could hear since she turned and said, "what about *Halwa puri*?" I nodded, and she walked in front of me. She took some keys off a key stand, and while she was planning to get out of the house, I looked at her back. I wanted to kiss her neck, and since I thought no one was home, I did. I grabbed her from the back, and kissed her on the neck. I slowly put my hands and moved them swiftly over her waist, and then I reached her chest. I was just about to grab her boob when she stopped me.

"Get some money. We have to go shopping." It stung me. I didn't know why, but I guessed it was because Zaib suddenly stopped me from getting to second base. It made me think for a moment, as I got back in the room to get my wallet. Is she serious with me about the whole relationship and all? Wait. Is she even in a relationship with me? Does kissing mean that? Is that a declaration, or do you have to say that *I'm in a relationship with you*? I didn't know, it made me anxious.

Anyway, as she was getting out of the house, she turned back to me suddenly.

"Almost forgot." She almost ran back upstairs, and I waited for her. When she came back, I saw her holding two black pieces of cloth. "Put this veil on." She handed me one of the veils, and it was long enough to cover my head and my chest. I didn't like the idea of veils, I had thought it was oppressive.

"No way." I shook my head, "I'm not wearing this."

Zaib stood still, and looked into my eyes, "I know, Mahnoor. I'm sorry, but this is not Islamabad, or a richer side of Lahore. We have to."

"Ugh." I rolled my eyes, and then looked at the veil. She was right, it wasn't a choice. I had to. "I hope this doesn't last long."

"It won't." She said as I put it on, asking *how I look. Fine.* She adjusted my veil, and said that again, "I swear it won't."

The slums were still pretty narrow, and it wasn't just a car effect. The smell was getting worse as we got into a deeper place, where we came across a market. It was huge, people selling all kinds of things on stalls - Vegetables, fruits, fish, chicken, beef, and then there were the general stores selling everyday items like detergents and soaps, and there were also cloth shops, selling dresses, shoes, and other stuff.

As we passed one stall after another, I heard people calling behind me, "Here, *baaji,* we have the best vegetables in the whole bazaar." "Come here *Baaji,* you won't see a better pair of shoes in the whole market." Some even used phrases which were just as cheesy as funny like *Wear clothes like you are noor of Taj Mahal.* I mean, it doesn't even make sense. What the hell was that? Suddenly, my eyes got stuck on a shade stall. I pulled Zaib's arm and whispered, "Can I get a pair of sunglasses?"

"Sure." She smiled, "anything you want. It's not like I'm paying."

I walked towards the guy selling them, and tried one on. I liked it. Zaib shivered slightly, and put her hand on my forehead, "you look beautiful even with the veil."

"You know, you can't really tell but I'm rolling my eyes Behind these." I said and she chuckled.

I had to bargain with the guy, but I eventually bought them. And then we moved on, when Zaib reached into her purse. "I almost forgot." She told me as she pulled out two lollipops. I nodded, and took one. I still couldn't open it, and Zaib helped me. Well, by helping I mean she opened it while I stood there watching.

So, we just roamed around, looked at a few things here and there, but didn't buy anything. I hadn't ever done anything like this… I had shopped before, obviously, but not in a stinking market 500 km away from home. And finally, we dug up some dresses. I had still thought of not buying any kurtas, but Zaib forced me to buy one. I told her *Only one*, and in the end, I did indeed buy one. It was beautiful, with a unique impression of tulips and lilies, and coloured almost brown. Zaib paid it for me, as a house leaving gift, but then I looked at my bracelet and asked, "what is this then?"

"Joining the Orion force welcome gift."

"Meh." Couldn't argue with that.

After wasting three hours at least, Zaib and I had a bought the following things:

- A pair of shades
- Two sets of chooriyan
- Three kurtas
- Five Henna cones

It didn't seem much to waste any time, maybe the whole thing was just an excuse to get a day off. Zaib took me to have breakfast at a local place, named *Butt naan chanay and halwa puri.*

We sat down at the table, and ordered what we had planned.

"Zaib." I noticed Zaib wasn't looking at me, she was staring at someplace else. I didn't know what she was thinking, so I had to snap my fingers to get attention, "Hey, Zaib, Zaib. Zaibo." She finally looked at me, "I was wondering…"

"What?" She asked as she shook her legs nervously. There was something going on.

"What happened?"

"Oh, nothing." She stopped shaking her legs, and somehow, she even stopped the sweat pouring out of her forehead, "What were you wondering."

"Anyway…" I continued, "I wanted to get a haircut, and a tattoo."

"Really?"

"Yeah." I made it sound obvious, even though my tone had been like I was kidding, "I'm serious."

She took a moment, and said, "I could arrange both of that for you." She smiled, and I nodded. The breakfast was pretty okay, I guess. Too oily for me, but I had changed after all. At home, mom once cooked something like that, and I didn't even take a bite. But today, I was actually liking it, maybe it was either that or the fact that I had no choice so my brain just forced me to think I liked it.

After Lunch, Zaib and I started walking back home. Was it okay to call it home? I guess any place with her was home. When she walked ahead of me, I had that craving to kiss her neck again and I remembered that incident at home. My mood suddenly changed, and it felt like I would throw up. To be fair, there was nothing worse than my own thoughts, because there was no proof they were true, and I would just overthink and overthink, until I can no longer bear it and end up crying. I couldn't cry there, not in front of Akmal and Zaib, and the chief and his wife.

"Zaib."

Zaib was texting on her phone, she ignored me. I said again, "Zaib?" She stopped, and turned around.

"Yeah?"

"Do you like me?"

Zaib's cheeks got red, she was blushing. I could feel her face getting hot from three feet away, and I could feel a rush of nervousness through her. "What is that supposed to mean?" She asked.

"Yeah, you are thinking right, *like* like."

Her face got even more red, and that was itself the answer. The way she smiled, and put her fingers in her hair, playing and all. I knew she was into me, now. That so fucking pretty goddess was into this ugly mortal. It all seemed like a fairy tale.

"Zaib." I stopped. I wanted to ask her something, but I didn't know if it was time.

"Yes. Glad you realized that's my name."

"Cliché." We both smiled, and then I decided to ask, "are we a couple?"

"Depends on your definition of couple." She said and started walking ahead of me again. Still texting.

"Umm… okay." I thought about the definition of a couple, "people who are committed? Like feel good when they are around each other, and want to stay in each other's arms forever, and eventually die there?"

"That's not a couple." I could see her muscles stretching, she was probably smirking. Her footsteps were steady, and she didn't care if a fast-moving motorbike or a car would pass by her, she won't even change her back posture, "You're trying to define love."

"Trying to?"

"No one can define love, dear." She turned back, did a round quick movement, and faced ahead again. Like a ballerina, "Not even you."

"Oh, and you can?" I stopped and folded my arms in front of me. My legs were starting to hurt a little too, but I stopped because it made me mad. She was this *know-it-all*, and she was trying to make me realize that.

"No." She stopped too, the moment she couldn't hear my footsteps any longer. She turned around, and got near me, "Neither can I. Neither could Shakespeare, or John Green, or I don't know Picasso? Because no one can."

"It's just oxytocin." I rolled my eyes at her.

"Human beings are so complicated." She argued, with her tone getting stronger. She fixed her foot into the ground, "You think it's all science. It's not. It's fucking not. There's a lot more than science, you know? If it was just oxytocin, it would have been a whole different story."

"Damn girls, chill!" I put my hands on her arms, and shook her a little. I saw something watery behind her spectacles. Tears. "I'm sorry. Okay?"

"I'm not mad." She continued walking, and now we were passing the narrow market. We were getting in a wider place, and the traffic was faster and more often here, "It's just that... Me and science don't get along."

"Science and *I*." I corrected her.

"Whatever." She stood at the end of a main road, where she looked around to see if any car was passing, "I don't wanna talk about it."

"Sure." I hugged her slightly, and patted her on the shoulder, "anything for you."

And suddenly I realized, I didn't see this place when we were coming to the market. Maybe Zaib was trying an alternative route. I had a lot to keep up with, like the directions, and this whole veil thing, and the prices, Lahore was surprisingly cheaper, and of course, work. I guess Zaib had everything planned out, but I was still worrying. Maybe worrying is just an instinct.

We walked a little more, and in the awkward silence that was inevitable, I realized I was sweating from the forehead. It was hot outside, okay, but it wasn't *that* hot, and I understood it was because of the veil. I tried but couldn't take my mind off it, and then it started itching. I scratched hard, so hard it made Zaib look back. She laughed softly, and I gave her an angry look.

"This is all new to me," I said forcefully, "while you guys seem to think it's nothing but funny."

"It's not funny." She laughed on the word *funny*.

"Contradicting much?"

"It's seriously not." Still laughing, "Okay, sorry, it is. But it's more cute than funny."

And then I caved, and smiled back. "Do you want to take a selfie?" She asked me, and then I realized. It was the first time she had asked me for a picture, we had taken no pictures at all, not even on our trip to Ayubia. It was weird for normal people, I guess, but I wasn't used to the idea of selfies since I was an ugly bitch.

"I don't want to take a picture in the veil." I told her as I lifted my veil slightly, "Maybe at home."

She nodded and kept walking.

In a few minutes, we came to a very narrow street, and I realized we had been walking for longer than when we were coming, and I finally asked, "We aren't going home, are we?"

"Depends on your definition of home."

"So, we are not." I rolled my eyes, kind of, and Zaib smirked.

"Maybe not."

Zaib stopped in front of a small building, it was almost crooked. It definitely needed repair, in fact it seemed as if it was abandoned years ago. If anything, it was giving me creeps like that of a horror movie, and when Zaib walked in, I remembered how the heroes always walk into danger. I didn't say anything though, I just followed her. And then finally I said, "what is this place?"

"Another home." She replied in a flash, without turning. There was an abandoned lift too, and she got on it. It was supported by only one wire, and I was afraid it would fall.

"No way I'm getting on this."

"Stop being so scared."

I didn't completely understand the term scared, maybe I never would have if I weren't afraid of heights, because to me being scared is like being high, or being drunk. It stays there for a moment, controls you, and makes you forget everything else for a while. Like Cannabis, or Marijuana. I hadn't ever taken drugs, but I wondered if taking them would be the same as facing your fears, and I imagined it was amazing, since I did jump, and all of it was worth the pain.

So, being high, I grabbed Zaib's hand and jumped onto the lift. There was no protection to the sides, so when the lift started moving, I grabbed onto Zaib really hard. I saw she was shaking a little too, but not as much as I was.

"Do you know the best thing about height?" She asked while looking at the building on the side. They were crooked too, abandoned. Like we were in some kind of a ghost town. "It is always high. Always up."

I just nodded, I didn't know how to respond to that, since I was shitting my pants. We finally reached the third floor, and to my surprise, the building wasn't crooked anymore. There were lights everywhere, of all colours, red, green, yellow. Like a disco, and a song was playing on the CD. I knew that song, I was so sure, but I couldn't remember. Beatles? Nay. Ugh… I couldn't remember.

The air smelt of smoke, and there was a faint mist. Artificial. The song made me want to dance at it, and I would have if I were any good at that. Zaib's expressions were cheerful as she texted, and then I heard a familiar voice.

"Girls, girls." The chief was standing right behind us, "you've come on your first day off. I'm impressed."

"Well, the whole shopping thing didn't work out, so, you know, we were bored." Zaib replied, `` *We?* I thought. "And then I decided to finally tell Mahnoor what was actually happening here."

"By the view of it," I said, "I suppose you're making meth and now you're gonna use me to smuggle it to Nigeria or something."

Zaib and the chief laughed hysterically, and for a moment I got concerned, but then I was like *Nah. That can't be true in a million years.* It was fun to imagine, though.

"So, you really are here." Another familiar voice. Akmal, "I thought you were messing with me."

"Why would I do that?" Zaib asked, "What's the poi- like, is this a government top secret? Sometimes, you don't make sense."

"Woah, easy there, cowboy."

Zaib rolled her eyes, and turned to me, "Do you wanna know what's the best job in the entire world?"

"Singing?"

"For you." She smiled, "but for Akmal, gaming for a living. Literally."

"What?"

And as I asked her, I could see beyond the mist. At least 15 sofas with LCDs hung on the wall, connected to PlayStations. Only one wire per screen, and each sofa had its own private cooler. There were drinks in each of them, and there were ashtrays. The walls were painted black, maybe to intensify the coloured lights, and there were posters of different video games. FIFA, Blur, Call of Duty, Resident Evil and what not. I wasn't particularly a fan of gaming, and I wondered how my singing could help.

"You see, we hold gaming tournaments and championships, whatever you wanna call it," The chief began explaining to me, "And though it is not that popular, yet, people are getting involved in all these, because everyone thinks they are a gamer, even if they play candy crush on their iPads. It doesn't matter to me, the more I participate, the better. The thing is, people have started copying us, so we needed something new to help us. And then Akmal told me about you, and I guess a girl singing would definitely boost my show since most gamers here are nerds who haven't talked to a girl past *No*."

"This seems promising..."

"We make enough money to do enough for ourselves, and I'm offering to pay you 5k per day."

5 grand per day?! Wow.

"Ahem." I cleared my throat, "Five thousand? Is this a one-day thing?"

"No. It actually depends on the number of participants, and at the moment we have enough to make it a 15-day long thing. Of-course, it can grow."

"How do you even make this much?"

"The winning prince is a hundred grand, and the participating fee is 20k. 20 players at the moment, 20 times 20 is about 400 grand. It's crazy." He continued, "and then the spectators pay enough money to get at least 5k at the end of each day, which we don't really need. I guess we can afford a singer."

"Hell yes!" I almost shouted, and then tried to keep my nerve, "If it makes you this much, why do you live in those slums?"

"Those *slums* have a name. Sanda." He almost scolded me, "And it's to keep myself low-key. Also, how often do you think I host tournaments? Not very."

I thought why would a gaming manager need to stay low key, but I nodded away anyway.

"So, what is Akmal's job?" As I asked him, I noticed he had turned his face away. He ignored me and went near one of the sofas, where a kid was playing *Injustice 2*. He told him his time was up, and asked him to pay. I figured it out, during non-tournament days, he would just charge kids coming to play video games for money. I read a notice, 100 rupees per half hour. That was a little expensive, but I guess that worked.

Akmal replied to me with a question, "I am an official manipulator."

"Whatever that means."

"It means I alter settings for different players." Akmal eyes were steady on me, while his hands kept circling, "You see, even before the tournament starts, we already know who's gonna win this time. All games are fixed. Everything has to go according to plan, and I ensure that."

"What do you mean?"

"Players bid, it's all black. The player who gets bid the highest, we never let him win. We try to bring the player who gets bid the lowest, but obviously usually they are not good players, so we just take someone mediocre."

"That's sick." Whatever I was, I wasn't a liar or a thief, "and what games are played?"

"Next month, it is FIFA. Last time it was COD, and they change it every time." He said as he picked up a box labelled *PS4 Games*, filled with CDs, and started walking towards a corner sofa. "This tournament is coming on 10th September, and I'll give you a complete schedule of songs." He turned to Zaib, "And oh, Zaib. When you're hosting, don't try to get too frank with the boys. They're mostly very weird. Like last time I met a guy who had a habit of sniffing his own armpits." Gross.

"How often are these tournaments?"

"Sometimes 6 months, sometimes 3. It depends a lot on the chief's mood really."

I nodded as Akmal stacked the CD box on a shelf. He wiped sweat off his forehead by his long sleeve, and turned back to me, "But you're supposed to come to work since tomorrow, because I'm supposed to teach you how to play FIFA, and if you get good enough by the end of the month, you'll be getting a chance to open the tournament, by playing with me." And he smirked.

When Zaib and I took off, I asked her, "do we have to wear this veil every day now?"

"Not really." Zaib told me as we still sucked on our lollipops, "We can remove the veil there."

"Why didn't we, then?"

"You tell me." Fair enough.

Now we took a rickshaw to home, because it was a long way. It turned out Zaib made me walk 5km before she gave her lame *surprise*. Just when we got home, I removed my veil very quickly. I almost ripped off the black cloth, before Zaib held my head and removed it herself, unpinning and unknotting whatever knot there was. My hair was all wet from the sweat, and then I remembered how I had planned to get a haircut and a tattoo.

"Hey, Zaib." I twitched her on the shoulder, "My haircut?"

"And the tattoo." She smirked, like she was being sarcastic. I couldn't really tell.

"Yes…"

"Tonight."

"Sure."

Zaib and I talked during the day, and napped, and watched Television, and looked stuff up on the internet. I looked up the most important thing I had to, *Orion's belt* on the internet:

"Orion's Belt or the Belt of Orion, also known as the Three Kings or Three Sisters, is an asterism in the constellation Orion. It consists of the three bright stars Alnitak, Alnilam and Mintaka.

Looking for Orion's Belt in the night sky is the easiest way to locate Orion in the sky. The stars are more or less evenly spaced in a straight line, and so can be visualized as the belt of the hunter's clothing. They are best visible in the early night sky during the Northern Winter/Southern Summer, in particular the month of January at around 9:00 pm.

The names of the three stars come from Arabic; Alnilam comes from النظام which means "string of pearls"; Mintaka (منطقة) has the same root as Alnitak (النطاق) and both mean "belt"."

Wikipedia was a little weird, but I liked how النظام meant *string of pearls*. It was both cool and anxious to know that, because I was supposed to be something far bigger than what I actually was. I was just a simple girl from nowhere, and Zaib was a goddess. But… now, it made me scared. Like I was high. My ocean was a little uncalm.

At night, maybe around 8 or 9, Zaib frightened me with a sudden pat on my shoulder when I was playing the guitar. I was getting used to the house, the rooms were smaller, the bathroom was smaller, the whole neighborhood was smaller, but it was livable I guess.

"How 'bout that haircut, eh?" Zaib smiled at me.

"I can get a haircut." I nodded, "But, please, take me to a good place."

"Meh. Nothing is as good as Islamabad or the southern side of Lahore here, but it'll be good enough." She pulled me up, and took my guitar from me. "How do you play this thing?" She held it in both her hands, and twisted it around trying to observe its every little detail.

"Yes, you keep rotating it and it will sing you a song."

Zaib smirked, "why don't you sing me one right now?"

"Haircut." I opened my eyes a little more, widening them. Zaib smiled, and she didn't ask me to sing anymore. She asked me to veil again, and I did. She asked me to walk again, and I did. She asked me what kind of haircut I wanted, and I told her *A boy cut*. I am not sure if she understood, but she nodded anyway.

Again, after walking enough area that made my legs hurt, we reached a parlor. The name was written in unreadable Urdu. I know, I know, I should know my mother tongue but Urdu wasn't common to me, because I didn't usually talk or write in Urdu. Also, Urdu was a very pronunciation language, the words would change meaning with a slight change in pronunciation. English is sometimes that too, like *read* rhymes with *lead,* but it doesn't rhyme with *lead* while the second *lead* rhymes with *read* but not with *read*. Pretty confusing when you look at it this way. But I was used to it, and Urdu? Not so much.

We got into the parlor through a reddish curtain, and behind me I saw a thin woman holding a pair of scissors.

"Ah, ladees, ladees." Her accent was funny, "I see you have come to get a haircut."

"Pretty sure about that." I nodded.

"Zo, do you both want one?"

"No, no." Zaib shook her head, "Just this beautiful Mahnoor, she wants to try a new hairstyle and that's why I brought her to the best hairstylist in the whole of Sanda." I noticed how Zaib was fake praising her.

"Ah, I see." The woman smiled, "vell, let's get you started. What do you want?"

Zaib helped me pull off my veil, and I showed her my ugly frizzy black hair. She stared at them for a moment, and then I told her, "See this area?" I took my hair behind my ears, and held them with my fore and middle finger, "I want you to cut all of them below this." And then I looked into the mirror, imagining how I would look, "yes. And let them rise from my neck. It would look cute."

"No problem-o." She told me, as she invited me to sit in the chair next to the mirror. She started cutting my hair, and I just stared at myself in the mirror. As the hair fell off, I noticed another thing – as my hair was getting shorter, my face was getting rounder.

Snap. Chukh. Trish. The hair falling off, and now… it wasn't quite like I had imagined, my freckles and a birth mark I had rarely spotted before was obvious on my neck. The hair had turned too much, because my roots were pulling them up. They lost strength, and the worst part was, my face had gotten even rounder than the chief's now. I could have cried, I almost did when Zaib whispered in my ear, "you look awesome." I didn't care if she lied, I didn't care if she was just keeping my heart, but it gave me a little self-esteem about myself. The tears stopped, and I gained the energy to turn my head and smile at her.

"Do you like it?" The stylist asked me, and I wanted to shout at her *NO. I HATE IT. I HATE MYSELF. I HATE YOU*, but I had a better plan – to just nod. "See? I told you, yu came to the right place."

"How much will it be?" I asked as I grabbed my purse.

"250."

What the hell? Am I a billionaire bitch? Does it look like I get 250-rupee haircuts for this shit? I thought, but I didn't say anything, just paid her and got out of there.

When we got home, I asked Zaib about the tattoo, and she told me there was no tattoo parlor there, plus it was super expensive so we would get that thing done on a weekend. Later that night, on the dinner table, Akmal and the chief were discussing the championship.

"I think it's going to be just 20 members this month." The chief said, looking at pages through a well-managed file. His eyes were tense, and disappointed. I noticed he hadn't even eaten, "we're dropping child. We need to bring our game up."

"Sir," Akmal replied after chewing his food and swallowing it. "To be honest, it is quite low. But, it is going to be the last time, since Mahnoor is going to keep singing and it's gonna attract people. Also, I have this super awesome plan. We should make a high bidding player win this time?"

"What good would that do?"

"Sir," He said again, "We will take a look. It could be no gain no loss kind of thing, but that won't really hurt us. We need to look forward, if we make a high bided player win, next time, more people would come. And maybe even this month, we can change the rules and alter binding statistics et cetera, and I don't know, make him win many games and then suddenly drop him. Winning a lot of money."

"I guess that could work." Chief calmed down a little, and began cutting his steak with a knife, "What do you think Mahnoor?"

Me? I think what you're doing is very manipulative and immoral, and if I weren't in a state of helplessness, I would never have said yes to that.

"seems like a good plan." I said, raising one eyebrow, "But I don't really know anything about gaming."

"Doesn't matter." The chief smiled.

Days passed by, and I was starting to get used to Lahore. I was loving the company of both Zaib and Akmal. I used to kiss her occasionally, when no one was looking. I only used to kiss her in front of Akmal, and the God, and no one else. When I first came there, everything looked small, but now everything was getting normal again. Life was getting a bit easier. It's a funny term, *easier*. Nothing really gets easier, you just get used to the difficulties.

I went to my daily song practice to the gaming zone, which was more learning to play FIFA than singing practice. Akmal told me first the rules of foot-ball, and what offside, red card, yellow card, fouls, free kick, goal kick, corner kick was. And different stuff like that. Everything was confusing, like when would I know what kick is corner and what is goal? They're both *kicks*. Ugh. I remembered Akmal telling me, "This is going to be harder than I thought." But by the end of August, I had gotten pretty okay at that, because all I did everyday was sing and play.

Meanwhile the chief was still worried about participants, which I guessed was nothing to worry about. Even if there were going to be 20 members, you're still earning 300 grand. What's the big deal? I noticed the chief's wife didn't use to talk much, but she cooked amazing food and she always had the veil on – even inside the house.

Oh, and we never took a selfie either. I had forgotten about it, but once I remembered, I didn't give it too much of a thought, because pictures weren't really my thing.

One night, when I was taking off my bracelet and my watch. I remembered Emaan again. I remembered him every day, of course, but this time it was different. I don't know what clicked that, but I also started missing Hania. She had gifted me a similar watch once too, and I didn't know what happened, but before I could realize it, I was crying. Zaib texted me *Dinner is ready*, but I couldn't go. I couldn't cry in front of her – I couldn't say that I'm sad about leaving… Because that would prove them right, won't it? That would prove that I was still a little girl, who thinks she can survive on her own but actually cannot.

I went to the roof, to cry. I hoped Zaib wouldn't come looking for me. The roof was smaller than my house, and the stairs were narrower. It was hard to climb, but I did. Almost trembling, I reached to the top and sweat was pouring out of my forehead.

I did the one thing I could do to cheer myself up: look at the stars. I looked up, but the sky was cloudy. I could barely see the moon, but a faint reflection was noticeable. Even the stars weren't there for me. I missed my home. I missed Emaan, I missed Hania, I even fucking missed my mother. To be honest, my mother was actually okay, it was my dad and my step-mom I really hated. I started crying like a little girl, sobbing in the corner, face in the palm of my hands.

Just before I felt like I would choke up, crying, I heard footsteps. Probably Zaib. I stopped crying immediately, and tried to wipe the tears that had covered my whole face. There was no way I could hide that. Zaib walked towards me quite calmly, and sat with me. She didn't say a word, she didn't ask *What happened?* Or *Are you okay?* No. She just sat there, feeling my breath, maybe hoping I would say something myself. Actually, I liked that. I liked how she didn't ask me anything, maybe because she already knew I was missing my family.

We just sat there, gazing at the moon. Zaib held my hand. The air was cold, but her hands were warm. I wanted to hold her hand forever, just sit there, waiting for the time to end. I started sobbing again, and this time Zaib didn't stay quiet. She asked me, "what happened?"

I shook my head. I couldn't actually say the words of how I miss my family. No. I just said "Emaan." And went back to crying. She kissed my slightly on the cheek, "Hey. Stop crying." I don't understand what people mean by *stopping crying.* Can we ever stop crying? Have you ever stopped crying by just thinking about not crying? It doesn't work that way. Zaib hadn't smoked once since we had come to Lahore, but this time she pulled a pack of cigarettes from her pocket again. I didn't hesitate, I took a cigarette. She took one, and put the rest of the packet back in her pocket.

"This cigarette is not for *Ishrat,*" She said loudly, loud enough for some God to hear, "This is for the bravest girl I have ever come across. Javeria Sultan."

She said my actual name. She said my real name. Not Mahnoor, Javeria. Javeria Sultan.

"Thanks." I told her, and lighted my cigarette with the same Van Gogh lighter. We smoked quietly, not even flinching, or moving, we just sat there, with my head rested on Zaib's shoulder. "Why Van Gogh?"

"Huh?"

I showed her the lighter, "why Van Gogh?"

"In his suicide note, Van Gogh said *the sadness will last forever.*" She told me, looking at the sky, "And I think that's beautiful."

"What?" I asked her, following her look towards the sky, "His words, or his death?"

"His art. Words, paintings, and death." She straightened her back, and flipped her hair very slightly, "All of it, it's beautiful."

"How do you know why I'm crying?"

"I don't."

"Then why aren't you asking me?" I almost frowned at her, realizing I now wanted her to ask me. "Just sitting here is never going to help me."

"You don't need help, Mahnoor." This time she said Mahnoor. "You're the most positive, most courageous, most beautiful girl I've ever met."

"None of that is true." And it actually wasn't. Because, yes, Zaib did change me, but not entirely. I was still mad at the world, I was still mad at everyone who thought I wasn't human, and how I deserved death, and how I wasn't happy. "I'm suicidal, and disgusting, and a coward who cries on the roofs of houses after running away from home, and --"

"Stop it." Zaib interrupted my speech about myself, "You're not that. You can keep lying to yourself, but you are not disgusting. You're beautiful. You're so beautiful, I can't even describe. Your hair, your eyes, your body, everything is perfect." *It's actually not* I thought, "You think you're suicidal, but you have a purpose. You are an amazing singer, and if I ask you to kill yourself, you won't. Maybe, you're right. Maybe you are a coward, because you actually care about yourself, and you actually ran away from home with a stranger to complete what you had realized was worth living for. Maybe it's okay to cry sometimes, but it's never okay to lie to yourself. Maybe it's okay to cry, but it's never okay to not kiss. Maybe it's fucking okay to cry, but it's never okay to doubt yourself."

The thing about Zaib was, even though she sounded unrealistic, she was honest. And, maybe, she was telling the truth. Actually, she was, because even after so many tragedies, I was still alive, I was still with a girl I loved to kiss, I was still with a person who made me feel what it's like to be actually alive.

"I miss Emaan." I finally lay my head on Zaib's shoulder, and couldn't think of anything else but my family. I couldn't stop complaining, "I miss Hania. I miss my mom. I miss home, I miss my college, I even miss my dad now. I miss Sana, I miss everyone. I'm a failure. I thought it was going to be easy, I'm such a coward, and an idiot."

"You're just insane." Zaib started lighting another cigarette, and after the third attempt, she finally lit it. "You see this cigarette? You see that end?" She eyed the red end, "Sometimes to get what you want, you need to burn some things up. But the thing is, not everything you want is good for you, sometimes it gives you cancer."

We stayed quiet for a while, smoking cigarettes after cigarettes. The smoke, whenever it flew away, I wondered: is this smoke like clouds too? would it cover us up? Would it cover the belt of Orion?

After a while, Zaib shook her shoulder and asked, "Are you hungry?"

"Not really." I closed my eyes. And that's the last thing I remembered, before I fell asleep.

Chapter 09:

The days passed normally. I was learning to play FIFA, and I was getting pretty good at it, actually. Zaib never got me a tattoo, even when I kept asking her to. Every weekend she would just give me some lame excuse, and she would actually get away with it – because, well I guess I'm soft at heart.

The real thing came on September 1, when during Zaib and mine kissing session, Akmal came thrashing in the room. His cheeks were red hot, and smoke was almost flying out of his ears. His body wasn't very tough, but it seemed as if he could take down a tank with that anger.

"Shit." He shouted, "Shit."

"What happened?" Zaib asked calmly, "Is everything alright?"

"Does this look like a face when everything's alright?" He leaned towards Zaib and pointed at himself, "No. Nothing's alright. The players have fucking called off the tournament and I have no idea what is going to happen."

"Wait, all of them?" I asked.

"All of them." Akmal replied as he walked around, trying to calm his own anger. Just like Zaib did at the bus station, "We're done."

"How can this happen?"

"I don't know." Akmal shook his head, "They all called it off at the same time. I, uh, have no idea why. There could be many reasons, maybe they somehow know it's all rigged or something. I have no idea. I don't know what to do."

"Hey, calm down." Zaib stood up and hugged Akmal from the back, grabbing his biceps, "Just calm down." And somehow, Akmal did calm down a little.

"I..." Akmal sat down with us on the bed, "I guess I need water."

I went downstairs to fetch water, and when I came back, Akmal was lying on the bed. He was thinking something, maybe trying to figure out what to do.

"Here's your water." I handed him the glass of water as he sat while sighing, "Are you better now?"

Swallowing the water, he said, "Yeah. I have no idea how to tell this to the chief."

"What exactly happened?"

"Today was the day of submission. Like submitting money, because you know it was ten days to the tournament. So, I called everyone. And I got the same reply from every single guy, 'I'm not participating', and I was shocked, I still am. I told them that cannot happen, but obviously couldn't force them."

"Has this ever happened before?"

"No. I mean, once, and only once before a single guy surrendered, but he did pay because I talked him into paying. But these guys... they were very keen to not mind anything. It was like they had already planned." Akmal put the glass on the side table, and laid down again, "Oh, how am I gonna tell the chief?"

"Look, you don't have to worry about the chief right now." Zaib told her, still keeping her calm. She was stronger than both of us. Akmal didn't say anything, he kept quiet, thinking *They don't understand, how am I gonna face the chief?* And once the silence started getting a little awkward, I started having selfish thoughts, like what about my money? I was getting 5k per day! Damn it. But I got over that thought – actually didn't get over it, but ignored it.

I noticed when the room was completely silent, the only sound anything was making was the ceiling fan. Grrr. It was impossible not to be intimidated by it. I know, it doesn't make much sense, even when Akmal is in such a problem. But it drew my attention, and I got a sudden idea just by thinking of it.

"Eureka!" I told Akmal, "you told me that members would love a girl singing in that nerdy place, right?"

"I guess." He replied, without giving much attention to my *eureka*.

"Have you told them that a *beautiful* girl like me was going to sing?" Even as I faked *beautiful*, I cringed. That was so unlike me.

"No. Where are you getting at?"

"I wanna sing in the streets. Near that place. We can hang posters and what not. It'd be awesome. I'm sure it'd draw some attention…" I stopped for a second, and that. The whole plan sounded way better in my head than it did by words, "I mean. I could perform in front of the gaming zone to raise awareness or whatever."

"A girl?" Akmal almost laughed, as he passed a smirk, "On the streets of Pakistan? Yeah, sure."

"Don't be sexist." I shook my head, "boys. What do you think, Zaib?" I turned towards Zaib, and finally I noticed she was more interested in her nails than she was in our conversation. "ZAIB?"

"I've been listening." She told me, without even looking up from her fingernails, "It might work."

"I'm a girl." I sounded ironic, "will that be okay?"

And Zaib finally looked at me, "Depends on what *you* think. Look, if you worry what others might say, if you don't do whatever you have your head stuck on, you'll never know. Saying that, I think there's a high probability that this will do nothing good to the tournament. It won't draw the *Attention*." Zaib made inverted commas with her fingers at the word *attention*.

"Well thanks." Akmal and I said at the same time, and at once he replied with *jinx* and I just rolled my eyes.

"It's not gonna work. They had planned this shit. I'm guessing your rival – if there's one – set this whole thing up. But I like the idea of Mahnoor singing on the streets. I would love to see that."

"What's the point if not the tournament?"

"How many seventeen-year-olds run away from their homes to sing?" She finally looked a lot serious, her jawline clenching and relaxing, her eyes dead straight at me, "What's the point of that? What's the point in any of this? What's the point of life? The thing is, there is no point. You just do what you want to do. You just be insane. Do I really have to say this again and again? Go, be insane, be poetic, leave a damn mark, because after 10 years you might not remember that you *thought* about doing something more than actually doing it. You might not remember the tournament that never happened, but you sure as hell will remember singing songs in the middle of a street where you're supposed to veil. I swear, you will."

"I guess you're forgetting this is not about me," I went back at her, with just as much aggression, "This is about Akmal."

"No. This is not about Akmal." Zaib said quickly enough to actually believe her, like I always did, "This is not about the chief, this is not about me, or the tournament. Hell, since last month, the whole thing has been about you. You need to get out of your anxiety bubble, and start doing stuff, because I'm sure as hell fed up with your…" Zaib stopped. She didn't say, but I wondered what. I could tell she was mad at me, mad at something I didn't even know. She stood up, and went out of the room. I stood up to follow her too, but Akmal grabbed my arm so tight it hurt. He shook his head, and I sighed. My head felt a little heavy, and I was perplexed. What just happened?

"What was that?" I asked Akmal, breathing very slowly, like I was getting out of oxygen, "What just happened?"

"You know, Mahnoor." Akmal let go of my arm, and lay down again, "I love her. I love Zaib. Not only because she's my sister. I would have loved her just like this even if she wasn't my sister, because the fact is, you'd never see a girl like her. She describes you like her, but I very much doubt that. She tries way too hard, you know? Way too hard."

I didn't understand, I could never understand what he was trying to say. Zaib was a mystery, and Akmal wasn't making it all any better. I just sighed in response. A moment later, I asked Akmal, "What are you gonna do about the championship?"

"What can I?" He said it was normal, "I will just say it to the chief and that's it. There's nothing any of us can do about it."

I sighed again. There was nothing we could do about it.

I didn't see Zaib after dinner that night. Akmal told the Chief about everything, and the chief's reaction was more normal than any of ours. He just looked down, and said, "I know what might have happened." But he never told it to me, or Zaib. I guess he might have told Akmal, but I didn't care anymore. Because I was more focused on Zaib's expression all through the dinner table, they didn't change. She was still mad, and she never got *not* mad. I felt bad, guilty, disgusted with myself. I wanted to apologize, but every time I almost opened my mouth to say something, my brain as if talking to me, saying *don't make it worse by saying something worse*, and I preferred being quiet.

Even when I was lying on the bed, Zaib didn't come. Akmal was sleeping to my right, and I left some space for Zaib on the right, even though we had managed a mattress on the floor, but I thought *I wanted to sleep with Zaib. I want to cuddle her.*

I couldn't sleep. Even when it struck 1 on my wristwatch, and then I got scared. I started shaking Akmal, who was still snorting even when he opened his eyes, "Wake up, WAKE UP!" He didn't wake up and I gave up. I wanted to go outside to look, I swear I did, but I don't know why, I thought that might not be a good idea. And finally, maybe another hour of insomnia, I started feeling heavy on the eyes. I still couldn't stop thinking about Zaib when I fell asleep.

I slept for two hours when I woke up again. It was still dark outside, and the sunrise was just to come. I yawned, and stretched my arms. I decided to go to the roof again, and I grabbed my guitar. When I climbed the roof again, I hoped Zaib would be there too, but she wasn't. So, instead I watched the sunrise by myself. It didn't feel normal. The sunrays weren't as warm, the light wasn't as bright, the whole thing was just not as magical without her.

When I came back to the room, I was glad. Zaib was sleeping, where I was before I went upstairs. It was a relief. I smiled. And then I went downstairs – the door of the chief and his wife's room was closed, and I yawned again. I smiled again. And then I got out of the house, with my guitar still in my hand. The morning seemed fresh, with a little rush of cold air. *It might be the first air stream of winter* I thought. And then I brought out my guitar again, and started playing with the C Major Chord.

Kodaline – All I want

All I want is nothing more than to hear you knocking at my door

'cause if I could see your face once more, I could die a happy woman I'm sure

I sang it as loud as I could, without trying to break my voice. I strummed the guitar hard, passionately, I could feel my pulse raising with every chord change. I could sense the air turning blue, I could hear my own voice echoing from different houses' walls.

And then I heard a strong humming from the back. Zaib. Definitely Zaib. I smiled, somehow still singing. I was bobbing my head and shaking my hips while making the voice from my larynx now, and I heard Zaib call before me "Wait there. I'm coming down." I still didn't look back, and kept bobbing my head. I knew I was disturbing people's sleep, but fuck that, I was enjoying it. I knew I wasn't even supposed to be out without a veil, *what would people think? A girl? SINGING IN THE STREETS? FUCK ALL OF YOU.* I saw people passing by me in the start, mumbling to each other at first. This would have been okay in the southern side of Lahore, or near my place in Islamabad, but doing this in this side of Lahore was worth the mumbles and whispers.

It wasn't long before people started gathering around me, and most of them were making videos of me. I was enjoying that, the center of a crowd. I was singing to an actual crowd, for the first time – actually the second, since I first sang at the bus station, but this was nothing like that. Zaib was busy having a lollipop behind me, and even Akmal was standing there, enjoying me singing. I closed my eyes, and focused on what note to hear and when. *Darkness. Sing. Yes, that was amazing. Yes, I can hear that, I hear myself. I am doing fucking great. Yes. That was a wow from the crowd. Yes, people are talking about me. Wait, yes, yes, yes, Mahnoor, Mahnoor, Mahnoor, clap, clap, clap.* With every beat, came a new light. Everyone was stunned by how well I could sing. Song after song. I was just singing
Noah Kahan – Young blood

Keep your time, keep your mind keep humble,

I was happy, too happy for anybody's convenience. I was almost crying, and it was all going okay on the streets before this happened: A few old guys came and shouted in front of me, scolding me like I was a 5-year-old child: "*Astagfirullah*! How dare you?" I stopped playing.

"What?" Zaib came in front of me, "What happened?"

And Akmal came in front of me too, like shielding me. I could barely see from over their heads, but the old men who had come did not look pleased.

"How dare this girl do something like this?" All four of those men had beards, but the one in the middle was probably the oldest and had the longest beard of them all, "Shame on you, shame on your infidel acts. You are playing music in the streets of Sanda?"

"Why do you even care?"

"I care because as a Muslim it is my duty to stop infidels from doing anything like singing or dancing," his face was getting even more hot, like he was boiling from the inside, "This stupid girl is not even wearing a veil."

"She… We are Muslims." Akmal kicked in, "And even if we were infidels, this is a free country. We can do anything we want."

"Not anything." Said a man from behind, "You think you can go against Islam?"

"Just mind your own business here, okay?" Zaib turned her back towards me, and shot me a look. A look that said *Go back inside*. I held my guitar, and turned too. I was just about to enter when I heard a voice from behind, "Oh not so quick, you don't." A man grabbed my hand, and pulled me towards himself. I let out a muffled cry, and tried to get away, but he pulled me even harder and for a second it felt as if my arm had come out. Akmal tried to help me, he grabbed the man's arm but another man reached for him. He wasn't stronger than these guys. The guys were pretty skinny themselves, but they were four against one boy and two teenage girls. And then it happened, one of the men grabbed my guitar, and jerked it. My guitar couldn't handle that jerk, its strap broke. The man bent his knee, and put the guitar on it. He was about to break it. Oh no. He was about to break it.

"Please don't!" I screamed, but the man holding me put his giant hand around my whole face, and pulled my ear. I couldn't scream, and hence the tears came out. I couldn't stop them, I didn't want to cry, but that's not how it works. I cried. I cried as I watched him break my guitar into pieces, one after another. The wood, and every time I heard a crack, it was a crack in my shallow heart. Akmal was screaming and shouting too, so was Zaib, but of no use. I saw Zaib's lollipop lying on the ground.

Just before I felt like I would pass out, the chief came out, running through the very narrow hallway, "What is happening here?" He looked at the guitar, and at its broken pieces. He looked at my face, and then at the broken strings. I bet he could relate to me with the broken strings, and at that moment, the men let me go, and the old people started talking to the chief, "I'm afraid, Mister uhh…"

"Akbar." His face was still frightened, his eyes still wide open, his forehead still sweating, but he shook his hand, "Akbar Khan."

"I'm afraid Mister Akbar, but we don't have good news." The old man's face was still expressionless, "Can we talk in a more private and sophisticated place?"

"Sophisticated my ass!" I shouted at them, but they seemed to ignore me, and went inside. To the small drawing room. I knelt down, and touched the broken pieces of guitar. Sharp ends of wood, broken strings, broken bridge. Everything is broken. I was still crying. I didn't care about that, but *that* was true.

"I'm sorry." Zaib knelt beside me, I didn't say anything. "I'm sorry." This time Akmal.

When I tried to control my sobbing for a millisecond, I said, "Sorry doesn't help."

"A sorry can heal a broken heart." Zaib touched my arm, and then slowly and lightly she pushed her palm against my chest, "Please don't cry."

"A sorry might heal a broken heart," I looked at her, my eyes red. My eyes were bleeding this salted water, "But it can't heal my broken guitar."

The men stood there watching. No one was helping me, none of them cared, none of them gave a fuck about me. To them, it was just a show, making fucking videos, probably upload them on the internet later, and maybe show their friends how they enjoyed this whole show live.

That guitar wasn't just a guitar. It was my life. Because, it was the only thing that kept me going through the past year of pain. It was the only thing that could make me truly happy before Zaib, and now it was gone. It was gone forever. I picked a broken piece of it, and put it in my side pocket. It stung a little when I was putting it, because it was pointed, but I didn't care.

My ocean wasn't calm, and neither was it uncalm. For the first time in my life, it was something in between. My nerves were controlling my body, and I was shaking, I was hurt. Anxiety had rose through my chest to my eyes and it felt as if I was swallowing my own tears to death. Zaib was talking, trying to calm me down. Her voice was soothing, but that was not enough. I already knew what was going to happen when the chief and the old men would come out again – they were gonna kick me out of there. Zaib knew that too, so did Akmal. But, they still tried to cheer me up a bit.

It's going to be alright. We'll get you a new guitar. Don't worry, the chief knows how to handle it. Like fuck no, I don't want a new guitar. I just want to fucking go home now, it's enough. It was stupid, it was all very stupid.

"I shouldn't have…" I tried to talk, but the words couldn't come out of my mouth, "I shouldn't have ever left Islamabad. I don't know what I was thinking. It's all very stupid."

"Hey." Zaib put her arm around me, and hugged me. Her chest against my shoulder, it felt good. I could almost feel her heartbeat, my headache was getting less worse than before, "Hey Don't you worry, okay? It's not stupid. You did the right thing, if we're blaming anyone, it should be me. I told you, you should sing in the street."

"Well, I went with that." I got her off me, because I was sweating. The air felt way hotter now, and I couldn't bear another body on my dirty body, "I shouldn't have."

Akmal and Zaib stayed quiet, and even though I wanted them to say something, I coped with the silence.

Finally, the chief and the old men came out. All of them were shaking hands, with smiles, and just for a second I felt relieved, but only for a second. When the old men left, I shot them a look saying *Go to hell*, but the chief's expressions changed dramatically. He seemed sad, his eyes were down, and he sighed. He went sweaty again, and he gestured to all three of us to come in. So, we went, only to find that my luggage was right in front of the chief's room.

"I'm sorry," The chief said, without meeting his eyes, "But you can't stay here anymore." And then he finally looked up at Akmal and Zaib, "you two can, but not her."

"This is ridiculous," I shouted at him, and he still didn't look at me, "All of this for a simple song out in the streets? What is this 1200 BC? Even that would have been a better time for us!"

"Please, chief, you gotta listen --", Akmal tried to speak, but the chief put his hand in the air, shutting him up.

"Leave, now." And he finally met his eyes with mine.

"What will I do?" I asked him, and then I turned to Zaib, "Where will I go?"

Zaib kept quiet. She was thinking, she was trying to figure something out. I kept screaming at both of them, but they were idle.

"Okay. Fine." I said, and came closer to my bag. I thought about how I picked both my guitar and bag at the bus, but now I only had my bag. I didn't say anything more, I kept quiet. I walked out, and the sound of the door closing behind me disappointed me. I hoped Zaib would say something, if not do anything. But she didn't. Outside, the people weren't there anymore. The hot air now felt much colder, like it was cutting my skin. Like I was being wounded by every strike. The narrowness of the streets was enclosing me, and I couldn't breathe anymore. I had to breathe manually again, but that was no help since I couldn't even force my brain to breathe. I kept walking, I didn't know where I was going. I didn't know what to do, all of a sudden, the air smelt much grosser, and the streets much filthier. I couldn't stay there for long, that was for sure.

I kept walking 'till my legs hurt. I didn't have a veil on, and everyone was staring at me like I was some sort of an alien. When my legs went numb, and I couldn't feel my weight anymore, I sat down on the footpath. The dust, the car and motorcycle horns, the filth, it didn't matter to me as much as the fact that *Zaib didn't do anything* mattered. I pictured her face, not replying to me. Like I was drowning, and she was right there. She had asked me to swim, but when I'm certain I'm gonna drown, I reach out my hand, but she doesn't grab it. She waves it, she laughs at me. Akmal is there too, laughing at me. I drown. And I passed out, right there on the footpath.

Chapter 10:

When I woke up, I was in a room surrounded by faint blue walls. A very dim light made it possible to see that I was on a single bed, which seemed like a hospital bed but there was no IV beside me. I looked around again, and the harder I looked, the more it seemed like a hospital. There was a very thin grey line of paint dividing the upper and bottom half of the room, and a white blanket was put on my feet. I noticed the room was colder than the room at the chief's house. I decided to sit up, and when I did, my bare feet touched the cold floor of the room and I shivered. There was a small chair at the corner of the room, on which my bag was resting. The dim light made it so hard to see that my eyes hurt, so I closed them. When I closed my eyes, I could smell something. Mashed potatoes, grilled, and the smell was getting stronger. My ears hurt too, like wind was rushing back and forth against it. The kind of pain you observe at heights.

I heard footsteps behind the door, and I opened my eyes. The door opened very slowly, making a crooked voice that stung in my ear. It was almost dark outside, but I could sense it was a hallway. Zaib and Akmal came in, and I was stunned. What happened? I just opened my mouth, and forgot to close it. My eyes were wide awake, when Zaib asked me, "Are you better now?"

I didn't reply, how could I? At first, it was just shock, and then I got angry, and finally I decided to lay down again and turn towards the wall. I made it obvious I didn't want to talk to her.

"I'm sorry, okay?" She was holding a plastic bag in her one hand, and lifted it up. I could hear the bag's chirp when she raised it, "I brought you a cake to make it up for you."

I shut my eyes as hard as I could, almost hurting myself, trying to not to give attention to any of them. I wrapped my pillow around my ears, but I could still hear her apologize and all. I clenched my teeth, but I could still listen to Zaib saying:

"Come on, now, Mahnoor."

"Hey, Alnitak."

"We're stars, *yaar*."

"I'm soooooooorrryyy."

"She's not gonna listen to you like that," Finally I heard Akmal's soft voice, "Let her hear this."

And then I heard a strum, a G-chord. But it wasn't a guitar chord, no, it was about three steps high. He got me there, because as soon as I heard him play that and sing some song I didn't recognize, it was impossible not to turn around, and I did that immediately. The voice felt nice on my ears, and when I turned back I was glad I guessed it right – He was holding a Ukulele.

"See?" Akmal stopped playing and faced Zaib, still pointing towards me, "Told you she'd like the Ukulele."

"For your information, I didn't like the Ukulele," Which was a total lie, because even though I loved guitar more, I still liked messing around with a Ukulele. One of my college friends had it once, and I knew how to play it – It was very much like playing a guitar, except easier. You wouldn't get calluses, since the strings are softer. And there are only four strings, but it made a beautiful sound, "I was just wondering how did you know how to play that thing."

"*That thing* was our mom's" Akmal told me, pulling the strap towards himself so the Ukulele would go towards his back, "And she used to sing like a Greek goddess. She sang even better than you." And I believed him, because Akmal's voice was surprisingly good. Very good actually. For a moment I thought if we could sing a duo together – yes, that's how good Akmal was. I guessed Zaib got his dad's voice, because she wasn't half as good as Akmal.

"I still haven't forgiven you." I shook my head, holding the bed's edge tightly. I clenched it harder, "neither of you."

"You don't have to." Zaib sat beside me, and put the cake behind me. She slowly patted me on the head, like I was some kind of a cat. I shrugged, and told her to get off me, but she kept being annoying, "But I'm sorry. You don't understand --".

"I don't understand?" I cut her in the middle of the sentence, my eyes and my cheeks both were as read as Akmal's shirt that day, "I *do* understand. It's you who doesn't understand, it's you who doesn't give a fuck and it's you --".

I was interrupted by another sudden opening of the door, and there was a tall and strong man. Very different from the chief, because he wasn't bald or fat. He stepped in without permission, so I guessed he was the owner of the room or the building or whatever.

"I suppose you're Miss Ahmad." The man came towards me, and I just turned my head in disgust, "I am Mr. Ehsan Mubarak, and I own this hostel, Miss Ahmad. And I assure you, you will not regret booking this flat."

"Booking this flat?" I finally asked.

"Yeah." Zaib replied to me instead of the owner, "We booked you this flat for you to stay. You'll stay here as long as we figure out where you're going to live."

I still didn't reply, but I was understanding the whole scenario little by little now. Zaib probably picked me up from the streets, and somehow got me into this hostel where they keep flats like freaking hospital rooms.

After having acknowledged my stay, Mr. Ehsan left the room without saying anything about the payment. Zaib was still sitting beside me, and Akmal was still standing in front of me. Zaib was still trying to make me talk to her, but in vain. Even when she cut the chocolate black forest cake, and placed a very huge slice on my plate, I refused. Not even saying anything, just shaking my head, in anger.

"I know what would get you to speak." Akmal said that phrase again, and I just rolled my eyes resting my chin on my hand. I was curious what we were going to do. He drummed on the side table of the bed, like he was doing an actual drum roll, and made the last *tishh* by his mouth and said as confidently as he could, "I declare my mom's Uke as yours from this day onwards. Uke is his name BTW."

I smiled. I didn't intend to, but it happened. And I looked at Zaib, and she looked beautiful, smirking as a reaction to my smile. She was overwhelmed, and she hugged me. She kissed me on the cheek, and hugged me again. Like she won a medal.

"Okay, okay." I got her away from myself, "Stop being so clingy." And then I turned to Akmal, "Thanks for Uke."

"Well, you deserve him." Zaib told me, almost whispering, "Since... you know, the guitar..."

"Yeah, I don't really wanna talk about it."

Akmal handed Uke over to me, and it felt even smaller in my arms. The guitar was way bigger, and Uke's strings were very soft. It almost made me want to keep touching it over and over. The wood was much more authentic, Uke was not cheap. It might have even been more expensive than my guitar. When I played it, it gave me a similar feeling nonetheless. The notes were still ringing in my ears the same, and it still felt magical.

"Thanks." I looked up from Uke, "Thanks both of you."

"Hey, Mahnoor." Zaib grabbed my face from both of his hands, and stared into my eyes, "Look, you are Alnitak now, okay? And you sing just as good as her. You're my *Ishrat*, okay? It's yours, not because we're giving it to you, but because it belongs to you."

I kissed Zaib on the lips, after a long while. I had almost forgotten how it had felt to kiss her, like I was kissing the moonlight, Pale, but strong. Bright, and beautiful.

Once we stopped kissing, I asked her, almost crying, "Why didn't you do something? I know it doesn't matter, but it hurts. It's stupid, but it fucking hurt."

"Mahnoor. Those men are strong people. They probably threatened the Chief, and I didn't know what to do. I panicked, okay? I'm sorry."

And even though I didn't say it, her face made me forgive her.

"What is going on now? I mean, where am I?"

"You're at a friend's hostel. They have given us a discount, it's just 5 thousand per month, but you're not gonna stay here forever. As soon as we figure out what we're going to do, we'll get you out. I promise. Until then, we're still staying with the chief, but since the tournament is still not happening, I am free and I'll come here every day. It's an hour of walking, but I'll manage." She smiled, so I smiled back.

"What about my singing career?"

"As I said," She said as she ate the cake, "We'll figure something out."

The way Zaib had told me, *figure something out,* I thought it would be an easy task. It was not. I was stuck there for God knew how many days now. But, after a while, I got used to the idea of living there, just like I did at the chief's house. I played Uke every day, and I thought he was liking me. It would always feel like he's gonna propose to me, before I realized he wasn't living. Zaib would come every morning, at exactly 11 O'clock, and she would leave late at night, sometimes at even 2 O'clock. What would we do? Nothing. Absolutely nothing, but talk. She'd still apologize in the first few visits, but other than that nothing unusual. I still asked her for that tattoo, and she was very irritated at that idea. I didn't want to do something she would be irritated by. I once brought up the idea of joining a gym too, but she laughed and embarrassed me, and I never thought of it again.

This kept going on for two weeks, and I started getting really worried. I asked her if she was somewhere with that whole *figure something out* thing, but she just shook her head every time.

Two weeks later, I remember I was still sleeping when my phone started ringing. It woke me up, it had been months before I was woken up by a phone call, but when I held my phone in my hand, it showed Zaib's name. I panicked when I checked the time – 5 in the morning. I immediately picked it up, and nervously said, "Hello?!"

"MAHNOOR." Her voice wasn't tragic, it sounded more excited. I let out a big sigh in relief, because I had imagined terrible things in my head. "MAHNOOR, MAHNOOR, MAHNOOR, MAHNOOR."

"God Zaib," I almost shouted at her, "you scared the fuck out of me." I whispered. Because the hostel had terrible rules, including no sound should reach the hallway from the room and like the residents can't leave or enter the hostel between 11 in the night and 7 in the morning. Those were the exact sleeping hours of Mr. Ehsan. He was a very strict person. "say what happened, already?"

"I'm sending you a video on WhatsApp, check it out!"

"Okay." And I hung up the phone, waiting for Zaib's text on my WhatsApp.

Zaib: *Fuck. You're famous.*

Me: *What do you mean?*

Zaib: *What I mean is, this video is viral all over the internet*

Zaib sent a video

I tapped on my screen, and it was a video of… me. Someone filmed me singing in the streets, but they cut the part where the men came in. I sounded so amazing, even on screen. I almost envied my voice, until I told myself – it is myself!

Zaib: *Check this link out. Check comments on your video.*

Zaib sent a link

When I tapped on the link, my internet almost died. Another problem of living in that shithole, and I head to lean against the door to get the signals right. I couldn't open my door, because you never know when Mr. Ehsan is out in the hallway, even at 5 in the morning. I almost gave up when my browser finally started to buffer, and a moment later I was on the webpage. My video was there, with the thumbnail. A *girl from a small town in Lahore sings like she was meant to fly* and for a second I thought how great that line was. I was getting ahead of myself, but still, I was flattered. I watched the video again, and this time with even greater enthusiasm. I was the next big thing on the internet, and I didn't understand what it meant until I said that.

At the end of the video, I read comments under it, by anonymous subscribers:

This girl has fucking nailed it!!!

Wow dis gal iz really owxem

I would definitely go out with her, with someone of that voice.

And the list continued, as I blushed. I didn't know exactly whether I was bushing of being flattered or of anger, because there were a few hate comments too:

What is this girl doing singing and all? La' haula, what the hell does she think she is doing?

Now girls will sing in the streets of ISLAMIC REPUBLIC of pakistan???

Ths s th rsn y v r so bhnd. Thse lbrls hv no valus

"Yeah bitch, go learn fifth grade English first." I thought.

Despite I liked that I *was* viral on the internet, I noticed how the hate comments were greater in number. It set my mood off. I put my mobile phone aside, and lay down again, trying not to think about it. But it was a paradox, the more I resisted the greater I was tempted. I tried to close my eyes again, and when even that didn't work, I plugged in to listen to a few songs. That did work for a while, and I almost fell asleep when my phone vibrated again. Obviously Zaib.

Zaib: *WHY AREN'T YOU SHOWING A REACTION?*

Me: *For what?*

Zaib: *Dude you're fucking famous. The moment they find your ID or something on the internet, they're gonna go crazy after you.*

I didn't reply at once, I just tapped the link again, and screenshotted a bunch of the hate comments, and sent it to Zaib. She replied with … *oh*, and I turned off my mobile data, and went back to listening to songs, and eventually fell asleep.

Apparently, I didn't wake up till 1pm. I wondered if I would have slept longer if it weren't for the very sudden and hard throbbing knock on the door. After a sudden tightening in my heart, I was wide awake in a second. When I woke up, I saw Zaib sitting in the chair, her head rested on the palm of her hand, smiling at me.

"I've been watching you for two hours." She continued her smile, ignoring the knocking at the door, she kept circling her head around my eyes. "Hope that isn't creepy."

"Dude!" I got up from the bed, and threw my blanket away. I went to the door with bare feet, and opened the door.

In came a very short man, not young, just short. Slightly below me, and he was wearing a long hat, the kind that magicians wear. He lifted it up, his small hands barely reaching the top of his forehead, "Hi, miss Mahnoor." He smiled at me, and with his other hand reached out for a handshake. I was confused, but conscious enough to shake my hand, "I'm someone you need to reach heights."

"I'm aerophobic, so…"

"The heights I'm talking about won't scare you," He rubbed his chin slightly and looked at the ceiling, "or it might. Can I come in?"

"I'm not sure if --"

"Let him in." Zaib shouted behind me, and I looked at her. She looked confident enough. I opened the door completely, and gestured to him to come in. He observed the room, and constantly kept saying "Nope. Nope. Definitely nope."

I made a circle with my finger right next to my brain, trying to tell Zaib how I think this guy is crazy, but when he jumped on the bed and turned towards me, I hid my hand behind my back

"This is not even close to where I want you to be." The man said to me, without even looking at me. His eyes were stuck on the ceiling, I guess he was trying to figure out how I could live in a place like that. Honestly, I didn't know. "You Mahnoor, are going places."

"Who even are you?" I shook my head and narrowed my eyes at him, "how do you even know about me?"

Zaib chuckled, but tried to hide it behind her hand. On her hands, her veins were clear, and it looked so beautiful.

"I." He stood up, "am." He strolled towards me, "Daniel Graystone."

"Daniel is an executive music producer, from Europe." Zaib told me, and reached in her bag. She brought only a single lollipop, and gave it to Daniel. I frowned. "He's actually from England, and he's here to find talented musicians from Pakistan." Zaib passed me a smile to which I couldn't reject smiling back.

"Let's just stay," he barely spoke with his mouth full of saliva, sucking on the lollipop, "I can change your world."

"Umm, okay?"

"Look, I looked at your video, and you are really good at singing. It's a shame you haven't heard of me." He explained to me, "I am conducting a singing contest in Lahore, next month. The winner gets a million rupees, and a chance to collaborate with another international singer. An album produced by me."

"What the hell?" I almost jumped in excitement, "Is this for real?" I almost fell down when I tried to run and hug Daniel, but then controlled my emotions, and folded my arms.

"Here's a list of songs produced by me." He handed me over a big list of songs from his pocket, "and if you still don't believe me, you can look me up on the internet. Also look up Daniel Graystone singing talent hunt in Pakistan. It will tell you about *Sing if you can*, my competition-audition thing. The contest. Here's my card," He placed his cards in my hand, "if you're interested, give me a call by Saturday. Have a nice day." And he was gone before I could stop daydreaming about winning the contest.

"This is so awesome." I shouted at Zaib, and she replied with as much enthusiasm *I know, right?* And we hugged. We kept hugging for a while, and then we kissed. And we kissed again, we kissed until we were tired.

"I can't believe this just happened," I had tears in my eyes, and probably Zaib had them too, but our eyes were shining like stars. "Some Daniel fucking Graystone AKA a well-known English music producer shows up at my door, and fucking asks me to sing at his contest, like is this even real?"

"You better believe it, Mahnoor, 'cause it's just as real as you and me. Imma go tell Akmal." And she got involved in her phone, while I imagined myself surrounded by a million lights, all shining on me. People cheered my name, and I was under the spotlight. I imagined my debut song becoming a worldwide hit, like I was born to be a singer. I was born to be a singer.

Until Saturday, the whole thing was a game plan. And now, with Zaib, Akmal used to come Akmal. We talked about how we would all go about this contest. I did call Daniel, but his answering machine said: *Hey, this is Daniel Graaaaaaaaystone, leave a message or sing a song. You can do whatever the fuck you want when you want and how you want. But right now, I am unavailable, and leaving a message is of no use because Imma delete it, but if I told you to call by Saturday, I meant call on Saturday. BEEP.* Daniel was an interesting man, and this could all have been just one of his eccentric tricks or something, but I got an Email that read

From: Danielthatkills765@pri.com

Subject: Just read it.

Hi, This should be Mahnoor Ahmed, yeah? Well well well well, I'm coming at your place on saturday, no need to call, no need to thank me. Our team gathered around, talked, and discussed how good you are, and like I must have told you, you are born to do greats. We have decided to take a low key audition of you, to start ahead of the programme in the contest. I'm sure you'd like that ;)

Uke was a nice Ukulele. He synced with me, and we were figuring each other out well enough. Sometimes I would play the wrong chord, because the whole difference of chord shapes was confusing, but he would never mind. Sometimes I would play it all night long, sharing my secrets with him. He was such a great listener. And then came the day I had been waiting for for a week.

Saturday morning, Daniel knocked on my room harder than what a bulldozer could have done to my room. I shouted "Coming!" but he never stopped. I opened the door, and he wasn't wearing his hat, he was in a totally different outfit. A light Miami shirt, and brown shorts. Like it was 40 degrees outside, even though the weather was getting cold now. It didn't seem to affect him.

Just then came Zaib and Akmal, and they both looked pretty excited, so I told them all to come in. Daniel walked with his hands in his pants, and jumped on the bed again, and almost screamed "Home, sweet home." I rolled my eyes, but I could see Akmal laughing from the corner of my eye.

"Who's gonna take my audition?" I asked him nervously, but he ignored me. He looked outside the window, towards a small park. For some reason, he smiled.

"Hello?" I asked him again, and then again, and finally when I shouted he replied, "Let's go."

"Right now?" Akmal asked, and Daniel nodded. I nodded along, and Zaib grabbed me from my shoulder. We followed Daniel downstairs, and I noticed how colder the weather had gotten. There was a 1980s car downstairs, I had no idea about. All I knew was that it wasn't common anymore.

The driver opened the door for us, and me, Akmal and Zaib sat in. The seats were made of leather, and they were very comfortable. I could almost jump on that bubbly seat, but I resisted. Zaib held my hand tight, it almost started hurting. "We're going to the southern side." Akmal told me, still looking ahead.

"There's a special place." Daniel smiled at me from the front mirror.

"Hard to guess."

The car stopped with a jerk, and Zaib was thrown at me, and I was thrown at Akmal. Daniel smirked as he opened the car door. The driver came out, and so did the rest of us. When I looked around I saw how everything was made of grass. The whole thing stretched as far as my look, and anything different I could see was a stone house in the middle.

Akmal leaned towards me a little and whispered, "Didn't see this coming."

"He's a multinational song producer." I told him, "What did you expect?"

I followed Daniel and the driver, as they kept talking to each other, like Zaib and Akmal. Whispering, but I was too busy focusing on the architectural beauty the place was. The shrubs were shaped like animals - lions, tigers, even birds like peacocks and ostriches. The whole place was amazing.

We were told to wait into a big lobby, with sofas as long as a limousine car. They were curved like palace sofas, it was the biggest room that I had ever been in before. Daniel and the driver moved on, but Zaib, Akmal and I sat and waited. The room was dome shaped, with the curved sofas placed around a big central table on which were present different decoration pieces. On the walls were paintings, but there was something different about them. Most likely, you'd see paintings of family members or old emperors or something like that, but they were all paintings of musical instruments and singers. Elvis Presley, Michael Jackson, Adele, Bob Marley and so on. My eyes were stuck on a guitar painting, it was so beautiful. Brown guitar, probably 22 fret, painted perfectly by every inch. I touched its cover, just when Akmal shouted from behind.

"Don't touch!"

I went back and sat between Zaib and Akmal, trying to annoy him, but he just smirked.

Zaib reached her bag, and started asking me, "bubble gum or lollipop?"

"Bubble gum," I told her, putting two fingers on my Adam's apple, "lollipop sours my throat."

She gave me once again a strawberry bubblegum, and I chewed it. I tried to keep my mouth shut, but the voice echoed inside my mouth. For the first time, I was annoyed by that. I didn't know why, maybe it was because I was sitting in a very sophisticated and large place. After a moment of awkward *silence*, a different man came into the lobby room.

"Mr Akmal, Miss Zaib and Miss Mahnoor," He called as loudly as he could from the other side of the room, "May you please follow me?"

We got up, almost together. Zaib moved in front, then me, and then Akmal. We were brought into another room, through the hallway, this time a smaller one. There was a window on my left side, through which I could see Daniel, and two other short guys. They looked awfully a lot like Daniel. In front of the window was a mic with a pop filter. At the opposite side was a sound controlling system, like the one used by our college DJ.

Akmal and Zaib waited at the door, and Zaib gestured to me to go on. Daniel's voice echoed around in the room, "Mahnoor, come in front of the camera, sing some shit, and play the Ukulele. We are going to make history."

"umm..." I told him, but I don't think he heard me so I just walked.

The man beside him told me to sing something *powerful*, and that picture of Adele clicked in my mind. So I just sang one of her songs, on the Uke, and somehow I made them consent.

I closed my eyes when I was singing. I gave it my everything, because it had something magical in it. When this song came out, I got a notification on my mobile, but I skipped it. Then I forgot about it, and two days later Usman told me how he heard the song, and how he loved it, and how he wanted to sing it with me. I was remembering all that, I closed my eyes, trying not to cry, but I was losing breath. I was giving it everything, and at the end of the song, when I opened my eyes, I saw through the window. Daniel and the guys were up from their seats. I turned my face, Zaib and Akmal were stunned. I touched my own face, it was wet. I was crying. not just your simple, delicate crying. Something far beyond that.

After a minute, when the atmosphere calmed down a little, I saw a smile on everyone's face. And then Claps. A whistle by Daniel, but I hadn't stopped crying. I left the room, went down the hallway, and got into the lobby. I was almost out of that too, when Zaib grabbed my arm. She pulled me closer to her, and turned me. She kissed me, on my wet face, and my ocean went very uncalm. Under her breath, she asked me very softly, "what happened?"

"Usman." The air was pushing my lungs out of the rib cage, my lips were like rocks, my body of a mannequin, "I miss him so much. I miss my brother."

"That's natural."

"Knowing that it's natural doesn't help, Zaib!" I screamed at her, pulling myself away, "I miss him."

She held me back in my arms, and slowly patted me on the head. Running her hand through my hair, it calmed me down a little, but didn't stop the tears. I put my arms on her chest, "why is it so hard?"

She crouched next to me, and swept my tears. She held my face in her hands, and moved my head towards her eyes, "You just sang a very hard song to its best. You know that that means?"

And at the moment came Daniel, in his own unique walk. He clapped around, saying "LIT. LIT. LIT."

I wiped any left tears, and told Zaib to stand up. Daniel came to me, and pointed between my eyes, "You, miss Mahnoor, are the greatest 17 year old singer I've ever listened to."

Akmal was talking to the other guys, and I shot a look at them. Daniel saw me, "let me introduce you to my humble fucking friends," He stretched his arm towards them, "Mr. John and Mr. Jameel."

It was clear who was who because one of them was white and the other was brown. They clapped when they saw me, and announced, "You, young lady, have a great voice. Cherish it."

Chapter 11:

Let me tell you what happened after I was praised for giving a good audition. Daniel told me he was hosting a singing contest in Pakistan, but he saw a greater potential in me than that. I was too big for that. Something happened, that changed my life forever. That day, when Daniel was driving me back to my hostel, he sat with me in the backseat.

"Girl, you're amazing." Daniel put his arm around my neck, and stretched his fingers in front of my eyes, "I'm talking big. I'm talking about TV interviews, fans, papers, news, money, fame, everything you have ever dreamt of."
"Yeah, right," I rolled my eyes like I didn't believe him, but honestly I did. I didn't know why, but I had a good feeling about that.
"Imagine..." as soon as he said "imagine", I didn't listen any further. Although he was still talking, I was lost in my day dreaming. My eyes again lost in all the camera flashes, I'm again wearing a black suit all the celebrities like Angelina or Katie. I imagined Zaib kissing me on screen, I imagined all the stuff I shouldn't be imagining, because imagining stuff leads to expectations and expectations always lead to despair.
When Akmal sitting beside me shook me a little, I woke up. I started listening to Daniel again.
"...and I am going to give you something that will make it all very possible."
"Like a dream-to-reality converter?"
"Better." He smirked, "An opportunity to participate in UK's *Singing for all*. You know, these small contests are too small for you, and I'm letting you have a go on one of the world's largest singing platforms."
"NO WAY." I gasped and screamed simultaneously, because what I was hearing was hard to believe in. *Singing for All* was a very successful show about young singers. It must have had hundreds of singers, and brought them into the real game. The winner was always a hit. They would give them a million pounds, and also an original song! I couldn't have dreamt of anything better, "STOP KIDDING WITH ME!" Zaib turned her head from the passenger seat and looked into my eyes, "he's not kidding." She smiled, and I can swear that was one of the most beautiful things I have seen in my life.
"STOP IT." I was still over the line of maximum excitement, because I wasn't believing him. I knew he could do something like that, and I knew how confident he was since he was laughing while I was screaming around. I even saw the driver smile from the front mirror, but I just covered my nose with my hands. I was shivering. "Oh My God." I panted, my breath was disrupted. I hugged Daniel, and somehow I hugged Zaib too. I turned to Daniel again, "Thank you, thank you, thank you so so much." I hugged him again. My short legs almost jumped in the air, if there were any.

On all of the rides, I just tried to make myself believe that it was all real, and not at all a dream. I couldn't convince myself, until we stopped. When I looked from the car window, I saw the sign of Lahore's most expensive hotel. *Pearl Continental*. When we all got out, Zaib leaned on me and said, "you're living here 'till you go to the UK."
And at that moment, I was entirely convinced that I was going to *Singing for All*, because I was starting to get the celebrity treatment.
"And it's all on Daniel." Zaib continued.
"My pleasure." Daniel patted me on the shoulder, "the world is yours if you want it to be."

"I don't even know why you're so impressed by me." I shook my head but he didn't reply. We walked in the hotel, and it was bigger than any hotel I had ever seen. I was brought to a room, it was bigger than two whole TV lounges of my Islamabad home. I didn't even know what I was supposed to do in such a space. It had a very large LCD screen on the front wall, a water bed, a small refrigerator, a fancy table, a large couch and whatnot. The walls were white, like I was already very famous.

"We could totally Netflix and chill with Pizza like it was meant to be in this room" I whispered Zaib and she chuckled, "Yes, chill like it was meant to be."

A man brought a trolley full of luggage with my stuff in the room, "your luggage is here, madame." He wore that perfect bell boy dress I had only seen in movies, red with a white line between the buttons, and that special extension from behind. A black dress, pants, and hand gestures are very professional.

"I'll leave you three be," Daniel told us as he turned around, hands in his pocket, "Good day." and he left the room.

I jumped on the bed, spreading my limbs as Zaib and Akmal stared at me. "What?" I asked them.

"Nothing" They replied together.

"You know what I like about you guys?"

"What?"

"We're in the same line."

"Duh." Zaib slapped her forehead, "Orion's belt. Remember?"

"Exactly." I smiled, looking at the fancy ceiling, "Orion's belt."

For a while, we talked about how great the UK opportunity was. And how it was both incredible, and amazing. They told me they believed that I could win that, and I believed they were telling me the truth. It was all very great. Akmal told me he had FIFA practice, so he went for that, and Zaib and I were all alone.

"This is very good." I told her as I touched her face, I slowly shaped my finger around her silk like cheeks. She shivered with every edge, and I got closer and closer to her. I leaned my lips towards her and she leaned back. Her lips on mine. Strawberries, like I was chewing one of her bubble gums or sucking one of her lollipops, or even better, smoking one of her cigarettes.

A sudden knock on the door broke us. And I almost hated my luck, but I told the person to come in. The same bellboy came in, and told me, "madame, Mr. Daniel told me to tell you that we'd be needing these documents of your personal to apply for a Visa in the UK." He handed me a paper, and as I looked at it, my face went blank. Zaib noticed I was either confused or scared or something like that, so she replied on my behalf, "That's fine. We'll get these as early as possible." The bellboy bowed and left, just like my expressions had. She asked me the matter, and I just told her, "I don't have these." I flickered the pair with my finger, "I mean, I do, obviously. B-Form, passport, and Parental or guardian permission letter, but that's all in Islamabad."

"Hmm." She rubbed her chin, "I'll text you tonight." And she started moving out of the room. I thought of stopping her, but then I realized it was of no use, and too late anyway, because she was out.

I tried watching TV, or reading a book, but it didn't help. I knew Zaib was figuring something out about my documents, so I didn't focus on it too bad. But I was bored, and curious, so I kept texting her. She didn't reply. The whole day.
At night, I waited for her text, and texted her too, but the text never came. I called her at about midnight, but she didn't pick up. I still decided to wait, and about at 2 O'clock, I got fed up, tired, mad, and sleepy. So, I went to sleep.

I was in deep sleep, when someone called me. I woke up on the third ring, and yawned. I tried to ignore it, but the bell hurt me ears. When I learned on my mobile. Zaib. I held up. But she called again, and after a while, I finally picked it up.
"No, I don't want to talk." I told her.
Zaib ignored me, "I'm coming at your place. Half hour. Be ready."
"For what?"
"We're going to Islamabad." and she hung up. Nothing more. Nothing less. And I was shocked for a second. What in the world was this girl up to this time? Such a mystery. What a beautiful mystery.

I brushed, both my teeth and hair. Didn't have the time to take a shower. Didn't pack anything. Just washed my hands and my face. Picked up Uke, obviously. And waited in the balcony as the cold wind rushed through my hair and hurt my skin. I liked it. I saw Zaib driving the same red Bentley coming through the driveway. At the same time Zaib called. I picked it up, told her I'm coming, and got in with her.
"Don't tell me you went to Sheikhupura just to get this car." I asked her. She just smirked, and I replied, "God. Poetic to be insane, eh?" I shook my head.

When we were on the motorway, I thought about how I could actually meet my family again. What would their reaction be? What could possibly be happening back there? A lot of things scrolled in my mind, but the answer was soon to come. Zaib drived calmly, so I decided to ask her the plan.
"We'll go to your house and pick up the documents and get your visa done, so we could apply and go." she replied.
"Just like that? With you?"
"Don't you want me to?"
"I didn't mean that." I rolled my eyes, "I was just asking."
She laughed, "stupid."
I narrowed my eyes.

Halfway through the ride, I decided to sing her a song. I decided to play Uke, it was easier to carry him in the car. The song I sang wasn't really romantic or anything, but it had a fun beat and nice to play on the Uke, so I sang:

Robert's got a quick hand
He'll look around the room, he won't tell you his plan
He's got a rolled cigarette, hanging out his mouth he's a cowboy kid

"I like Pumped up kicks." Zaib told me as she sang along with me, we both bobbing our heads.

The trip was long, and I kept on looking at my watch again and again. It made me remember Emaan. And with that, I looked at my bracelet. It made me want to kiss Zaib more and more. But when the city was really close to us, I started panicking a little. I didn't really understand why, but I told Zaib about it.
"Zaib." I shook her shoulder nervously, "I can't face my family."
"Look, Mahnoor." Zaib hesitated on *Mahnoor*, because in Islamabad I might as well be Javeria back, "Don't worry."
"So helpful, thanks."
"Sarcasm should be illegal."
"Not until I'm alive." I laughed, and Zaib laughed back.

When I looked at my watch again, just before we entered the same police check post. 11 O'clock. Hania would be in college. I decided, after all that, Hania deserved to know what's been happening.
"Zaib." I looked at her, sudden, eyes flashing. "College." She nodded.
I searched my phone for Hania's number, I felt a little embarrassed for not remembering it. I texted Hania.

Me: *Hi… okay, this is awkward, but umm… can we meet?*
Hania: *wru?*
Me: *Oh, yeah, forgot I got a new number. It's me, Hania. Mah-* I erased back three letters- *Javeria.*
Hania: *r u srios?!?!*
Me: *Yeah, sorry.*
Hania: *no no where can v meet?*
Me: *I'm coming to college. Obviously, I won't come inside, you have to come outside*
Hania: *cming. missed u Jia. missed u a lot.*
Me: *I know, and my stupid brain missed you too.*
Hania: *cum quick*
Me: *come***

I told Zaib to step on it, and she accelerated like driving a bullet. Every sharp turn told me I'm getting closer to Hania. How was I even going to face her. Guilt was filling up my heart, my head was circling. Zaib still looked firm, but I was delicate. I felt as if I would throw up.
        We finally reached the place. My college, I could see its building from a mile away. Throbbing in my heart, as I got nearer to the parking. I saw Hania, and my heart left a heartbeat in. I swallowed, and sighed. Hania just stood there, expressionless, even when I offered her to sit inside. She sat on the backseat, and I told Zaib to drive to a Café shop. Hania didn't say a word to me, she didn't even look at

me for too long. Her hands folded, her eyes at the window. I looked back, and forward, and back, and forward. Hania didn't look at me once.

Outside a coffee shop, I asked Zaib to give me and Hania a minute. She nodded, and when I asked Hania, "shall we go?" she didn't reply. She just got out of the car, and I followed her. She sat on a chair, and I sat at the same table.

"You won't hear me say this much, but…" I curled my eyebrows, trying to give a friendly look to her, but her eyes were dark. Narrow. Focused. "I'm sorry."

"Sorry for what, exactly?"

"For… uhh…" I took a moment to think about it, but Hania cut me off. "For Fuck's sake, javeria. For God's sake please." She shook her head and slammed her fist on the table, almost making me shake with fear, "It doesn't matter anymore. I cared about you, okay? And you left me, alone-"

"You were not alone, you had Sana." I got a little upset myself, "Don't you dare use that BS on me."

"NO." Hania opened her eyes, scaring me a lot more now, "Do you really think Sana could ever take your place? Or Sana could ever be half as good a friend as you used to be? NO. I don't *love* Sana, I loved you. I needed you, not because I wanted to help you, or because you seemed lonely or sad. I needed you because you were my oxygen. When we first hugged, you told me it wasn't common, and I thought I was something special to be your friend. To me, being your friend made me feel special. And you left, it didn't matter, Javeria. It really didn't, I swear. What mattered was realizing you never thought of me as a friend. You never loved me the way I loved you."

I was stunned. I couldn't speak, I couldn't move, not after that. My head was hurting, my eyes almost bleeding. She was crying, and I was too. She didn't want to look towards me, and I wanted to stare at her fucking beautiful green eyes. She was my bestfriend. Not Zaib. Zaib was my lover. Hania was my bestfriend. Not Akmal, Not Daniel, Not anyone else in the whole wide world. Hania.

I put my palm on my burning left eye, but it started stinging more, "I'm really sorry, Hania. I love you. I never realized how much I needed you until I moved to Lahore."

"It's too late, Jia." Hania stood up, "a little too late."

She started going out of the Café, and I wanted to follow her, but my legs couldn't move, like they were cemented to the floor. My eyes stuck on her, and I hoped she would turn. She didn't. She opened the door without hesitating. She walked without hesitating. She got on a bus, without hesitating. I cried behind her. That is just how it goes, you reach a person you had to leave after two months, with hopes, and they leave you forever. I really did love Hania. Just when I got a little consciousness, I tried to text Hania, but she had blocked me. It broke my heart.

Somehow, I got back into the car, but barely held myself up. Zaib knew I was struggling, but she couldn't do anything either.

"Is everything okay?" She asked me as she pulled me into the car. I shook my head.

"Oh, dear." Zaib hugged me. Her hands about my back, but they couldn't stop my racing heart, "What happened?"

"I don't know. I don't even care." Lies. Lies. Lies.

"Do you want to go to your home?" Trick question, do I? What if the reaction is worse? What if it doesn't work out the way I'm supposing it should have. What if they don't accept me? What if Amazon doesn't accept me? That's my worst nightmare. No. But I had to, so I just nodded, but my stomach ached. I grabbed it, but it still hurt. It didn't matter.

Zaib drove to the end of my street, and I told her to slow it down.
"Actually, go around it." I told her, pointing and circling my finger around my house. "Quick."
"Sure."
She parked the car right in front of the back door, but I told her to move it a little forward so no one would suspect. I told Zaib to wait in the car, while I get the necessary documents. My room was able to be climbed by using the pipe, but I hadn't climbed it in a long time. For someone as short heighted as me, you had to jump to grab on it. I jumped, and missed it. I jumped again, my fingers brushed against the pipe but missed it. I finally grabbed it in the third attempt, but the jerk made my arm hurt. I was hanging off the pipe, and prayed no one would see me. I tried to pull myself up, but I was just too heavy. Somehow, I was able to rest one leg on the shed, and I could see Zaib in the car.

In a moment, I started climbing again, and I reached my window. Just enough that I could see inside it. It was still tidy, still neat. My guitar stood right in the corner. And my closet. And the study table. They had to be there, in the drawer. I opened the window, leg after leg, and got in. I tried to keep as quiet as possible, and I opened the drawer. It had my passport, and my B-Form. But I still needed that parental approval letter. I had already got one, but it was to be signed by my parents. I could easily copy it - it didn't matter. But I had to get my Dad's CNIC number, so I opened my room's door very slightly. My heart was racing, but somehow, being at home made my ocean very calm.

I realized it was still office time, that meant no one was home. I opened the door calmly, let the *creek* echo. I strolled down, and got into Dad's room. Took out a photocopy of his national ID card, and just as I turned, I almost lost my breath. It almost gave me a heart attack. It was Emaan, he was still in his Pajamas. He looked ill, he was yellow, and he was coughing. I dropped in front of him, and hugged him. His body temperature was high, how could my parents leave him like this?!
"Oh God." I kissed him on the forehead, "are you okay?"
"Jia aapi," He coughed twice, "you're back? I was singing songs to you."
"Yes. I am. Why are you alone?"
"Moms, dad, they had to go." He coughed again, "they called a nanny but she's sleeping."
"We need to get you to hospital." I hugged him harder and held him up. I almost ran as I got out of the front door. I had to go around the house to get to Zaib, who was listening to songs.
"GO. GO. GO." I jumped into the car, still holding Emaan, "he's very sick. We need to get to a hospital."
Zaib drived as fast she could, but Emaan was smiling. He tried to speak, but he didn't have enough energy. I told him to go to sleep, but he was too excited to see me. Another paradox. Like my ocean paradox.

At the hospital, the doctors put him on nebuliser, and I calmed down a little when he fell asleep. The cute little thing, a little angel.
"Brothers." Zaib stood next to me and Emaan, folding arms like me, elbowing me slightly, "you love them, don't you?"

"Brothers are one of the best things about family." I looked up at her, but she was looking at Emaan, "I mean, he's not even that sick but it got me so worried."

"That's how you know he's precious."

She and I stood silent, just watching him breathe. His stomach going in and out, in and out. His body tensed, but he still looked better.

A little while later, Zaib turned to me and asked, "do you have everything?"

"You mean the documents?" I reached in my back pocket. Everything there. "Yes."

"I think we should go." Zaib nodded firmly, but I shook my head, "we can't leave Emaan alone."

"The hospital has already called your parents." Zaib looked impatient, "we better go. We need to apply for a Visa as quickly as possible."

Zaib's phone started ringing in her pocket, and she took it out rather nervously. "I need to get this." She told me, waving the phone at me, "You can talk to Emaan while I come back if you want to." She eyed me to look at Emaan, and he was waking up. By the time I looked back, she was gone, so I just crouched next to Emaan. I could hear him breathe through the nebuliser, but I put my finger between my lips to gesture him to keep quiet.

"Look, Emaan, brother." I hesitated, and sighed, but then spoke again, "I'm sorry I had to leave you like that. I'm still leaving you, and I apologize. Emaan, I love you. I really do, but I had to go away. You might not understand it yet, but you will in some time. I'm not coming back, Emaan. I'm sorry. I don't even know what to say to you." My vision got blurry, the tears scattered the light. My cheeks were hurting, my body was red, "I don't know. Don't even... I have to go." I stood up, still facing Emaan, I walked backward. Emaan's face was expressionless. He couldn't speak, of course, but he didn't move either. He just stared at me, calmly, like this was normal. I almost tripped over the door, but somehow got out. I was hurt.

Zaib came to me, but I didn't see her coming. She walked like a fantasy, and she was smiling yet again. She got closer to me, and said, "Shall we go?

I sighed, she pulled me closer to her, saying, "Now, now, it's okay. It happens."

"I might not even come back, ever."

"Or you might." She pulled my chin towards her, looking down at me, "You still have a chance."

We got back into the car. It was night now, but it was cloudy. I looked up to see any stars or moon, but there was only darkness. No Orion's belt, no happiness, no *Ishrat*. Zaib's hands were firm, but tensed on the wheel. Her looks were staring at the road. Even though there was no traffic. I noticed we weren't going back at the motorway, not from the same route at least.

"Where are we going?" I asked her, trying to calm her down a little, but she didn't reply. Her face was just like Emaan's, expressionless.

A little while later, I read the same board again, *Daman e koh 3600 ft*. "Wow." I told her, but she didn't reply. She accelerated the car, even though the climb was just ahead. She should have slowed down the car, but instead she made me scream, "What are you doing?!" She didn't reply. Just when I thought we were going to fall off the cliff, she took a sharp turn. SCREECH. We almost hit the mountain side, but she controlled the car. Still speeding.

"ZAIB." I shouted at her, "YOU'RE GONNA KILL US."

Finally she slowed down the car, and I could relax a little. My heart was still racing, it was all still very ugly, but better than before. Zaib remained quiet, and we got at the top. "Please, not Pir Sohawa." I told her, but she didn't say anything, she just got out of the car. She started walking, and I cried behind her, "wait!" but she didn't stop. She continued walking. Just at the edge, she stopped. Looked back, and smiled. I smiled back at her. But then she reached into her pocket, and brought out another pack of cigarettes. She lit up two cigarettes at once, and put one of them in her mouth. I got near her, and she gave me the other one.
"The sky is cloudy tonight." Zaib let out a large stream of smoke in the air, facing the clouds, "Can't see any stars."
"Yeah."
"Do you know what's so great about the stars? Zaib smoked again. The smoke circling around her.
"What?"
"They're from the past."
"What do you mean?"
"They are so far away, that it takes light millions of years to travel. The stars you see in the sky, are actually dead by now, but since they were far away, it took millions of years to be able to see them." Zaib's eyes were starstruck, "If you place a large mirror on the stars, you could actually see Dinosaurs. Live, real dinosaurs. Speaking theoretically of course. But that's how big the mystery of star is. It's amazing."
"Stars. The belt of Orion. Alnitak, Alnilam, Mintaka." I said. Telling it to myself, actually.
"The stars are dead, Mahnoor. Exactly from today, millions of years later, Orion's belt will end." Tears dropped on my shirt as Zaib rested her head on my shoulder, "It has already ended actually. There's no point in trying to hold them together."
"What do you mean?" I smelled her brown hair. Tobacco. Fucking amazing. "What happened?"
Zaib looked up to me, and she was almost crying blood. Her face was red, and I could feel her temperature rising. Like Emaan. She was either mad, or very sad. Very sad, I figured. I held her in my arms, and asked again, pulling her even closer. "What happened?" I patted on her back, but she said something under her breath. I couldn't hear her, so I asked again, "what happened?" She finally told me. "Akmal's dead."
The ground moved from my feet, and I fell down with Zaib. For a moment I couldn't believe she had just said this. Like the gravity was pulling me inside the Earth, because even in the cold wind, the fire from down below was making me scream internally. I didn't say anything, maybe because I was in shock, or maybe because I thought it was a dream, a nightmare.
"I received a phone call just now." Zaib continued. She started explaining, "It was from National Hospital, Lahore. They asked me if I was Zaib Abbasi, sister of Akmal Abbasi." She was crying with every word. Almost drowning in her tears, "I told them," She swallowed, "Yes. They told me they brought him two hours ago. He was in a car accident. Santro. Broke most of his bones. They tried to save him, but it was too late. He lost a huge amount of blood and some other medical shit was not complete or whatever the fuck. But he died. He died. I told them I'm in Islamabad, I told them I'd be there in the morning. So, I came here to smoke."
"Za... Zaib..." I tried to speak, but the words didn't come out of my mouth. "I..."
"You know what's the worst part? Both of them died in a car accident."

"I'm so… sorry…"

"I loved him." She was still crying, smoking, looking at the city in front of us. Covered in light, "It's over. My life's over. He was all I had."

I got a little selfish, I thought, "what about me?" But obviously, it wasn't about me, it was about Zaib and Akmal. It was about them.

I decided to sing a song, again. Maybe that wasn't the best thing, but I had to do something. I did the best I could: I sang *Sleeping at last - Saturn:*

You taught me the courage of stars before you left
How light carries on endlessly, even after death.
With shortness of breath, you explained the infinite.
How rare and beautiful it is to even exist.

For a second, there was silent crying by both of us. I didn't understand how that could happen. I thought if I was bad luck, because I certainly brought misery to everyone who cared about me. There was Hania, and Emaan, and now Zaib.

"Zaib." I finally spoke up, "Akmal… he was one of the best people to have ever lived. I…"

"You don't have to explain anything." Zaib told me, "I know who he was. The thing is, he is not there anymore. He was too young to die. Fuck. He was too young to die." another smoke, but this time she coughed. She coughed hard. "I want to die."

"You don't deserve to die."

"NEITHER DID HE!" She shouted at me, but lost her breath. "Neither did he." She sobbed like a little child. I realized, now, silence was the best thing. I remained quiet, let the silence talk, because sometimes it's the best you can do. Not sing, not talk, not move. Just smoke in silence. Zaib was breaking down with every smoke, and I could see that. I could see her pain staying with her. But… I was useless, I couldn't do anything. Seeing her hurt made me hurt. I wished I could do something.

Chapter 12:

See, that's how life is. Unexpected, sudden, and certain to end. When Akmal left the world, Zaib broke down. She couldn't imagine living the rest of her life without him. To her, to me, I didn't matter half as Akmal, because Akmal was her brother. He had been with her when no one else in this world was. Zaib was a lot like me, because she loved her brother as much I did, but she wasn't entirely me - She wouldn't have left her brother for the world.

On our way back, I drove the car. Zaib was shaking constantly, and I decided it was best to let her clear her mind up a little. We didn't talk when I was driving back. It was a long way, and it seemed longer than ever now. I did want to talk to her, but seeing her eyes dying behind her spectacles scared me, and I couldn't utter a word.

Halfway through our journey, I was finally able to speak, because I had a few questions in mind. "When is his funeral?"

"Today." She could barely speak, laying in the back seat, "at Asar."

"Who's arranging everything?"

"The chief." Her voice was stubborn, like she didn't want to talk, but she had to. "He's done everything. Insurance. And other stuff, blah blah." She waved with her hand.

"I am sorry…" I didn't know what to say anymore, "…again."

Zaib didn't reply, she just closed her eyes, and pretended she was asleep. I kept silent, and drove the car at the speed limit. Another thought struck in my mind, what about the UK singing contest now? Would Zaib travel with me? Or would I even go at all? Should I go? A lot was going on, and it wasn't the best time to be selfish, but that was it. Javeria Sultan. Selfish, arrogant, heartless. I wanted Zaib to go with me, but how could I ever ask her to?

When we reached Lahore, I went back to PC instead of Sanda. Zaib was fast asleep, so I just sat in the car in the parking lot. Waiting for her to wake up, and thinking about how cruel God was to take Akmal away from this angel. I kissed Zaib on the forehead, barely reaching her from the front seat. She shivered, but then went still again. I felt her breathing, seeing her chest contract and relaxing. I could see her hair moving a little with every breath she took, and her eyebrows slanting, like she was having a nightmare. I decided to wake her up, I shook her a little. "Zaib, Zaib." She woke up, her eyes red. She yawned, and stretched, and then sat up.

"Where are we?" She asked, still half asleep, "what's happening?"

"In Lahore."

"Oh." She lifted her head up, "right."

We walked into the elevator, and on the third floor. I got into my room, and she followed. The bellboy must have seen me come, because he came just as we got into the room.

"Madame. Mr. Graystone was calling on your mobile phone."

I checked my mobile phone, "Sorry. Battery dead."

"Madame, we need your documents so we can apply." and then he turned to Zaib, "yours too, madame."

This was it, what was going to be her reply?

"Sure." She said, and I was relieved, "They're back home. I just need to go and grab them."

I sighed, and brought out my documents. I gave them to the bellboy, and he bowed. Then he left the room, and the atmosphere started feeling kind of awkward. Zaib sat on the sofa, staring at the blank television screen.

"We should probably go to Sanda." I told her, but she waited a second. I think she was about to say something, but she didn't. She waited. Hesitated, and then just nodded. She stood up, and walked ahead of me. I followed her, while looking at her neck. I wanted to kiss her, but it wasn't the best time.

She got in the driver's seat, and I sat on the passenger's seat. I asked her if she was okay to drive, and she replied, "why wouldn't I be okay?" I couldn't understand her. Why was she faking it? Why was she pretending it was okay? Why was it okay to lose your brother?

We reached the chief's home. I was afraid to enter, but figured it wouldn't be such a problem since Akmal had died. I knew his dead body was here. Probably ready for his death bath. I didn't want to think of it much, bust the more I resented, the more I did it. I couldn't believe it, with every passing second I thought Akmal would jump from the back, hug me and say something like October fools or something, but who was I kidding?

And then I saw it. There he was, Akmal. His dead body laying on a bed, people surrounding him. People I hadn't seen before. People who didn't have to do anything with Akmal. Zaib stood still, for a moment, and then she cried again. She cried like she had never cried before. She screamed, and jumped towards his body. People got away from him, but Zaib didn't seem to care. She hugged his dead body, and let the tears fall on him. She was hurting herself, twisting against the bed so hard. But that pain was nothing compared to her loss.

"Poor chap." The chief was standing right behind me, and I could notice he was sad too. Of course he was. "He was very young."

"What happened?" I could barely speak.

"I don't know. He told me he was going somewhere to get something, and I told him he better hurry. We were planning another gaming tournament. But he never came back. The hospital called me, and then Zaib. He was a good kid, you know. Obedient, and better than most. God really does call them early who he loves."

"That is true." My body was shivering. I had goosebumps. "God is very selfish."

At Asar, the rituals were to be completed. And as the men lifted the bunk on their shoulders, that was the last time Zaib saw him. She reached out her hand, but she couldn't touch him. He was moving away from her, going away. He was never going to return. He was never going to return.

That was the last of Akmal we saw. The air wasn't easy after that. People were coming up to Zaib and telling her how sorry they were, and how Akmal didn't deserve to die. But that was it, wasn't it? One day thing. This would end, they will forget Akmal, Everything will become shitty, and it would make Zaib smoke more, make her more sad.

Finally, when it was all over, and everybody had lied how they'd miss Akmal, Zaib and I got back into the car. She drove. I knew it wasn't going to be alright, but when she parked the car at the hotel, I told her, "Hey, Zaib." I slowly massaged her arm, "Everything is going to be alright?" Lies. She shook her head, "No. It is not. Not everything."

She looked beautiful in the yellow car light. The reflection from her spectacles fell behind her eyes, and her brown eyes were shining from the tears. It was the time I wanted to tell her how I loved her. She already knew that, I'm sure she did. But I wanted to say it. In the car. Where the air was tight, but breathable. I wanted to say it, because I knew how much it mattered to her. Maybe not as much as Akmal, but as much as it mattered to me, because when I'm alone at night, or when I have a nightmare, all I want to hear is Zaib calling me and telling me how she loves me, and how everything will be alright, because my life, or her life is going to end, like Akmal, what shouldn't end is our love, because it doesn't matter how many times we say, we need to be there. I need to love her. I loved her. I loved her more than anything in the world.

We got back in my room, and I noticed her walk had gotten slower, and tired. She wanted to smoke, and I told her to come to the balcony, where we lit up our cigarettes once again. We smoked as long as the night was young, and we had love in our hearts. We smoked till our lungs gave out, and our hearts screamed. Zaib didn't seem to stop any time soon, neither did I. And after we had smoked like we had planned, we kissed. Her soft lips on mine, the pinkness of hers spreading onto my lips. Her hands on my neck, mine on her back. I felt something wet on my nose, it was Zaib's tear. Her eyes closed, but tears hadn't stopped coming.

The next few days were a bit hard. Actually, they were very hard. Zaib didn't go back to Sanda, she lived with me. She didn't care about her stuff, but she was scared, she was alone. Daniel told me that our Visas were applied on Fast tracks, so we'd get Visas in no time. That no time was one week, one long week. Finally, our Visas arrived.

Daniel, Zaib and I went to pick up our Visas. We didn't have to stand in Queue because apparently I was still getting the celebrity treatment. Zaib didn't smile at all, I did though. Because it was my dream coming true, but it didn't matter to her. She was sad. I didn't blame her.

"*Singing for All* starts on 20th of October." Daniel started explaining to me the whole trip to the UK, "It's in London. We'll depart Lahore on 15th, and reach there on 16th. If you win, which I'm sure you will, we'd stay there 20 days. You will have four performances, every five days. If you survive them all, you would be voted by the people of Britain to make you the winner. Between the days, you can explore London, and practice your singing, or do Whatever you want."

"Where would we be staying?"

"In a hotel of course." Daniel continued, "we have the best for the best."

"Can you arrange a small flat or house instead?" I didn't really know why I was asking this, but suddenly I just didn't want the celebrity treatment. I wanted to be a little normal.

"I'll look forward to that." He nodded, "Anyway, I want you to do a favour." As he said, the car stopped at a PC hotel. We all got out of the car, but Daniel held my arm. Zaib stopped in front of me. Daniel went around the car, and opened its back. He brought out an acoustic guitar. A Taylor Gs mini. I almost screamed as he lifted it up, I could swear I was crying when he was handing it over to me, "But, my favour." He continued, "I want you to write a song for the finale."

"Write a song?" I tucked my hair behind my ear, and held the guitar high, "I've never written songs... well good songs before."

"But you should!" Daniel almost fell on the ground, but his excitement was cheerful, "And anyway if it doesn't work out, we can dismiss the idea."

"Hmm. writing a song." I thought. "I'll look forward to it." I told him sarcastically, and he just smiled and nodded. But in all that, Zaib was already gone. Even us getting over Akmal's death wasn't acceptable. Even my future wasn't acceptable. I felt bad for her.

Part 2:

The Flight:

Although Zaib was sad, she knew she couldn't back away from the UK tour or whatever you wanna call it, because to her it wasn't my future, or a tour, or a voyage. To her it was just some social work she was doing for me. "I am sorry Zaib" became my new motto, but she would never reply. Even when I showed her my bracelet - it would just make it worse. The results of post Akmal's death were obvious - the world had gotten a lot more depressing. But until one day before our flight to England. Zaib and I were packing, and I was asking her what would we need or what would we not. Zaib was always the wiser one.
"It's not that cold." Zaib told me, as she saw me packing those thick overcoats, "you're packing like you're going to climb the everest or something."
"Sorry."
And finally Zaib replied to that, "stop saying sorry." She dropped the pink shirt she was holding, and I picked it up for her, "Why are you sorry?"
"I'm just... a generally bad person."
"You're not." She shook her head and she slammed the suitcase's kid, "You have no idea do you?"
"About what?"
"About Akmal." She sat down on the bed, "Look. I understand he's gone, but I can't stay sad forever, can I? No. I miss him, I do, but I need to get over it." And then she finally smiled. It stung me, seeing her trying to fake a smile. I said beside her, "He's gone. Dead. He's in the dust. Maybe with a God, maybe there's no God and he's gone forever. For now, it doesn't matter. He's gone, and soon I'll be gone too. And you will go away too."
"I guess, the only certainty in life is death? I mean, you start dying the minute you are born."
"Exactly." She stood up excitedly, and pulled me up too. "I made a promise. I won't talk about him on this tour, okay?"
"You don't have to do that."
"Of course I do." She hugged me, probably still trying to smile, "This is about you, Mahnoor--"
"Javeria." I interrupted her, "from now on, only Javeria."
"Okay, Javeria. This is about you. Akmal's stories and my depression can wait."

On 15th, we went to the airport with Daniel, who, as usual, was very talkative. He told me how great England was, and how much I would love London. I believed him, because I knew anywhere was better than the hell I was living in.

Our flight was a direct flight to London Heathrow, which was about 9 hours long. When we were boarding, we were stopped at the airport multiple times. I mean, okay, okay, it's about security and all, but really? Just check me once and throw me in. I can't wait to go to the UK! I was wearing those long black boots - kind of like cowboy boots, and it was a mistake. I was asked to take them off like a million times. It was so very tiring. My passport was checked at least five times, my luggage was checked that much too. But I was still somehow very glad, I was going to a city I could be whatever I wanted to be.

I thought about it. London, where I could be open about my sexuality. London, where I could complete my dream of becoming a singer. London, where I could kiss Zaib in public and no one would judge.

Once on the plane, the crew met us with smiles. I asked Zaib if she wanted the window seat - she declined, so I sat on the window seat. I was excited, because a) It was my first time in London and b) I was acrophobic, but I wasn't under any immediate threat. I had wondered how it would be like to fly when you know you're not gonna fall down, and of course I didn't know. But I was about to know.

The flight attendant made an announcement to put our seatbelts on, and be attentive as they flew the aeroplane. The plane started, and it shook. I got scared, because it was about to fly. I held Zaib's hand sitting left to me. I was pressing her very hard, but she was smiling. My face was out of breath, ironically the flight attendant was telling us how to put our oxygen masks on.

"You know, Javeria." Zaib leaned in and whispered in my left ear, "You're not as scared as you think you are."

"The plane hasn't even started moving." I told her, "and I'm scared to death."

"No." She put her other hand up, "observe. It is moving."

I didn't feel it the first time, but when I looked out the window, I realized it was moving. I felt a little scared, my ocean was uncalm.

A moment later, it's movement got obvious. It picked up speed, very suddenly. It was about to take off. I looked out the window, I was almost going to choke up.

"I'm scared." I barely said.

"No you're not." She put her other hand on our intertwined fingers, "Wait."

As I was looking out the window, the land started getting away from me. The people started getting smaller. I was pushed back a little. We were in the air. I was... I was in the air. I was flying. And I wasn't scared, I wasn't afraid. I was actually calmer now, even my ocean was. I didn't feel any fear from the height. Obviously because I was in an aeroplane, but I really didn't think it would be that easy. Zaib noticed this all.

"Told you." She smiled at me, but I wasn't looking. I was looking at the beautiful scene below me. Everything so little. We were in the air. I wasn't falling. "Haha. Told you, you are even more brave than I am."

"Shut up." I laughed, and she laughed back. Our frequencies started to match again, "Stop flirting."

"Never."

In short, the flight was less interesting than I had imagined it to be. I mean, I sat in the same place for ten hours, what do you expect? For most of the flight, Zaib was asleep. I watched movies, slept and talked with Zaib. That was all I could do (not including the toilet, if). Zaib and I talked about a lot of things, but most importantly she talked about how she believed in me.

"Javeria." She told me, "I know you're going to be a star. I know you're going to be awesome. I know you're the next big thing."

"I hope."

"Javeria. Your voice is… is something I know isn't ordinary. I don't know how to put it in words…" She looked deep into my eyes, "But… I know you're going to shake this world."

"I hope." I nodded sarcastically and she laughed. Although, I really did hope. Even though it went against my own rule: to never hope. I guess, sometimes hope is all you have.

Between the flight, it started hurting in my ear. I rubbed my pinky in it, and then it hurt my ear drum. I rubbed my whole palm against it, and now I looked funny. Zaib cared enough to notice, but not help. She kept laughing, and I snapped. "Shut up."

She continued laughing and held my hand. "Have this." She said, handing me over a pink pack of bubblegum. Strawberries. "It helps me. It might help you to. At least take your mind off it."

I chewed on the bubble gum, and it helped me a little. Not much though, and I still had to rub it for a couple of minutes.

"You know?" Zaib elbowed me looking outside the window, trying to focus on the wings, "The plane isn't actually flying."

"What do you mean?"

"What I mean is, look!" She pointed outside the window, and I looked at the wings too. The flaps moved up and down. "The plane got its initial run from the runway. There is no friction anymore once we're in the air. All there is, is the air thrust. The whole power for this 10 hour journey was provided by that single run, and once it had the speed, all it uses is the air thrust to keep *gliding* it, not actually flying like birds."

"Are you supposed to be Newton or something?" I focused my eyes on the wings, and thought about what she had said. It was actually pretty true. We were not flying, we were gliding.

"Just curious." She smiled at me. "Man has always intended to fly. One of his greatest dreams. He invented helicopters, and aeroplanes and parachutes and shit, but he could never fly. Not at least like a bird. That's what a man could achieve with his ego - only half truth. But with a little love and art, you could achieve the completeness of truth."

"It doesn't even make any sense." I pointed my index finger upwards and closed my eyes as if beginning to explain. "Science is always better than art."

"Oh, science is an art." She smirked. Her signature smirk. She was finally back. And then I asked her to explain, but she just ignored me and went back to reading a book about an Afghan boy. I rolled my eyes, and I knew she noticed, the way she smiled told me she wasn't smiling at something in the book.

I had slept for a while before the passenger announcement woke me up. I shook my head, and straightened my hair. Saliva had been coming out of my mouth which I had hopped no one noticed. I yawned. Drank some water that was put on my tray when I was unconscious. And sat still, still trying to adjust to the light.

I heard a sound. *THUD.* It took my breath. We were crashing, were we? I shouted, "Oh My God!" All the passengers looked back at me. They were staring like no one had seen a girl before. Zaib held my hand, and then she began to laugh. "The gears just opened, doofus." and suddenly I heard roars of laughter around me. I felt embarrassed, and I blushed, trying to keep my head down. "Stupid Javeria. Stupid." I said to myself.

"We're now approaching London Heathrow. Please keep seated and fasten your seat belt. Also keep your window shields open… *blah blah blah.*"

I heard another *thud*. This time I knew, we were landing. The gears just touched the ground. Screech. It didn't scare me much, but Zaib tightened her grip around my hand. We Pulled out our hand-carried bags from the compartment, and started walking in the queue. "Curse you Javeria for asking Daniel to book economy class." Zaib whispered in my air while standing in the aisle. I smirked.

"Just as salty as my blood during ascend and descend." I told her.

"Fair." She lifted her shoulders, and I patted her on the back. We finally moved, and heard the crew telling everybody, "Thank you for flying with us. We hope you had an amazing journey." Their smiles were charming.

Day 1:

Through the tube-like area, we entered into a large hall. I'd heard how big the airport was, and I was only in one terminal. Terminal 4, and it was huge. We had to look at the signs like we hadn't ever read English before. I saw Daniel standing there, already holding ours and his bags. He had been in the first class, we passed a smile to each other.

The way Daniel guided the way, I knew he had travelled a lot. Obviously. He was an international music producer, and knowing he was travelling with me felt good. Zaib was looking around like she had just gotten new eyes. "It's just the airport." Daniel had told her, but she had ignored him. We kept walking, until at the end of the queue, some guy called us and asked me, "The purpose of your visit?" I felt proud telling him I was participating in *singing for all*. Now, if it were Pakistan he would give me a look, trying to keep me shut, but this man said, "Oh, that's fantastic! Good luck. I hope you win." And he smiled, brighter than any man had ever smiled at me, except maybe Akmal or Daniel. But this guy was a stranger. That was my first impression about London. It was amazing.

At departures, we got out of the doors, wheeling our bags behind us. Just as we got out, a lot of things changed by one single act of nature. The air was cold - and like very cold. It pressed against my face, giving me a chill. It took me by force, and I stood still. My heart beat raised, because it wasn't just the air, I felt something I couldn't describe, I felt for the first time in my life *homelike*.

I looked around, and everything was different. Of course, the air was clearer. The men were not all brown, there were all kinds of races. White, brown, black, asian. I liked that, diversity. Women roamed around the roads, some even in short dresses in that cold, but no one was staring at anyone. I realized, no one was staring at me either, and that felt a bit odd since in Pakistan, everyone was staring at me and Zaib when we were out. Here, girls were wearing tights, and skin-fit shirts, but no one thought that was odd or "Slutty".

"I like the weather." I told Zaib, as Daniel called for a taxi. A black cab, the one I used to see in *Sherlock* stopped in front of us. "I already like London."

Zaib nodded in agreement, and we sat in the back. Daniel sat on the passenger seat, and he told the Driver to go to Shirley. Bridle street. 150.

The cab moved, and I looked around. Zaib and I looked out from our respective windows, and what I saw was beautiful. Men and women everywhere, some couples, some had pets, some were single. People were riding bicycles, and driving cars. Everybody was following the traffic rules. The roads were cleaner, there was no litter. Everything seemed better. I saw the union Jack, and it stuck in my mind. I liked even the flag.

I saw maple and oak trees everywhere. Much more greenery, and even in autumn, I could see all shades of green. It stretched as far as my look. The roads were narrower, but no long traffic jams. Everybody seemed calm and excited, both at the same time, like Zaib.

"Look at that!" Daniel pointed outside his window, addressing me and Zaib. We looked. "Do you see that guy with those dogs?"

I saw a 25 year old guy, and he was holding three dogs. Poodle, shepherd and a husky. "Yeah." Zaib said, and Daniel replied, "Look at that bag in his hand?" I looked. A very small green coloured bag. He was holding it by the edge, and threw it in a nearby dustbin.

"Do you know what was in it?" he half laughed. I understood, I remembered Professor Hanif telling us about it. That was actual Dog shit. I hadn't believed the Professor, but now I was stunned. My eyes wide, and I hoped Zaib guessed it right.

"That's dog shit." Daniel continued the laugh, "that's how clean these guys are, and people say the *angrez* are dirty. Short dresses don't make you dirty." He winked, and I smiled.

The cab stopped at a house. When I got out, I could see everything even more clearer. All houses were exactly the same, same infrastructure, same design, same colour. It looked pretty, and not dull. I stretched my arms, and grabbed my bag and guitar when Daniel knocked at the door.

A black woman came out. She had funny hair, curly. She was fat, twice as much as me - which was a lot. But I didn't judge, no one judged anyone in London. She talked in a funny accent, which was very hard to understand. Daniel introduced us, and the lady jumped.

"I've been waiting for you!" She hugged me, and my head got stuck between her breasts. I tried to pull away but in vain. "Welcome, welcome."

"Umm..." I could barely speak in lack of air, "Thanks."

Zaib giggled behind me, but tried to not. I shot her a look, and she couldn't even hide it anymore.

"Come child, come." The black woman told us, "I am Maria."

"Highfive Maria." Zaib held her hand in the air, and Maria just stared at her. A moment later she held her hand and told Zaib, "No highfives." and she pulled us in.

When Maria told us to wait, it turned out she was very fond of Pakistani food.

"Who's she?" Zaib asked as we smelled the obvious aroma of Sindhi biryani.

"Just a friend." Daniel told me, folding his hands and shaking his head. "She was with me in our music school. Now she's a church singer. An *okay* one. I told her I had guests coming and she was delighted to know that."

Maria came in holding a big pot covered with a cloth. The steam was still visible, and she had gloves on. The smell got stronger, and Maria's expression told me she had given it her everything.

I had noticed the houses were smaller here from the outside, but there was enough room once you were inside them. In fact, it would get a little too big for a middle aged single woman, but not very lonely. I hoped.

To be a little honest, the food wasn't exactly like home, but it was a good effort. I admired her. Once we had eaten, Daniel left and I started feeling tired. I asked Maria, "where do I sleep?"

"Upstairs, second room." she pointed upwards, swirling her fingers, "There's two rooms. Take your bags with ya."

I barely took my bag and guitar with me, and asked Zaib if she wanted to come. She shook her head. To my relief, the stairs were smaller, and I didn't die before reaching the bed. I jumped on it, without even taking my shoes off, which reminded me of Akmal. Oh, Akmal.

Akmal's was the last thought I had on my day 1, before my eyes started feeling heavy. I closed them, and before I could plug in my earphones to listen to some songs, I fell asleep.

Day 2:

Well, the excitement of London shouldn't have let me sleep this long, but it did. I was tired, and the amount of sleep I had was very unusual, even by my standards. I don't know the exact time, but I came in the afternoon, slept the whole day, the whole night, and still didn't wake up in the morning until Zaib started playing my guitar horribly.

"What are you doing?" I shook a little, and sat up. She gave me a look, stunned.

"I didn't think you'd wake up." She tried to smile, but she was kind of scared of me.

"Stop bullying my guitar," I said as I fell on the bed. Kind of like a trust fall, except I trusted beds more than anything, "my ears bleed."

Zaib stood up, and put the guitar aside. She got into the bed with me, and I could feel the weight increasing. She hugged me from behind, and kissed me slowly on the neck. My hair stood on edge, and suddenly my sleepiness went away. I smiled, but she didn't see, she just rubbed her hand slightly against my arm.

"I have planned everything." She slowly whispered in my ear. I was feeling good, she was touching my chest, my belly, my thighs. She was hearing my breathing, she was smelling my hair. I tried to ignore her, but I was curious.

"Planned what?"

"Well." She stood up, jumping away. She threw the blanket so hard it fell off me. She held a pamphlet in her hand, and kept shaking her finger on the top right corner.

London eye, Madame Tussauds, Parliament house & Big Ben, etc etc. "Daniel gave me a credit card, saying we should spend as much as possible, and I have already booked these tickets."

"Wow." I chuckled sarcastically, "You like London already, huh?"

"I do." She smiled brightly. "As a matter of fact I am british by blood." She said in her fake, crooked british accent and I laughed. She blushed, and I said, "don't do that again." but she did, and I said, "please." She laughed.

As we sat on the table for a fine English breakfast, toast with hot beans and mango juice, Maria told us to eat properly while I was busy on the mobile. It reminded me of one thing - since Akmal's death, I hadn't seen Zaib text anyone. Not even call, actually. She might have in my absence, never in my presence. I put down my mobile, and grabbed the ticket. I read the booking dates - all of them were within the first few days of our travel. It was kind of strange, but I ignored it thinking it was just Zaib's excitement.

"London eye, today?" Maria put some more beans on my plate, and I held my hands in the air telling her to stop, but she widened her eyes. I stopped the urge to refuse. "It's a great child. Great. Take a camera with you."

"We will." Zaib nodded, "Daniel gave us a camera by the way." Zaib elbowed me.

I started to have a feeling of a little jealousy, but it wasn't too bad, since she was gay too.

"Why not take Daniel with you instead of me?" I rolled my eyes.

Zaib smirked, "That's a good idea. We could do--" I slammed my foot on hers, and she jerked her leg hitting the table. *Oww.*

"Clear this up when you're done." Maria stood up very slowly, foot after foot. She gestured her fingers towards the table. She walked funny too, side after side, like a penguin.

Once she was gone, and we had done eating, I started picking up the plates.

"When are we leaving?" I asked zaib while we washed the dishes. She smiled, and told me, "at 4."

"How are you so confident?" I asked her, still scrubbing hard, "Like... I don't know."

"I checked everything out last night." She told me, finally looking at me. She had done washing her dishes. "I didn't sleep like a pig." She referred me. "I even bought you a dress for today. I hope you like it." She winked, and I smiled. And then she went away when I went back to the dishes.

After the dishes I thought about what Daniel had asked me to do. Write a song. After a shower, I sat in the room alone. I tried to get my mind off the fact that I was in London, or I was at a singing contest, or even that Zaib had bought me a new dress. I took a pen I saw on the dressing table, and started looking for a paper. When I couldn't find one, my stupid brain thought of writing on my hand instead of on the phone. But I wrote.

In the dim light of moon spark, I saw your face
The empty seats of your car, the fire of your grace
We couldn't ask for something --

I wrote that in about fifteen minutes. Just that. I knew I wasn't made for writing songs, but I was still trying. I thought, and thought again. I did eventually get more lyrics, but none of them were good enough.

Zaib knocked at my door, and her way of knocking told me it was her. I opened the door and she said, "do you want me to bring you your dress?"
"Sure."
Zaib turned around from the toes of her feet, and moved quickly. I smiled. I waited for her to return, thinking what the dress would be like. I thought about her, I thought about how amazing she was, and how much she cared about me. At that moment, Zaib came back. A black dress. She was holding it in a hanger, and as soon as she came back upstairs, she held it high.
"Tadaa." She held a black dress, the one you'd normally see on western weddings. It reached just above your knee, and it had no arms. The area above cleavage was hidden and *not actually* hidden by a very light and see through black cloth. It was skin fit, and totally *Haram*. I didn't care. When in Rome, do as the Romans do. "It was on sale. 50 £ only."
"What?!" I almost shouted, counting in my head, "that's like 7000 rupees."
"You're going to be an international celebrity." She grunted, and I shrugged, "get used to it." I shook my head, but she continued, "I'm going to get changed. You change, too."
I nodded, and took the dress. When I wore it on, I got a little insecure, because it was skin fit. My pouch belly was obvious, and I bent my back to hide it. I tried to swallow it, but I couldn't take my mind off it. I wanted to take the dress off, but how could I? I hoped no one could see, but that was impossible.
        When Zaib knocked at my door again asking, "you ready, yet?" My head was between my palms. I was worried she might think I'm ugly, so I didn't reply. I kind of hoped she wouldn't come in, but she did. She saw me, and I don't know what she was thinking, but she crouched next to me.
"What happened?" She inquired softly, "didn't like the dress?"
"Actually." Something about her voice made me want to tell her the truth, "No. I'm fat and ugly, and it is too pretty for me."
Zaib raised my head from my palms, and put her hands on my cheeks. She jerked my head, and tilted it slightly. "Javeria." She said, focusing her eyes on mine. "I swear, there's nothing prettier than you. Not the universe, not the stars, not existence itself." I can say she meant it, I saw it in her eyes.
Her words made me a little confident about myself. I sighed, in relief of course, and tried to smile. She kissed me on my forehead, and I shivered.
"Come on." She winked, "It's time to leave."

"London eye, please." She told the cabbie, after waiting on the road for at least fifteen minutes.
"What a beautiful day." The cabbie smiled at us, looking through the front mirror. "It's october!" he cried, "and look..." He left the steering wheel and danced his arms around, "...what a beautiful day!"
"Somebody's glad to be in London." Zaib whispered in my ears, and I smiled.
"London... is london."

When we were nearing the London eye, I could already see the huge ferris wheel from miles away. Zaib was smirking, and when I opened the window slightly, cold air went through the car. Fresh air smelling of hope and beauty. Trees, everywhere, maple, peach, and apple. Again, seeing London like I got new eyes.

When we finally reached the London eye, Zaib told me she had VIP tickets.
"Aren't they crazy expensive?" I asked her, my eyes wide. "Don't waste Daniel's money."
"It's no worry."

It was a big and scary queue, but thanks to Daniel, we didn't have to stand and wait in that. It was easy peasy, once we confirmed the doubtful guard that we *were* VIP. Still getting that celebrity treatment. "Stand in this lane, please." The operator stretched his arms symmetrically, as we stood alone on the VIP lane. "Thank you."
We watched the cabin coming down at us, and Zaib was too excited. She almost tripped over the yellow line we were told not to cross. The door opened, and I looked behind. No one. Zaib and I got in, quickly enough, because they never really stopped the car. We had to get on it while it was still moving, and guess what I remembered then again? I was acrophobic.

The car moved very slowly, but it was getting a little scary. We were lifting up, and my blood was going down. My brain was shifting down, and even though I knew I was safe, my fear gained control over my senses. Maybe it was because the whole car was made of glass.

Zaib looked at me, and kept quiet. I frowned, but she shrugged. She started staring out from the glass, and I noticed she was cold. Not literally, but she was frozen. She was standing at the edge, looking, and really looking, her eyes never tiring, her mouth never shaking.
"Is everything alright?" I asked her. She looked over from her shoulder, but her eyes were watery.
I stood up from my wooden bench, and held her shoulders from behind. I was short, but I could do that still. I rubbed her arms, but now she was crying more intensely, and the worst part of it was I knew why.
"Do you know what's the worst part of death?" She swallowed, and I smelt something uncomfortable. Like the air was thinning. "Death doesn't end beauty." She looked down at the beautiful city of London down us. The river thames went on and on, as far as we looked. Surrounded by a million buildings built by a million people, like a large lego town. Joined together as a masterpiece, to show people that the world is not just about sadness, there is beauty even after death. "I swore I won't talk about him… but…" She cried a little more, biting her lips, one after another. Her face all blushed, like she was out of breath. A squeak, and then another. "I miss him. I wish he could see this. I wish we could see this, together. It didn't last much long. I loved him, more than anything else in this world. Sometimes, he used to tease me." She half cried, half laughed, "and I told him I wish he was dead." She started crying again, "And I never knew it would be this bad. I thought… I thought I…" She went silent. Didn't speak another word, she didn't want to hear another word. She wasn't feeling well, she wanted to get answers. She wanted to know why Akmal had to leave, and why God had to be that selfish.
I didn't know what to do, so I did the only thing I knew how to do. *Passenger - let her go*

Well, you only need the light when it's burning low.
Only miss the sun when it starts to snow.
Only know you love her when you let it go… and you let it go.

Zaib smiled. "Thank you, Jia." She wiped her eyes, and her tears fell on my like blood drops. She was smiling, yet sad. I wanted to hold her, I hugged her. I kissed her, on her upper lips. Biting it slightly. The tears she couldn't wipe touched my cheeks, and I blushed. I kept kissing her, it was amazing. Strawberries. Everything seemed unreal.

Just before we were on top, the sky went yellow. Sunset. All shades of yellow and orange, like it was some sort of a movie. The sky stretched over everything, the tall skyscrapers, the parliament house and Big Ben, river Thames. Even above us. The whole city of London seemed like one giant piece of cloth, going to be painted yellow and orange. An artist of taste. A lemon sky, with a peach tree.

"Let's take a selfie." She said in her dim but surprisingly cute voice. I nodded. She took out her phone, and through the front camera's snap, I could see *The* London behind us, and us, beautiful and adorable. Red and black. Left and right. Pieces of a puzzle, a book to be written, a song to be heard.

Just before our car was at the bottom again, a sign said *Smile for your picture*, and I turned. I saw a camera, facing Zaib and I. we both smiled, and I could feel it. I could feel it being the best smile I had ever made since I was born.

When we got out, and went to the souvenir shop, they told us to wait in a scary-ass line for the picture. I couldn't do that, neither could Zaib, and we already had our selfie, so we just skipped that. We got home. Changed. Went to our rooms. And tried to sleep. I couldn't sleep, because in my mind, I was thinking about a song. I was trying to come up with ideas, but I was blank. The two lines I had written made no sense, and I had nothing else to come up with. My irrationalities told me to stay awake, and there I was, still an insomniac in London, even though Zaib had told me this would happen. She told me it was jet lag. She didn't know, terrible nights don't have jet lag.

Day 3:

The next morning was a little awkward. Because I couldn't sleep almost all night, I had taken off my trousers and my panties. And I was shirtless, so when Maria started screaming, I knew why. Zaib was lying next to me, completely naked herself, and the blanket was off us. Maria cried, "Lord forgive these children." and all I could say was, "We didn't do anything. I swear. I swear." while still getting a little insecure about my naked body, and Zaib lying next to me. Zaib was still asleep, her face towards the ground. But her back and her butt was visible. The thought of touching her got control of me, and when Maria closed her eyes, I pulled the blanket above us, secretly touching her from all the way from the toe to the shoulder.

"I'm going to make breakfast!" She shouted, "you better get dressed." she moved her eyes to Zaib, "both of you." She circled her fingers around us, and shot us a shunt look.

I hid my chuckle behind my hands.

Once she walked out in her penguin style, and shut the door, I took the blanket off us. I stared at her lifeless back, but she was breathing. She was moving up and down, her bare arms to each side. I touched her back again, slowly, like a cloth running against her. She shook her shoulders, and tried to open her eyes. She saw me, and I saw her. I was completely naked, without anything covering up my breasts, or my stomach, or my any other area. But then she turned, and her breast was bare too. Her boobs, they were right in front of me. A goddess, a greek goddess of beauty. Her stomach shaped perfectly from both sides, like a boomerang. Her belly button, and the stretched line above it 'till her sternum. Her eyes, brown, chocolaty. Her hair, a little golden now, coloured, icing on the cake. Her heart, beating, and I could feel it in my heart. I leaned forward, and she didn't hesitate, even though she was stunned. I kissed her, and I kissed her again. I forced my weight on her, it was like I was choking her, but she didn't stop.

I stopped for a second, "why are we naked in the bed, though?"

She laughed, she started laughing louder. And it broke the whole mood, and now I got back, and started feeling insecure again. I covered myself with the blanket again, and funnily enough, I started feeling a little cold.

"Funny story." Zaib told me, "Last night…"

I rolled my eyes.

"I got drunk." I stared at her. Please, not you. I know you're not stupid, and you won't start doing stuff like my mom, but please don't drink. I can't take risks. "And I came up stairs, forgot which room I was supposed to sleep in. saw you naked, got naked, and slept with you."

"*Slept* slept?"

"No." She shook her head, still smiling, "Not yet. I can't even do that while you're asleep."

We both laughed.

Before we headed to Madame Tussauds today, I wore a complete black outfit. Black Jeans, Black shirt, and a black upper Zaib got from Primark on our way back last night. We still left pretty early today, at 2. I read a sign that said *Baker street* and I almost jumped, patting Zaib on the arm hard.

"Isn't that where Sherlock lives?" I told her, looking out the window, "I thought it was a made up street."

"Do you like Sherlock Holmes?"

"Just curious." I smiled at her. She nodded.

"221B Baker street." she corrected me, "there's a Sherlock holmes museum there now. Do you want to see it?"

"Maybe." I shrugged.

We finally reached Madame Tussauds, and it was actually smaller than I had thought, because all I was seeing was the gate. There were big lines, on each gate, but a smaller one on gate 5, where we were supposed to be. Celebrity treatment.

We got in, through a red coloured tube. Like we were boarding on a plane. The people would move, stop, and again move in the same line. The red light falling on Zaib, making a silhouette on the wall, still red. Her eyes shining behind her glasses, her lips turning more pink. The more she walked, the more beautiful she got, and the closer we got to all the wax statues inside.

A middle-aged man told us to wait behind a yellow line, before he checked the tickets. "Sorry girls." He said as he lifted his QRCode reader, and lasered above the tickets, "this'll only take a minute."

"No problem." Zaib said in a beautiful british accent, and I had no idea she could speak in that accent that well before. She might have been practicing. It was silly.

"Thank you for waiting." He gave us back the tickets and stretched his arms towards the last elevator of the five, "Please go the elevator, it'll take you to the top floor where you will start your journey among the celebrities."

The top floor was *Party*. It was a large hall, with statues of the best actors across the world. A red light, over each of them. Curtains behind everyone, and white spotlight over each of them. A faint scent of an unknown but beautiful perfume under my nose, and Zaib. Shahrukh khan, Brad Pitt, Morgan Freeman, Benedict Cumberbatch, you name it, they had it. Zaib almost stood at each mannequin, asking me to take her photo, and I took hers. I didn't take any of mine, still, because I thought it was stupid to be pretending these people to have met for real. It wasn't very charming.

The floor below us was of film study. There was a huge Shrek, and Steven spielberg dressed in the iconic Jurassic park clothes. Again, Zaib is taking photos, and not me.

And below that floor, was the floor of my taste. Singers. Just as I entered, to my left, I saw a sturdy Elvis Presley, holding a guitar. I was starstruck, and I knew how good the work was when he had a perfect G-chord on his hand. Next to him, was the original band of One direction, including Zayn Malik, which was funny because at the party, they put Angelina and Brad away, and here they put the whole band together.

Next to One direction was Miley Cyrus, in the same dress she wore in *We can't stop* music video, sliding down a red slide. Her tongue out, her hair short, her hands in the air. She looked sexy, even though she had changed now, her latest single *Malibu* was so majestic. I liked her that way.

Next to her, was the king himself, Michael Jackson, in his very famous and trademark end dance stance. This time, I told Zaib to take a picture of me. I stood against Mike, and tried to copy his action. It might not have been perfect, but it was still okay.

Next to the king, was an artificial stage of the voice. Where people were hearing music auditions on the screen behind them, and the instructor told them to roll the wheel next to them. They did after a white light splashed on them, and a sound of *Dhush* came. As they rolled the wheels, the seats moved around, just like in the show, I would've got on it, if I had had any interest in the show.

Next to the Voice stage, was the Queen. The queen of vocals. The lady. Adele Laurie Blue Adkins. Her left hand on her chest, her right bent towards the ceiling. Her mouth open, like she was making a vibrato out of a high vocal. Her short hair tucked behind her ear, she was wearing a similar dress to what I had worn last night, the kind of one she wears in her live performances of *when we were young*.

Next to her, last but not the least was one of the best singers to have ever lived. Bob Marley, sitting on a chair, head under a headphone, his eyes closed, mouth open like singing something. I sat on my knees next to him, and hugged him. I could have cried if I hadn't heard his *No woman no cry*. No woman, no cry.

Everything else was boring to me. Sherlock Holmes, Marvel 3D and something else I totally forgot about. The whole time nothing was better than taking Zaib's pictures, and telling her how beautiful she looked, and how the other celebrity was nothing against her. Telling her how amazing she was, and how wonderful life was with her. She didn't even talk about Akmal. A beautiful soul.

When we got out after the Marvel 4D experience, it was still day. It was just above 5, and I looked at Zaib confused, I already knew we were going somewhere else.

"Where?" I asked her, and she winked, saying, "just follow me."

We got to a cab,Zaib told the driver some address, and we got there. Zaib got out, I got out, and I stared at the board. A tattoo parlour. She remembered.

"I told you I could work it out."

I smiled and shook my head. "You're so amazing."

"I know." She flipped her hair, "Now, come on. I have an appointment."

A guy, who was less human and had more tattoos, told me to sit in a seat. The kind of one dentists have, except that this chair had only one needle. The tattoo needle.

"This won't hurt a bit." the man lied as he put some chemical over the wrist end of my forearm. It smelt like chloroform. The mean first drew the tattoo with a marker. A star with a bolt, just like the one on Akmal's neck. Zaib told me she'd get one too, it relieved me a little of the fear.

The needle touched my skin. Ouch. My hand almost drew back, but I held it there, helped by the artist's own hand. He did it calmly, not uttering a word. His eyes focused, his forehead tensed. But my pain was getting a little unbearable, until Zaib held my shoulder. She whispered in my ear, "Fun. Right?"

"To you." I barely spoke. Shaking my head.

Once I was done, my whole forearm had gotten red, but the tattoo was fresh. And it made me a little happy, even though it was still stinging. By the time Zaib had finished getting one over her shoulder, the pain had lessened a little. It was bearable. I'm sure Zaib would have felt the same, but she didn't say anything. To my surprise, she didn't even talk about Akmal. I didn't know why, because it was obvious. The three stars. But I got to know about it soon, a little too soon.

Day 4:

At breakfast, I asked Zaib what was the plan for today, and she told me "Daniel." I was confused, until I realized it was one day before my audition.

"It's more of a performance than an audition." Daniel had come, and now he was telling me all about tomorrow. His voice was soothing and determined, but I was nervous. My throat had a frog before I caught it. I usually am never nervous of singing, like *nervous* nervous, even in front of a large audience. But this was different. This was big, and I could guess it from Daniel's seriousness towards it. He continued, "You need to be at your best, you understand?"

I nodded. My cheeks were hot, my lips unsteady as I spoke, "I guess."
Daniel grabbed both my arms and jerked me, "You have to be certain." He looked into my eyes, and I was almost going to cry. I had never seen Daniel this serious before, not even when I told him about Akmal's death.

Daniel took me, only me, without Zaib to central london. He came in his own car, a black Audi. It was a short car, kind of comfortable for me. Daniel sat on the back seat with me, but he was quiet. Quieter than usual. His eyebrows tensed, his temples strong, his forehead bleeding tears.
"What's wrong?"
"Let's just say, I know a lot more than I should have." Daniel wasn't joking. He knew something he shouldn't have known, but why was it related to me?
"Why do you think I am not going to perform well tomorrow?" I asked, rubbing the palm of my hands, even though my chest was warm, my hands were cold. "Don't you think I'm not good enough?"
"It's not like that." Daniel looked away. Out of the window, at the streets, at the people, at the trees. Like I did when I first came here. "You have to perform the best of yours, okay? There are reasons. Reasons I can't tell you. It won't matter to your audition. You're going through, I'm sure of it. But I want you to perform your best."
"Okay." I shrugged, even though I was still a little curious.

Daniel took me to a huuuuge skyscraper, and I hoped he would say something like "That top is where you should be" or "you could be" or "you are going to be." But he didn't say anything. He just walked, and I followed. It didn't help my mind tremors though, because I was even nervous to go to the band practice I was gonna play with.
The 5th floor was an enormous hall, with green and white lights on the ceiling. Chandeliers and ribbons coming down off it, and the glass windows reflecting the sunlight onto the instruments. I tried to imagine how Zaib would look in that light. Beautiful.
"This is your band. *The mockers.*" Daniel stretched his arm towards them, and I was starstruck. My first band. "You guys can play any song you like. Just make it awesome for tomorrow." He took a huge sigh, his hat falling off his head, "please."
I nodded.

A young and tall man stood firm next to the rest of the musicians. He had a goatee, no mustache, and long hair tucked behind his ears. He was wearing a check shirt, with standing collars. His sleeves rolled up, and baggy jeans going lower than his underwear. He smelled of tobacco, not like Zaib, the disgusting kind. He held a Les Paul in his hand.
"I'm ya boy." He sniffed. Sniffed air, I guess. "Johnny."
"Even Johnny Bravo is disgusted by that." I contracted one half of my face in disgust. He shrugged.
Then there was a girl. Short hair, but longer than mine, not trimmed. Her eyes were beautiful. Blue eyes. Her hair was ginger, and she was wearing bold rectangle glasses. She was short, almost of the same height as me, and she had freckles on both of her cheeks.
"I'm the keyboardist." She smiled awkwardly. I liked her. "Joana."
"That's cool." I smiled back, "I'm Javeria, the vocalist of course."

"Of course." Said a heavy and dark voice behind me. I turned back. A middle-aged man, going bald was standing there. His shirt half tucked into his khaki pants. He was a sturdy man, with a Bass-guitar strapped around him. His eyes were narrow, his shadow behind him was tall. His left hair was half black and half grey. His appearance was older than his face, maybe it was because of his fat nose.

"I'm Aron. Aron Dawn." His hands came above me for a handshake. He must have been twice as tall as me. "The bassist." After the handshake which I barely manage to tolerate, he moved his hands around his cuffs. "You know kid, they say you're good. Prove it."

"No drummer?" I asked. He frowned, and I immediately regretted my question.

"We don't need one. We will play beats on the keyboard." He shot a look at Joana and she made a nervous face.

I started playing on my own acoustic guitar I had brought.

Well you done done me and you bet I felt it
I tried to be chill but you're so hot I melted
I fell right through the cracks
And now I'm trying to get back
Before the cool done run out
I'll be giving it my best-est
And nothing's going to stop me but divine intervention
I reckon it's again my turn,
To win some or learn some

After I had finished the song, he just gave a simple *hmph*. But it was a relief. He knew it, I knew it. I could sing. His eyes knew it, he saw me that way. He moved his head a little, smiled at me, finally. Daniel smiled at the both of us, and started clapping. Finally, he looked a bit calm himself.

"You can sing." Aron nodded. "Let's get practicing."

For two hours straight, we decided what to sing. Aron was stubborn, and he wanted me to sing something that suited me. He didn't want me to sing strong vocals, because I was a *short sweet girl*, but he didn't want me to sing a high pitched song either because that was too *mainstream*. I didn't know what he wanted me to sing, maybe something jolly, but no. Not that either.

"Sing something that will make the audience nostalgic." He asked me, and I got the idea at once. There was a thing about all Coldplay songs, they were always making me nostalgic. Their music was always best composed, and their vocals always had a great taste.

"What about Coldplay's fix you?" I asked. Aron smirked at me, and I knew he liked the idea.

To my surprise and relief, all of them knew about this song, so it wasn't much about practice. They all plugged in their instruments, and Aron told me to play chord on my own guitar too. I started singing.

When you try your best, but you don't succeed
When you get what you want, but not what you need
When you feel so tired, but you can't sleep
Stuck in reverse

At the last note, everyone stopped playing, but I stretched it. I stretched it higher than I thought I could have. It rang on my ears, my larynx never tiring, my throat never stopping. A vibrato, I felt like Adele giving a Coldplay cover. I was trying to define what I was, trying to say I can do it. I could do it. They all stared at me, but my eyes were closed, my pulse strong, my blood cold. I was shivering, but not my band. Not The Mockers. They were clapping, and cheering. Shouting. They knew I was born to sing. I remember Aron saying, "This girl is going to win."

Day 5:

Zaib and I were brought out to the suburbs of London, where the competition was held at a large auditorium. Daniel drove us there, not with the driver this time. He parked his Black Audi in the VIP Parking, and we got off.
"I will watch you from the audience." Zaib smiled at me, but this time her smile didn't seem wholehearted.
"Are you sure?" I asked her, trying to understand what she was up to.
"Yeah." She rubbed her hands nervously. "I guess, I just want to watch you like the whole world is going to. You're so amazing."
I shrugged, "Well, thanks."
"We should go." Daniel told me, pushing me slightly from the back. But Zaib half shouted from behind. "Hey!"
"What?" I turned back. I saw her in the morning light. Her brown eyes screaming, her red cheeks firing love. Her lips cold, and her face burning. Her white hoodie covering the back of her hair, and her hands skinny, but in air. She looked like the first time I had seen her, strange, mystical, and beautiful. Her smell was attracting, her voice was drowning. "I want to tell you something."
Her hands were slightly shaking, her nose was pink from the cold. Her glasses were getting off her face, and finally, a tear dropped off her eye. "What happened?" I asked her, but she was too crying to reply. She hugged me, forcefully. She almost crushed my ribs, and pulled my back. Her head was on my left shoulder, and her tears kept falling. I hugged her back, she felt warm. It felt like I was smoking again, She felt like my heart was in a garden full of daisies and sunflowers. A violin music playing behind us, she finally said. She whispered in my ear, and I swear I could have died at that moment. "I love you. I love you so much."

I couldn't speak. I couldn't utter another word, I couldn't breathe. I wanted to say something, but by the time I had realized this wasn't a dream, Daniel was pushing me away from her. I saw her once again, She was waving at me. "Good luck." She shouted behind me, and just before the backstage gate closed, I saw a half sight of her, pulling out one last cigarette from her pack.

Between the all other singers, who were going to audition, I was the only one who had wrapped her head between her arms. I was thinking about Zaib, and how she told me she loved me, and how I was going to love her back. I was planning how to tell her I loved her too, and that we can move to England, and marry, and adopt a kid, and live happily ever after. I imagined travelling the whole world with Zaib, I imagined us growing old. I imagined living with her scent for the rest of my life, for fifty or even more years. I imagined smiling at her, and her smiling back at me. I imagined my whole dream, I imagined it was coming true. I opened my eyes, and Daniel was standing next to me.
"You're next. Give it your best." He tried to smile, but failed miserably.

I heard the crowd roar when the host told them the next contestant had come from a different continent, and I stood up. But before going on the stage, I went to Aron.
"I'm not singing Fix you." I told him. And he widened his eyes.
"What are you talking about?"
"I'm singing *how would you feel* by Ed Sheeran." It was the first song I had sung to Zaib. Whenever I listened to that album, it would make me nostalgic. All the memories coming back. Nostalgia is such a beautiful and sad feeling, like you feel good to have lived that moment but can't bear the fact that you're never gonna live that moment again. "I don't care if you guys can play it or not, but I'm singing it."
"I can play it." Joana told me, "but these guys can't. You sure you can go with just the piano?"
"I do have my guitar too." I raised my guitar from the strap. I heard the crowd going silent, and Daniel telling me to go on the stage now. "I gotta go." Joana nodded.

When I arrived at the stage, the whole crowd went silent. They handed me a mic, and I tapped on it to check if it was on. The whole auditorium went *roar*, and I got a little scared. My legs were shaking, and I hoped no one noticed. I swallowed, my head was hurting slightly, but it didn't matter. What mattered was what was about to happen next.
        A little away from me, were three large sofa seats, on each was sitting a singer who was going to judge my singing. From the right to left: Ed Sheeran, Ellie Goulding and Sam Smith.
"Hi. What's your name?" Ellie asked me.
"Javeria. Javeria Ubaid."
"And where are you from?"
"Islma- Lahore, Pakistan."
"Alright, and what are you going to sing for us today?"
"I'm actually singing an Ed's song." Ed smiled at me, and I half chuckled, "It's *how you would feel*."
"Good luck." Ed raised his right hand. I nodded towards Joana, and she nodded back, and then she played it on the keyboard. I strummed the first chord right on point.

You are the one girl
And you know that it's true
I'm feeling younger
Every time that I'm alone with you
We were sitting in a parked car
Stealing kisses in the front yard
We got questions we should not ask but
How would you feel, if I told you I loved you?

The song ended, with me crying. The judges went on their feet, clapping. Clapping like they had never clapped before, smiling and cheering. I looked at the VIP panel at my left, and Daniel was standing, clapping too. "Amazing." He mouthed, and I nodded. And then my eyes began searching the audience, I was looking for Zaib. To the left, to the right. But she was nowhere to be found, my eyes wanted to see her. Where was she? Ugh.

"Your voice is remarkable." Ed told me, "Hell, you sang it better than me. Hands down." The crowd roared, but I didn't care. I was still looking for Zaib, my eyes still searching.
"Your voice is charming. I've never heard anyone sing better than that. Well done." Ellie.
"What I like about you is you sing it from your heart, and that's when you know this girl is special. I really think you are going to make a name for yourself." Sam.

Just after the auditions, I came out from the backstage. Daniel had told me I would get a chance to take pictures with the judges, but it didn't matter to me. I wanted to find Zaib, I wanted to tell her I loved her too, and I wanted to ask her about my performance. I ran to the audience, but the guards stopped me, saying "you can't go there. The crowd will be out of control."
"But I am looking for somebody."
"Ma'am, you can meet them after the show."
"Ugh."
Daniel shouted from behind, and I turned my head. "What are you doing here?" He asked me, but I didn't reply. He asked me again and told me, "you need to go back."
"No. I want to find Zaib."
"It's getting dark." He looked at the sky. A lilac sky, now being covered by grey clouds. A single tear drop fell from the sky, and it bit my cheek. It stung, but I stood stubborn, "It's about to rain."
I pulled my black hoodie over my hair, "not yet. Not until I find Zaib."

A Dark Tremor

Always together and never apart.

My phone vibrated in my pocket. Zoom. Zoom again. I pulled it out, my hand slid against the pocket button and got itself cut. An unknown number. For the third time this month, a hospital got involved in my life.

"Miss Javeria?" A small voice told me, but I was already hearing ambulance sirens in my ears. They felt like killing me.

"Yeah?" My voice was still ignorant, so calm, so stupid.

"This is BMI Shirley Oaks Hospital." The voice got a little more dull, and dark. The sky just got a little more grey, and the ambulance siren was lost. My cheeks were hurting, they were too hot. The inside of my hoodie had started stinging my muscles. "You were in Miss Zaib Abbasi's emergency contacts. I must inform you of this tragic news. Miss Zaib was brought half an hour ago in the emergency ward of our hospital by Miss Maria Trang, but she is now declared clinically dead at 5:58 P.M. I am sorry for your loss; the case seems to be suicide. There were massive blade cuts on both of her wrists, and according to Miss Maria, she found her in the bathroom tub. She was still breathing then, but she had lost a massive amount of blood. The doctors tried their best, but we couldn't save her. I'm sorry."

The phone fell off my hand, and Daniel asked, "What happened?" I couldn't hear him properly, I stumbled and fell down on the ground. The bracelet on my arms broke. Rain started pouring, and Daniel looked at my phone. He ran. He left me there, but I didn't care. I lay down on the ground, the hard pitch hurt my ribs, and I remembered Zaib's hug once again. I wanted to tell her that I loved her, but now I couldn't get up. My ears were getting hot, my breaths were not complete. Something inside me went missing. My heart couldn't save itself from drowning into an ocean of thoughts. Thoughts of suicide and love. Thoughts that were both psychotic and idiotic, thoughts which meant the end of world to me. I imagined what Zaib would have thought before she had gone through with it. Would have she thought about me? Of course she would have. She told me she loved me, but why did she leave me? Was it because I didn't tell her I loved her back? That's a hole I lived with forever. Why did she have to leave me? Why did she even kill herself? Why did she think she wasn't good enough to live in this world? I knew her, I knew her a little too well. She wasn't suicidal. I was! She shouldn't have killed herself, it should have been me! Zaib. Why couldn't you understand? Without you, I was Javeria. With you, I was Mahnoor! I am not a single person. My story has had two sides. This fucking depressed weirdo who knows nothing and this super awesome singer who knows how to love, and who knows how to be loved. You asked me to jump, and I did jump, is this how you pay me back? You meant the world to me, was that a mistake? You told me I was brave, and yes, I am. But you're not. You're a coward. You're such a coward!

Once I was finally able to get up, I ran to find a cab. I ran in the rain, but after quarter a mile I slipped. I dropped hard on the ground once again, and my elbows stung, my face was burning. I tried to get up once again, but I could barely get up half an inch. I turned my head towards the right, my hair fell back. I saw a pack of cigarettes ten meters away from me. Zaib's pack. Just getting wet in the rain. I got up, and somehow, I felt majestically a lot more powerful. I ran towards the pack of cigarettes, and crouched next to it. There were no cigarettes in them, but I put the pack in my pocket. My elbows were still burning, I was still having a migraine, my body was on self-destruct. My chest was calling me back, and making me spin like a whirlpool.

I somehow got to a busy road. Blood was flowing from my arms now, but I didn't focus on that. I called for a taxi, and one stopped in front of me. I tried to speak, but I was shivering. "Shir... Shirley.... Shirley Hospital." I fell down on the ground once again. I felt a sudden pain in my chest again. I blacked out.

Beep.

Sometimes what you want in life, is not what you need in life. A simple cigarette can kill you, the most probable death is lung cancer. But does it matter? The whole of my life has been just about getting closer to death. Smoking gave me a lot more than the risk I had taken, it gave me a feeling. Whenever I used to smoke next to Zaib, she would have a feeling. It's such a cliché to call that love, because it's not. Love is what Akmal and Zaib had, or what I and Emaan have, what Zaib and I had, didn't have words. You want to know what it felt like? Take a cigarette, burn it, place the burning end on your palms, and then smoke it from there. Try to wet that smoke from your tears, and then try again to not let it get wet. That was it. That was my feeling for Zaib.

Beep.

Life ends, it doesn't matter whether you go on to win a stupid competition. Five performances are nothing, it was bullshit. It always had been bullshit. Another cliché is to try to win, because it doesn't work like that. Winning in life is winning only when you fall in love, but I hope you don't fall in love. Trust me, I've made that mistake, it sucks. The competition was so easy for me, I felt I would break down with the boredom and stupidity of it. I did win, if that matters. It doesn't matter to me anymore. I did write a stupid song, if that matters too.

One day will come, when I'll leave a tear in your eye.
I will hurt you, with a blade on your smile.
Nothing will be left, but a note by my side.
Or the jokes for the laugh I tried.
Days will come and days will go.
I know it won't be an unexpected blow.
For all I think is death and life.
Would it ease my pain if I died?
No it won't, says someone from beyond.
Or maybe it would, but not for long.
And all the songs I write or not.
Do we, or do we not belong?
We don't really love, we don't really hate.
We don't feel anything, we just keep making mistakes.
And I can't understand.
Why cry When you can die?

Beep.

I went back to Pakistan, after winning the tournament. I didn't have to, I had planned it like that, but without Zaib no plan made any sense. I called Hania, and she was still mad. I told her everything, about how I was homosexual, and how I loved Zaib, and how I wanted to spend my life with her. She forgave me, but I could never forgive myself. I went back to my family, and between this whole time, my dad had divorced my step-mom. My real mom was glad that I came back, but the most of all was Emaan. As it turned out, he was never really mad at me, but I was mad at myself. Almost a year later, after my first album was a hit, I took Emaan and moved to the UK. Life is fun here, but depressing.

Beep.

I took Zaib's dead body back in Pakistan, and got it buried with Akmal's. I have got a place for my dead body too, and I hope to join them soon. I am not going to kill myself, never, but whenever I go out, I keep on hoping some car would run me over, or I would fall off a building. Interesting story is that I have also lost my fear of heights.

Beep.

Beep.

Beep.

I woke up in a hospital room, which reminded me of my hostel, but I was now sure this was a hospital because there was an IV beside me. My thumb and index finger had plugs, which were attached to a CRO, which kept on making the same sound over and over. Beep. Beep. Beep. My fingers were itching, but I couldn't move. Plugs were also all over my chest and belly, but they were hidden under a cloth.

Daniel was sitting across the room, his arms folded in front of him, his head looking down. He hadn't noticed I had woken up. I tried to make a voice, but it came out as a muffled cry.

Daniel looked at me worriedly, and asked me if I was okay. I tried to nod. He calmed down a little, I had noticed I had calmed down myself. The doctors must have given me some sort of anesthesia or some other drug that had calmed my ocean. It still hurt. My heart beat was slower. And I noticed the CRO graph. It wasn't normal, I had seen Emaan's. The slope should have been a little wider.

"You knew it, didn't you?" My head was still hurting. I wanted to sleep, but more importantly, I wanted answers. "You knew she was going to suicide."

"A few days ago, Zaib told me she would suicide." Daniel started explaining, his voice shallow, and he was sighing after almost every word. "I tried to fight her, I swear I did. But you know how stubborn she was. She tried to explain to me why she was doing it, and she was going to do it anyway. I tried to stop her, I even almost called the police, but she said she would kill herself the moment the police arrived. She told me it was for the best, and that she wanted to do one last thing before she departs. She didn't tell me when exactly, but I kind of knew it would come soon."

"Why didn't you tell me?" I thought of shouting, but I couldn't. My hands were shivering, my eyes were bleeding. I had barely any energy. "What happened?"

"You just had a heart attack, Javeria. You should --"

"I don't care." I screamed. I was furious. "Why?" A simple question can leave you speechless.

"Because she told me not to." He stood up again, kicking his seat away. He stood tall, and I remembered how small I was. Just another ordinary girl from an ordinary place, "You think I like this? You think I wanted Zaib to kill herself? I would rather have myself killed. NO!"

"Why did she do it?" My voice went low again. It was dull, and depressing. My whole life was going to be one big ball of depression.

"I think you should have this." Daniel handed me over a white envelope. "Her name is written with her blood."

I looked at it, and I could barely see it. My vision was blurry, and my migraine had still not gone, but I tried to focus. Zaib.

"Is that her…?" I asked, looking up and pointing at the envelope. Daniel nodded. "I should give you some privacy." He patted me on the back, and left the room.

I hesitated to open the letter, I was thinking about all sorts of stuff. I did want to know, and I didn't want to know. Both were true. My nose smelled fear, but My eyes were excited. I opened it, still.

Hey Jiya,

How are you? So stupid of me to ask that, I know you're doing great because you're a warrior. I hope I'm doing fine in heaven, or even if I'm in hell, I'm probably drinking booze and making out with naked chicks. Hope that doesn't make you jealous.

Jiya, I'm sorry. I know, you have a lot of questions in mind. I can predict that, but the first one and the most important one is, why. Right? Javeria, Akmal was my brother. When my mom left, I attempted suicide, and guess who saved me? Akmal did. He didn't say anything, he just saved me, and cried. He cried for two nights, thinking what would happen if he lost me. Well, he didn't lose me, but I lost him. You must know how I'm feeling, after all I'm gone too. I told you, we were three stars, we were meant to be together. Me, Akmal, and my mom. I know, I called you a star too, and you are, and we will be together too, but my mom was with me for fourteen years, Jiya. And my brother was with me for seventeen years. I tried to imagine my life without them, but I couldn't, even though I love you. I really do. You have no idea how much I thought about this, and now you're probably mad at me and all, but you know, Jiya, I couldn't. I just couldn't. I'm sorry. I miss him, I told you I couldn't stay sad forever, I had to get over it. This is the only way to get over it.

I would have killed myself the day I got to know about Akmal's death, but I didn't. You. You were stopping me from dying, but it got unbearable in the next weak, and that was when I decided I would do it. The only thing I wanted to do was hear you perform in front of a large audience at least once. Hey, that was the same song you sang to me in Ayubia, right? See? I remember stuff too.

When I saw you for the first time, I hoped you were homosexual too. I kind of knew. This is not the reason why I helped you, if I did or anything, but God Jiya, you were a fantasy. I wish I was just a fantasy, and you were real, so I'd be the girl you'd be reading books about. But it doesn't work that way, does it? I wanted to leave a mark. Maybe I did. Hey, did I? I love you, and if you love me back, then that's it. I have, I have left my mark. Each time I kissed you, I fell for you deeper and deeper. I hesitated every time before telling you. I wasn't sure if our relationship was love or not, but believe me, girls like you are special, and I don't know why but I always tend to be attracted to specials.

Sometimes, at night I get dreams. Most of them are nightmares, but some of them are about Art, and literature, and when I say art and literature, I always mean you. Because Javeria

Sultan aka Mahnoor Ahmad is the best fucking piece of art I've ever seen.

You know, I told you but it's worth writing it again. Van Gogh in his suicide note said, "The sadness will last forever." Do you know what he really meant? Death doesn't cure sadness, it only prolongs it. When my mom was alive, only she was sad. Not us, at least not that much. But when she died, her sadness transferred to me, and now mine is going to transfer to you. I know that, I'm sorry. Suicide is selfish. Van Gogh died pretty early, you know. At 37, it's still young for a philosophical painter. Maybe I'm going to meet him, and tell him how beautiful his paintings were. Or maybe not. I would tell him his paintings were depressing pieces of shit and we'll laugh smoking more and more cigarettes every day.

Also, hey. Please don't stop smoking. I know, it gives you lung cancer, but I told you about Cherophobia, right? If you stop smoking, you'll get cherophobia and then it'll haunt you for the rest of your life. We don't want that, do we? We want you to be happy. Remember, it's poetic to be insane.

Do you remember the time we hid in the same cupboard? God, I swear it was so awkward, but here's a secret. I came in front of Danish's mom myself, just to hide with you in the cupboard. It's stupid, I know, but I wanted an excuse for us to touch as much as possible. This is so awkward right now. You know, when I came back to Lahore with you, it reminded me a hell lot of my mom. I had always remembered her, but this was different. This was the place where she died, where she took care of me, and grew me up. She had big dreams for me, and I turned out as a disappointment. Shame. But they were all crazy moments, and you know, you never know the true value of a moment until it becomes a memory.

The first time I thought of telling that I loved you was when I was going to say I'd write a book with the title of your name. But I didn't. I made a lame joke instead. OMG that's my life in a nutshell.

Hey, also, please bury my body with Akmal. Promise, okay? In Maria's house, under my bed, there is Uke. It doesn't matter if you have forgotten about him, but please, can you bury it with me? Please. And go on to win singing for all. Okay? I'm sorry again, but I have to. I have to do this. Bye. I love you, I have always loved you.

With love,
Zaib Abbasi

I love you too Zaib. I love you so much.